Saltaire Blonde

To Anne, with best wishes

Saltaire Blonde

Alan Hall

Alan Hall

07/09/18

http://www.fast-print.net/bookshop

Saltaire Blonde

A catalogue record for this book is available from the British Library

ISBN 978-178456-557-2

First Published 2018 by
Fast-Print Publishing of Peterborough, England.

CHAPTER ONE

It was just as breakfast was being served that the hotel dining room and adjoining kitchen were blown up by a bomb. At first it was thought that partisans may have been responsible, but that was always going to be unlikely, for there had been no recent evidence of partisan activity in that region. Later it was confirmed that a solitary aircraft had flown low over the hotel and dropped the bomb. Probably the pilot had intended to target the nearby barracks and had missed his aim, or perhaps he had mistakenly thought that the hotel was somehow connected with the barracks. In a sense this was true, for the Hotel Lew – the Lion Hotel – was regularly used to accommodate visitors who had come to inspect the camp and its facilities. Ferenc Kovacs was such a visitor. He had been sent from Budapest to ascertain the suitability of the camp for possible future transports from Hungary. Before the bomb dropped he had been partaking of an exceptionally good breakfast of strong coffee with local ham, cheese and warm bread rolls. Hospitality for guests at the Hotel Lew was always of a high standard, even in those difficult times.

Ferenc Kovacs was killed instantly by the explosion, although his body was relatively unmarked when it was dug out of the rubble. A waitress was also killed, as was the hotel's cook, whose body was so torn to pieces by the blast it was difficult to appreciate that it had ever been a human being.

The Hotel Lew had enjoyed a good reputation in peacetime. Well-heeled tourists would come by motorcar from Krakow, or even from as far away as Warsaw, for although the hotel was not large it was well-appointed and in very pleasant countryside. There were some excellent walks to be enjoyed in nearby woods, and there was even a lake not too far away, where one could fish for carp and pike. Of course, that was before the camp and the barracks were constructed. Soon after that, the hotel was requisitioned for the sole use of visitors whose business was with the camp authorities.

Not everyone from the Hotel Lew's staff was killed in the explosion. The manager had stayed the previous night with a woman, as he sometimes did, so he was not on the premises that morning. When he returned, summoned by an urgent telephone call, he stood stock-still, holding his bicycle and staring at the still-smoking ruin of the hotel, before he was ordered to get out of the way. A hastily-assembled team from the barracks was busy; some men were damping down the area with stirrup pumps, whilst others searched for bodies among the debris.

The hotel receptionist had also survived. She was a young woman called Elsa Muller who at the time of the explosion had been walking the manager's dog in the woods a little distance from the hotel. This was something she had to do whenever the manager was absent, visiting his woman. When she heard the explosion Elsa had run back to the hotel with the dog at her side and her little companion in her arms. Later she told the authorities that she had heard the sound of an aircraft and it seemed to be flying low. No, she had not seen it because of the trees, but she had thought at the time that it didn't sound like a German machine, not that she was too familiar with their various sounds. Anyway, before she'd had time to consider the matter any further there had been a very loud bang which had caused the leaves on the branches of the nearby trees to shake quite violently. The noise had frightened the dog, which started to whimper, and Elsa's little companion had screamed and clung to Elsa's leg.

Elsa's little companion? Oh yes, that was Ferenc Kovacs' daughter. God knows why he had brought her with him; she was only four years old – scarcely more than a toddler; a pretty little thing with blonde hair. Elsa, whose receptionist duties were not particularly onerous, had taken the little girl under her wing almost as soon as Kovacs had signed the hotel register. She had played with her during the times when Kovacs was in meetings with the camp administrators, and on that particular morning she had taken her along to help exercise the manager's big friendly dog, Pluto. When questioned by the authorities Elsa said Kovacs had mentioned to her that he had brought his daughter with him in the hope of combining his official business at the camp with a couple of days' holiday, as he didn't see enough of his child in Budapest. He was so busy. His wife had recently died and the little girl was cared for by an elderly neighbour when Kovacs was at his office, but that arrangement was not really satisfactory. Two days with his daughter in a nice spot was what Kovacs had anticipated.

7

Instead he was blown up by a stray Russian bomb and his daughter was left an orphan.

All this was quite awkward for the camp administrators. It was true that Ferenc Kovacs could hardly be said to be a VIP. Nevertheless, he was a representative (albeit a middle-ranking one) of the government of a friendly country. For him to be killed by a random Bolshevik bomb whilst a guest of the Reich was horribly bad luck all round. Embarrassing too. And what on earth was he doing bringing an infant along with him? Who was responsible for permitting that? And what was this nonsense about a holiday? Didn't he realise that they were engaged in a titanic struggle against a ruthless enemy? This was no time for holidays, and certainly no time to bring along a small child to an important conference, as if the whole thing was a Sunday afternoon treat! Ally or not, Ferenc Kovacs was clearly an irresponsible idiot.

And equally clearly the child, suddenly an orphan, could not go back to Budapest. Decent standards of behaviour had to prevail; Kovacs' daughter must be adopted by the right kind of step-parents and brought up accordingly. What about the hotel receptionist girl? Would she be appropriate, or would it be better, bearing in mind that the child was Hungarian, if she were adopted by a non-German who nevertheless had the right attitudes and could be trusted? There must surely be someone who would be suitable. All these issues vexed the camp administrators for a short while, but they were keen to get things settled quickly, for this was no time to be bogged down with trivial matters. They had much more important things to attend to.

CHAPTER TWO

Alison's friends were rather surprised to hear about her intention of moving from London to Yorkshire. What! Living among Yorkshire people? Good God! That was what some had said when she told them. Others had made annoying jokes about flat caps, ferrets, whippets. Then they would chortle and say "Ee, bah gum." Then they would say it again. Quite tiresome really. Of course, few of them had actually visited Yorkshire, though some vaguely recalled passing through it on a train going to the Edinburgh Festival. Or was that Lancashire?

Alison herself had once stayed for a weekend in a youth hostel near Kettlewell in the Yorkshire Dales. That had been on a geography field trip when she was studying for her A Levels. The scenery had impressed her, but she had read somewhere that the towns in other parts of Yorkshire were impoverished, bleak and joyless – just as they doubtless were everywhere in the north of England, she supposed.

Now, almost twenty years later, and rather to her own surprise, she had taken a job with a design consultancy in Leeds. Why leave London? If you are tired of London, you must be tired of life, as Dr Johnson had once said, and that surely still held true today, didn't it? Alison wondered if

Johnson would have been quite so enthusiastic if he'd had her daily commute to put up with, or the rip-off rent for a miniscule flat – above all, if he'd had Ed as his consort rather than Boswell. Ed was tall, skinny and quite ridiculously style-aware. If bushy beards were in, he grew a bushy beard; when stubble was fashionable, he had stubble. He tweeted constantly and always knew what was trending before anyone else. It was quite easy to grow tired of Ed.

Alison reckoned that moving to Yorkshire was not necessarily an irrevocable step. She was good at her job, and she had the kind of skills and flair which would always be in demand. If Yorkshire was as dull and hopeless as most of her friends said it would be, then she could always move back to London, or perhaps even try Brighton or Bristol; both said to be acceptable.

Leeds turned out to be better than Alison thought it would be – scarcely a flat cap or whippet in sight. Her work colleagues were friendly and welcoming; her new boss showed from the start that he valued her, and he gave her a lot of scope to do things in her own way. She'd taken a cut in salary, it was true, but she soon found that her living expenses were nothing like they had been in London. For the first couple of months she rented a small flat on a temporary basis near the city centre. Then at the weekends she would usually return to London and stay with an old friend from her university days. Alison saw these early weeks as something of an interim period of adjustment; a foot in both camps, as it were. But soon she decided that she had best give herself more fully to this new northern experience. Besides, it was hardly fair to impose on her London friend almost every weekend. She started to look for a more permanent home. And that's when someone told her about Saltaire.

Titus Salt was not just one of the most successful of Britain's textile manufacturers, but also one of the great philanthropists of the Victorian age, especially with the building of Saltaire, a model village designed to provide his workers with a much healthier environment than they had previously had in the middle of Bradford. In 1853 to celebrate his fiftieth birthday and the grand opening of Salts Mill he laid on a banquet for 3,500 of his workers. This took place in the mill itself and contemporary reports deemed it to be perhaps the largest dinner party ever set down at one time. Salts Mill ceased textile production in 1986, and for a time was threatened with demolition. But by the twenty-first century the mill had been refurbished and transformed. Nowadays it houses an art gallery, IT companies, restaurants and a range of upmarket shops. Saltaire itself has become a sought-after place to live. It is now a UNESCO World Heritage Site, a fitting tribute to Titus Salt, a man of vision.

This footnote to an estate agent's blurb tempted Alison to undertake the twenty-minute train ride from Leeds to explore Saltaire, and not many weeks later she moved into a small, tastefully modernised terrace house on Caroline Street. (Most of the streets, she discovered, were named after members of Salt's family). She found that Saltaire suited her; it was definitely Yorkshire – stone-built, solid and unfussy – but it also had a certain charm and style which belied the stereotype of Yorkshire as a boring place full of boorish people. There were some older residents, who had clearly lived in the village for years, but there were also many newcomers who, like Alison, were usually pursuing professional careers in Leeds or Bradford, or were developing start-ups, working from home.

One Saturday morning in October, perhaps two months after she had moved to Saltaire, Alison visited the 1853 Gallery in Salts Mill. The gallery occupies a very long room on the ground floor of the mill, and Alison assumed that it would have once housed looms or spinning machines. The noise of the machinery would have been deafening in those days; now there was a Mozart opera (Alison didn't know which one) playing in the background.

Alison was pleased to have this gallery almost on her doorstep. It boasted a large collection of works by David Hockney, an artist she particularly liked, although she had always associated him with California and its gay scene rather than with Yorkshire. Her particular favourite Hockney was *Mr and Mrs Clark and Percy*, which hangs in the Tate Britain gallery. As someone who worked in design, it was understandable that Alison would have some interest in Ossie Clark and Celia Birtwell, those flamboyant style gurus of the 1960s and 1970s. On one occasion she had visited Tate Britain with Ed specifically to show him the picture, but he had merely dismissed it with, "Oh my God, check out the fucking flares! Hee hee. Nah, it's just miserable hippies with a moggy." It was pointless trying to tell Ed about the influence of Van Eyck's *Arnolfini Portrait* on Hockney's picture; how the dog in the one symbolised fidelity, and the cat Ossie Clark was holding symbolised infidelity – all stuff she knew from the art appreciation module of her degree course. Ed of course didn't listen; he was always tweeting and texting rather than listening. Anyway, fidelity was never his strong suit, any more than it had been Ossie Clark's.

Alison looked for a time at *Tennis 1989*, a huge black and white affair, constructed out of 144 sheets of paper, which Hockney had apparently faxed to the gallery and had reassembled there. She decided that she didn't really like it. In a way it reminded her of Picasso's *Guernica*; she didn't like that either. She much preferred a small painting on the opposite wall, *My Parents 1977*. Here was Hockney's mother, seated to the left on what looked like a folding wooden chair. She was wearing a plain blue dress and flat brown shoes, her toes turned slightly inwards, her hands in her lap. Opposite was her husband, seated on a matching chair. Whereas mum was looking straight at you, dad had turned to one side, bent almost double over the pages of a large open book. More books were stacked on the shelf of a piece of furniture, which was painted bright green and stood centre-stage between the old couple. A small mirror and a vase of tulips were on top…

"You seem to like this picture very much, I think." Alison's almost forensic scrutiny of the picture was interrupted by this comment, which came from behind her. She turned to face a woman who was standing about four feet away.

"Am I blocking your view? I do apologise if I am," she said.

"No, no," the woman said and she smiled. "I just noticed that you were looking at this picture very closely. Do you like Hockney's work?"

"Yes, most of it," Alison said, turning back to look at the picture, as the woman came and stood beside her. "I'm not too sure about the sketches of dogs, or some of his designs for stage sets, but most of it I like, yes." Out of politeness she asked, "What do you like?"

She turned to look at the woman, noticing that she was probably in her seventies, but still rather striking, despite her age – careful make-up and good hair, with tasteful blonde streaks, an expensive coat and shoes; her hands still quite smooth, with three large rings on her fingers. All this Alison took in as the woman spoke to her in quite a cultured voice, with just a hint of a local accent.

"Yes, I like him. Though like you, there are some things of his I care less about. For me, I always preferred his portraits, like this one of his parents in their old age. And I have a particular liking for the very early one over there, the scene in the fish-and-chip shop." She gestured towards the opposite wall. "I think that was his local fish shop, when he was a boy in Eccleshill."

"Eccleshill?" Alison said. "Where's that?" She wasn't really interested, but felt that there was no point in being impolite.

"It's a suburb of Bradford where Hockney was brought up. Not very far from here. He was born in Bradford. You know, they say that when he was a pupil at Bradford Grammar School he made sure that he was always in the very bottom class. You know why?" Alison shook her head. Her companion smiled once more and shook her head too. "It was because you could only study art if you were in the bottom class. It wasn't considered a suitable subject for the supposedly brainier boys, you see." She shook her head again, without smiling this time. "Only in England, eh? Only in England is art seen as…" She pulled a face and didn't finish the sentence.

Alison couldn't think of a reply, so she turned back to look once more at the portrait of the old couple. One thing Alison had noticed about the woman was a particular timbre to her voice, and a certain formality of expression. Beneath her cultured English, with its slight Yorkshire undertone, there was a hint of something else. It made Alison think that perhaps English was not the woman's first language – or at least she was used to speaking another language. Alison looked at her again. By now the woman was in her stride, pointing out features of the painting, rather like a gallery guide, informing her audience that Hockney had spent his time at Bradford Art College developing an expertise in figure drawing which, in her opinion, was the foundation of his genius. Alison was only half-listening to all this. Instead she was looking closely at the woman's face, noting her refined features, the high cheekbones and slightly slanting eyes. Definitely not English, she thought.

"So if you like this picture of his parents, would you now like to see a picture of one of my parents? Of my father? It's here," the woman said, concluding her mini-lecture about Hockney.

"Really?" Alison said, politely. The woman reached out and patted her arm and laughed.

"Oh, it's not in this gallery, but it is here in the mill. Follow me if you want to see it. I think you'll find it interesting." She turned and headed towards the heavy wooden door which was the entrance to the gallery. After a few paces she turned and beckoned. "Come on," she called.

Alison, a touch reluctantly, followed her. Oh, the woman was harmless enough, that was clear, and she was even quite interesting in a way, but Alison didn't want to be lumbered with her for the rest of the Saturday morning. This was not what she had planned for her day. And like many people, Alison generally avoided getting into casual conversation with strangers. Still, when in Rome...

At the other side of the exit door there was a wide flight of stone steps leading up to the other floors of the building, where there were smaller galleries, shops and places to eat. Alison wondered which of these she was being led to, but it turned out to be none of them, for on the landing a couple of floors up the woman stopped by a large window. Covering the window was a fabric blind, about eight feet in height and four feet in width. Printed on the blind was a giant-size black and white photograph of workers leaving Salts Mill at the end of their shift. A nearby caption informed you that the photograph had been taken in the early 1950s. This was not like a Lowry painting, with the famous matchstick figures all looking the same as they swarmed out of a Salford factory. Here, the camera had been positioned a little above the crowd of people, and they were coming directly towards you, about a hundred of them. Anyone from that era who knew the workforce would have had little difficulty in identifying just about everyone.

Several things struck Alison as she looked closely at the photograph. Everybody looked older than they probably were, but this did not surprise her; she had once been shown an old photograph of the England football team of 1950 or thereabouts, and had initially wondered why a bunch of middle-aged men had been selected for the national squad.

Some of the men in the Salts Mill photograph looked to be wearing old army battle-dress blouses, but she assumed that may have been common enough so soon after the war. About half of the crowd were women, most of whom were bareheaded; just a few wearing headscarves. Nearly all the men were bare-headed too; she could only spot one flat cap and a couple of trilbies. Nobody looked particularly animated or happy, even though they had finished work for the day. They looked preoccupied with their own thoughts, and only a few of the women seemed to be talking to each other.

"So, which do you think? Which is my father?" the woman said, taking up a position next to the photograph and turning to face Alison. For a second she was like a teacher at the blackboard, ready to fire questions at her class.

"Oh, I'm hopeless at things like this. I'm bound to choose the wrong one," Alison said, peering at the men to see if she could spot one with high cheekbones and slightly slanting eyes, but no luck. "I give up. Tell me."

"There he is," the woman said. "That's my father." No wonder that Alison had been unable to pick out the right man, for the one the woman indicated bore no resemblance to his daughter. Whereas the daughter had a certain elegant poise and fine features, the father was squat and had the rather coarse appearance of a Russian peasant, or some such. Still, perhaps nobody would look their best after a day working in a textile mill in a foreign country – Alison presumed the man was a foreigner. And if he was, God knows what horrid experiences he might have recently suffered during the war and its aftermath.

"And now," the woman said. "Will you allow me to buy you a cup of tea? The café here is quite good."

"That's very kind of you," Alison said, "but I'm afraid I have to go. I've got quite a lot of things to do today." As soon as she had said it Alison could see what a weak excuse this was. Someone with a lot of things to do would hardly be whiling away their time in an art gallery. She knew too that the woman was shrewd enough to have spotted the fib.

"I understand, my dear. Perhaps another time. Do you live locally?"

"Just round the corner, in Caroline Street. I've moved here quite recently," Alison said, giving more information than was necessary in order to compensate for her earlier feeble lie.

"Really? How nice!" the woman said. "I live in George Street, quite close to you, so we are neighbours. May I ask your name?"

In for a penny, thought Alison. "It's Alison, Alison Booth."

"So nice to have met you, Alison," said the woman, taking Alison's hand in hers. "I am Marta. Marta Nowakowski. I do hope that we will meet again soon. I am sure that we will."

"Yes, I hope so," Alison said, not sure if this was strictly true. She reclaimed her hand and started to descend the stairs. When she turned at the next landing she glanced back and saw that Marta was watching her from above. She gave her a little wave and Marta raised her own hand in reply.

Reaching the bottom of the stairs Alison went back through the door into the main gallery. She wanted to have just one last quick look at *My Parents 1977*. It only took a minute. Then, as she started to make her exit, she noticed an old sign fixed high up on the door itself, almost as it were one of the gallery's exhibits, which in a way it was, she thought.

SMOKING IS FORBIDDEN

PATENIE WZBRONIONE

RAUCHEN VERBOTEN

NON FUMARE

By order Salts (Saltaire) Limited

Alison recognised the German and the Italian, but was unsure about the other one. It was likely to be a Slavonic language, she thought, probably Polish. Marta's surname, Nowakowski, sounded as if it might be Polish, so Alison surmised that she and her father, the man in the big photograph, could be Poles, post-war refugees most likely, who had come to England and settled here in Yorkshire. Clearly the mill must have once employed people from all manner of countries.

She went out of the mill into the open air and walked to nearby Victoria Road, Saltaire's principal thoroughfare. Here there were antique shops, vintage clothes shops and tearooms, the things one would expect in a place which wanted to appeal to a certain kind of person – not the theme-park fan, still less the lager and kebab crowd – rather the more discerning visitor, who might appreciate the architecture, history and heritage of a somewhat low-key tourist destination. Few, if any, hen-parties would target Saltaire. Alison was pleased about that.

Instead of going back to her house Alison walked up Victoria Road towards the stone lions *couchant* on their plinths outside the rather grand Victoria Hall, built by Salt as a concert hall, library and community centre, in an attempt to keep his workers away from the temptations of the public house. Not that Alison knew it at the time, but the lions had originally been intended to grace Trafalgar Square, but they were considered to be too small, so Salt got them at a knock-down price. He was a shrewd businessman as well as a great philanthropist.

There was a notice board outside Victoria Hall, giving details of forthcoming events. Alison's eye was drawn to an invitation for people to join a new community choir which was to be based at the hall. Rehearsals were to be every Wednesday evening. She had sung in her school choir, but that was years ago. Was it time to do it again? She was not sure. Just then her mobile phone rang and she took it out of her jacket pocket. It was Ed.

"Hi Ali, how are you? I'm giving you the undoubted honour of receiving a call on this very latest top-of-the-range phone…" For a second or two she wondered if she was the recipient of an unsolicited advert somehow utilising Ed's voice, an impression further enhanced by Ed burbling on at some length about the cutting-edge features of his new toy. Eventually he reverted to his more usual version of English. "I queued nearly all fucking night to get it. I think I was the fifth person to get to the counter when the shop opened this morning. Wow! Anyway, how the fuck are you? Where is it you've gone?"

"Saltaire."

"Salt...what? Never heard of it. Where the fuck is that?"

"Saltaire. It's near Bradford. You've heard of Bradford?"

"Sure I have. Somewhere up near Newcastle, isn't it? So you're up there among the Geordies? Cool."

"Oh yes, very near to Newcastle. Just the odd hundred miles away." Alison knew the sarcasm would be wasted; Ed wouldn't be listening. And indeed for the next few minutes he did all the talking. He gave her minute details of various hip new bars and restaurants he'd recently visited and the amazingly cool people he'd been hanging out with. As he rattled on, each sentence ending on an up note, as if he were asking a series of questions, Alison wondered, not for the first time, what on earth she had ever seen in him. He was the same age as she was, well over thirty, but much of the time he acted and sounded like an overgrown teenager. And so self-obsessed. Eventually he remembered she was there.

"So what the fuck do you do up in Salty whatever-it's-called? Sounds like salt mines, huh? Yeah, you're exiled in Siberia, working in the salt mines, that's it. You must be bored rigid."

"Oh, it's hell, but I manage," Alison said.

"No, but seriously, what is there to do for fun, for fuck's sake?"

"I've joined a choir," Alison replied and she ended the call.

21

CHAPTER THREE

It was true that he had been given a choice. Of sorts. He remembered how he had been standing to attention in the office while the German, Arschloch, lounged behind his desk, smoking a cigarette and trying to look sophisticated.

"My dear chap, of course you have a choice," Arschloch had said. "And there is no need to remain standing. Do please sit." He had sat down on the upright wooden chair that Arschloch languidly pointed to. Arschloch had been doing that stereotypically Teutonic thing of being outwardly courteous and civilized, yet all the while making it clear that if you did not concur with his wishes your life would not be worth living. That's if you still had a life.

"Now, let us just go through it again, to make sure everything is clear, shall we?" Arschloch said pleasantly. "You will have the privilege of married quarters, and the girl Elsa Muller will move in with you. Whether or not you have an intimate relationship with her will be up to you. She is only partly German. Half-Ukrainian, I believe, but she seems sound enough. The important thing is that Kovacs' daughter will live with you, and the pair of you will look after her as if she were your own child. It is not fully clear how important Kovacs was in the Hungarian administration, probably a higher rank than we at first thought, so Budapest (with the full backing of Berlin, unfortunately) has insisted that it is we who must make provision for his orphaned daughter. They don't want her back in Budapest. They seem to think that we were somehow responsible for Kovacs' death, simply because he was staying with us. If I had my way..." He sighed, then leaned forward in his chair and adopted a more official tone. "So that's the arrangement. We were careless enough to let him get killed; consequently we must look after his brat, and nothing more will be said. Ridiculous, I know, but there we are. Do you understand?"

"Yes sir."

"Good. So let us move on. Now that you no longer have a hotel to manage, (and there is no plan to rebuild it), we must find you another job. Obviously the Muller girl will be the one actually looking after Kovacs' child, and you will be the one who has to bring home the bacon to the... family home, let us call it. So, it has been decided that you will take up a position here in the camp. In administration. We know that you ran the hotel efficiently enough, and that in addition to fluent German you obviously speak your own Ukrainian language, and I believe you can understand Polish and Russian. Is that the case?

"Yes sir."

"Good. You will wear the uniform of the Ukrainian Auxiliary Police, and you will have junior officer status. I am aware that you have no military training or experience, but under the circumstances, we shall have to overlook that. Any questions?"

"Yes sir. You did mention a choice."

"I did indeed. You are volunteering to do this important task of your own free will. Nobody is forcing you to do it," Arschloch said, lighting a fresh cigarette from the stub of an almost spent one.

"So is there an alternative?"

"Oh yes, there is always an alternative." Arschloch grinned. "In this case the alternative is that you will be conscripted into the Galicia Division and sent to the front, where you might receive some rudimentary military training before going into combat, but I doubt it. You might even survive for a month or two, but I doubt that too. Understood?"

"Perfectly, sir."

"Excellent. Oh, and one final thing," Arschloch said, with a sneer. "You will have to stop seeing the woman from the village. We know all about it. It would be most inappropriate for you to be carrying on with another woman when you are supposed to be creating a secure, moral home environment for your new… spouse and your adopted daughter…"

Where did these old memories come from? A scene like this, from years ago, would come out of the blue and career through his mind, with every detail as clear as if it had taken place that very morning. And as he got older he found that it was happening more frequently.

When he had first come to England everything about his life had been so confused that the past – even the immediate

24

past – only occasionally impinged on his consciousness. He was a DP, a displaced person, and that described him perfectly, for he was not simply geographically displaced, a refugee from the still-smouldering wreckage of a war-torn Europe. No, his entire mental state was totally displaced too. If the times were indeed out of joint, then so was he. The harshness of his working life in those early years at Salts Mill had, in a perverse way, been a boon, for the deafening racket of hundreds of looms and spinning machines drove everything out of his head, so that by the end of a shift he would trudge away from the mill more like a stunned beast than a thinking and feeling human being.

Not that he would have wanted to stay any longer on the shop floor – good God, no! Those years were behind him. Little by little he'd become a human again. He had to, for his own sanity, and for the sake of his daughter. He had worked like a slave for several years, doing all that was asked of him, and more, so that when the opportunities came for promotion he had grabbed them eagerly. And now, twenty years after starting at Salts he could wear a suit to work instead of overalls, and he worked from an office with a desk and a telephone and a shared secretary, called Katherine Riley. That was who he was going to see now.

He visited Katherine fairly regularly. Not that there was anything of a romantic nature between them, you understand, not so far as he was concerned anyway. He supposed that they were "Just good friends," as the expression goes. Katherine Riley was a widow, though she was only forty. He counted himself as widowed too, so they had that in common, and they both had the burden of loneliness that accompanies the widowed state. Elsa, whom he generally thought of as his wife, had died in 1945, as he had eventually discovered from the Red Cross. That was nearly twenty-five years ago. They had been together for less than a year in the married quarters, close enough to the camp so that he never needed to use his bicycle to get to work.

The quickest way for him to get to Katherine's house near Hirst Lock was to walk the half-mile along the canal towpath, past the bowling-green and the tennis courts and the cricket field and the football pitch. Were these facilities here right from the start, when Saltaire was built? If so, Titus Salt had made damn sure that his workers had plenty of sports to occupy them! No time for the pub! The walk was pleasant enough in summer and in daylight, but it was now November and eight o' clock of a gloomy evening, and there was no lighting on the towpath. It was so dark that he wished he'd had the foresight to bring a torch with him to light his way. Perhaps it might have been more sensible to have gone the longer way, via the road.

Katherine had come to work at Salts in the spring of that year. She was a competent secretary with a pleasant personality, which he considered to be important when you had to work closely with someone every day. She was no beauty, but that was of little consequence to him – he was hardly Paul Newman himself. When he was young his lack of good looks had never seemed to be a hindrance. His friends frequently used to tease him, saying that if an ugly chap like him could have such success with women, it must mean that he had some sort of magic power over them. And it was true that from his youth he had never gone short of sex. But since Elsa he had scarcely been with a woman, and now he sometimes wondered if he would ever again enjoy an intimate relationship.

It had been in June that Katherine had plucked up the courage to invite him to tea at the house near Hirst Lock that she shared with her mother. Although he was aware that there might be a hidden agenda, he had been glad to accept. After that first visit they saw each other socially once a week or so; sometimes they went for a walk or to a pub for a drink, sometimes they just watched television together.

He remembered clearly the fine Saturday morning in late July when he had gone to her house to help her tidy her garden. As the two of them trimmed and weeded in the warm sunshine they had become aware of something happening nearby, so they had stopped their work and had gone to the garden gate. Across the road two young men were posing for photographs next to an open-top red vintage sports car. They were in full morning dress, flowers in their buttonholes, and they were holding grey top hats, so it was clear that one of them was going to be married and the other, the driver of the car, was to be his best man. Some of the other neighbours had come out of their houses and were standing on the pavement to watch as the young men made ready to set off. The two of them were in high spirits, joking with each other about their somewhat comical wedding outfits as they settled into the soft leather seats of the sports car.

"Still time to change your mind," the best man said as he started the motor, and the groom laughed and told him to shut up and drive on. The best man tooted the horn and the sports car roared away. The neighbours gave them a farewell wave before going back into their houses.

He and Katherine returned to their gardening, but now his thoughts were elsewhere. That groom and his best man; they looked so young and innocent. How much did they know of the world? He thought of himself at that age – early twenties – and how devoid of innocence he and so many young men of his generation had been. The world had been too much with them. History and geography could play cruel tricks, he thought. Born in the right country and at the right time and you could enjoy a carefree life, as the young men in the red sports car would no doubt continue to do; born at the wrong time and in the wrong country and your life could be so blighted that you might even envy the dead.

Why was he thinking of that day now? Was it because he was going towards Katherine's house? He was approaching Hirst Lock. God, but it was dark! Next time he would definitely go on the road, or bring a torch with him, like the sensible person who was coming along the towpath towards him. The torchlight was directed down onto the towpath to light the way, then, for a moment it flicked upwards and he had to blink as it shone directly into his face.

"Now then. Be coming on to rain again soon, I think," the man with the torch said, as he drew level.

"Yes, I think it will," he replied. He couldn't see the man at all clearly, nor did he recognise the voice. Neither had he realised that there was a dog there, until he nearly tripped over it, and he heard the animal growl a warning. "Ah, sorry, I didn't see your dog," he said.

"Take no notice of him. He growls at owt. He's harmless. 'Appen lick you to death, but not bite you," said the man. "Have you no torch?"

"No, I left it at home."

"Well, best take care not to fall in the canal. There's a street lamp once you get to the lock."

"Yes, thank you, I know."

"Well, look after thissen. Goodneet," the man said, and he walked on, the torchlight bobbing in front of him.

These days he could understand everything that was said to him in English, even when a speaker used an occasional local dialect word. He'd always had a knack of picking up a language quickly. He'd been brought up on a farm in an area where many people had spoken both Polish and Ukrainian. At school he'd had to learn Russian of course, but his paternal grandmother, who lived with them, spoke only German, so from an early age he could speak that language too.

There had been a terrible famine in Ukraine before the war, but it had not affected their part of the country too badly. Besides, his father had made sure that he was on good terms with the local party secretary, so they had never suffered any real hardship. This party secretary, a Russian, admired his father because he was half-German, so the presumption was that he had some German efficiency and know-how, unlike the others in the district. But the admiration was not reciprocated; in fact his father hated the party secretary, just as he hated all Russians, Stalin most of all. When the Germans arrived in the summer of 1941, it was his father who had directed them to the house in the village where the party secretary was in hiding. German soldiers dragged him into the street and shot him dead. Some of the onlookers applauded, and a woman gave the German officer in charge a bunch of flowers that she'd gathered from her garden.

At that time many Ukrainians had welcomed the Germans with the traditional gifts of bread and salt. They thought the Germans were the liberators who would free them from Stalin's communist regime, and thus enable the creation of a free and independent Ukraine. Some hope! Before many months had passed it was hard to tell who was worse, the Russians or the Germans. But you had to survive, and when the opportunity came for him to work for the Germans he had followed his father's advice and taken what was on offer. What choice did he have?

By then he'd had several years' experience of farm management and that, along with his fluency in several languages, led him to a job as the under-manager of the Hotel Lew, not far from Krakow. Before long, the manager, who was a Pole, was dismissed. He had been in charge of the Hotel Lew right from pre-war times, but it was thought that he might not be suitable once the camp and the barracks had been built nearby. So Petro Semeniuk, aged twenty-two, three-quarters Ukrainian and one quarter German, had become the manager of the Hotel Lew.

It was raining by the time Petro got to Kathleen Riley's house, so there was no question of them venturing out that evening. Anyway, Kathleen had prepared a light supper, especially for him, with some Polish sausage and cheese which she had bought from a delicatessen stall in the market. Her mother had, as usual, retired to bed early; she was virtually bed-ridden these days. They sat in front of the television and ate the food from plates on their knees. A programme started. It was a documentary about the Second World War, perhaps made to commemorate the thirtieth anniversary of the start of the conflict, though it seemed to Petro that the British were always making documentaries about the war, whether there was an anniversary or not. They seemed obsessed by it, whereas people in most other countries were trying their best to forget it.

Tactful as ever, Kathleen suggested that they could watch a programme on the other channel, but Petro said he was fine watching the documentary. As was usual with such programmes, the focus was almost all on Britain's involvement – Churchill, Dunkirk, the Blitz, the Battle of Britain – and there was hardly any mention at all of events in Eastern Europe.

"Do you have any strong memories of the war, Kathleen?" he asked, when the programme had finished.

"I was at school most of the time," she replied. "I can remember rationing and shortages, but not much more. We lived in Bradford then. I don't think we had many air raids, not like London and Coventry. It must have been much harder for you in Poland. Was it?"

He had never disabused anyone who mistakenly thought he was Polish. In the immediate aftermath of the war, when he had first come to England, he'd thought that people would be more sympathetic to a Pole than a Ukrainian – in those very early post-war years he'd even carried Polish identity papers, taken from one of the bodies he'd come across during that dreadful time. He soon discovered, however, that the English made no distinction whatsoever between people from Poland, Ukraine, Latvia, Estonia, or anywhere else in Eastern Europe – they were all just "foreigners," and some English people were none too keen on any of them.

"I was lucky enough to escape the worst," he said. He knew this reply would be sufficient. Kathleen was an intelligent woman and she would be sensitive enough not to dig for any further details. "Polish people did feel quite let down in 1939, though," he continued. "As it said in the programme, Britain went to war specifically because the Germans had invaded Poland. So the Poles gave three cheers. I think they fully expected the Royal Navy to steam up the Baltic and rescue them. No such luck! The British did absolutely nothing." .

"I'm sorry about that," Kathleen said.

"Hardly your fault, you were just a schoolgirl in Bradford."

"Still…" she said.

The two of them watched part of another television programme, and then Petro helped Kathleen to wash up. It had stopped raining when the time came for him to leave, a little after ten-thirty, but Kathleen insisted that he take an umbrella with him, just in case. When he said that he was going to return home via the canal towpath she tried to dissuade him, but finding that he was adamant, she rummaged in a kitchen drawer until she found a torch for him. On the doorstep, rather to his surprise, she kissed him lightly on the cheek, saying that she would see him in the office the next day.

Now that the rain had stopped the sky was a little clearer as Petro walked away from Kathleen's house towards the solitary lamp post at Hirst Lock. Once there, he crossed the footbridge over the canal and started to walk along the towpath. The lights of Saltaire were ahead of him, about a ten-minute walk away. He didn't think that he needed the torch, but he switched it on anyway. As far as he could tell he was alone on the towpath; no solitary dog-walkers this time.

He must have gone less than fifty metres towards Saltaire, and would have been just at the point where a row of ash and sycamore trees stands between the towpath and the football pitch. He would no doubt have been completely unaware of what hit him so hard on the back of his skull, and he would have been dead by the time that his body was pushed into the canal. He wouldn't have heard the splash.

CHAPTER FOUR

A lison had been delayed in Leeds. There had been an issue with a client, and it had taken a good deal of her diplomatic skill and trouble-shooting experience to work things towards a satisfactory conclusion. The upshot was that she'd had to take a later train than usual, and then she'd had to run the short distance between Saltaire station and Victoria Hall. Alison hated being late for anything, but she needn't have worried. People were still filing into the large rehearsal room in the basement of the hall, even though it was a few minutes after the scheduled start-time of 7:30 pm.

A little out of breath she entered the room and joined the crowd of people who were milling around several rows of chairs facing a piano. At times like these it is always nice to spot a familiar face and have a friend to sit next to, she thought, but she could hardly expect that. Then, as she hesitated over where best to sit, she became aware of a woman seated on the far side of the room who seemed to be waving in her direction. Was the wave meant for her or for someone else? Alison wasn't sure. Now the woman was waving both hands in the air in a beckoning motion, rather like someone helping a driver to reverse a car into a tight space. Alison suddenly realised that it was the woman who'd spoken to her earlier that month in Salts Mill, the one who'd shown her the big old photograph with her father in the crowd of workers. What was her name? Maria? No. Now she remembered that it was Marta, Marta-something-or-other-in-Polish.

Well, she wasn't necessarily the person whom Alison would have ideally chosen to join, but any port in a storm, she thought. Then she mentally upbraided herself for her lack of charity – the woman was only trying to be friendly, for goodness sake. So she smiled and waved back, and Marta indicated that there was a seat free next to her. Alison crossed the room, still smiling, and held out her hand, but to her surprise, instead of accepting the proffered handshake Marta rose from her chair, gripped Alison's two arms rather firmly above the elbow and planted kisses on both her cheeks.

"How very nice to see you, my dear," she said, and Alison caught the hint of an expensive perfume. Marta released her hold. "I wondered when I might see you again."

"Hello Marta," said Alison. "How are you?"

"I am fine," Marta replied. "So, I see you are a music lover as well as being an art expert?"

"I'm hardly a …" Alison began, but the choirmaster had now clapped his hands to bring the meeting to order, and there was soon a silence in the room, as the members of the newly-formed Titus Salt Community Choir settled down and waited for their inaugural rehearsal to get under way.

"The thing I want to stress," the choirmaster said, "is that this is a community choir, open to anyone who wants to come along and sing. You don't have to have been in a choir in the past, and you certainly don't have to have had singing lessons or anything like that. Even if the only singing you've ever done has been in the bath, that will be fine. I know that some of you may be anxious because you can't read music. Don't worry about that. It's my belief that everyone can read music; it's just that some people have had more practice at it than others. Even if you've never done it, you'll find that you'll quickly pick up the basics, and that's all you'll need. Can I say as well how encouraging it is to see so many of you? We've had to get some extra chairs from the room next door, though I have to say that you won't be sitting down much once we get started. In this first session I'll introduce you to some exercises to get us going, then we'll sing a couple of songs that I'm sure you'll know. (Have they all got the words and music packs, Arthur? Good man.) We won't be dividing you up into tenors, sopranos, or whatever tonight, that'll come next week probably. Righto, if there are no questions, let's stand up and have some fun…"

After an hour of breathing drills and singing exercises, culminating in an attempt at a sea-shanty, there was a short break. Marta had come well-prepared, and she opened her bag and took out a bottle of spring water which she offered to Alison, who shook her head.

"No thanks," she said.

"It's not been opened," said Marta. "You should always have water with you when you are singing."

"I know," said Alison. "I should have brought some. It's just that I had to work late, so I didn't have time to get any. I haven't been home yet. I came here straight from the train."

"I see," Marta said. "Well, the water is there if you wish it. And do tell me, what is this work that you do, which keeps you so late?"

"I work for a design consultancy in Leeds."

"Ah, design. So, you are an art expert after all."

"Not really," said Alison.

"Oh yes, all design is art…"

"And all art is design. Yes, I've heard that too," was Alison's reply.

"Very good," said Marta. "And very true, I think. So, what area of design?" she asked.

"Some of it is graphic design, but I work mainly as a consultant, not much hands-on stuff these days. It's a bit difficult to expl…" Here she was interrupted once more by the choirmaster who was keen to bring his fledgling choir members to order and commence the second half of the rehearsal.

An hour later the rehearsal was at an end. Alison was about to leave and go home, but Marta was not going to let her escape so easily.

"You have not had time to eat anything, Alison. It would be wrong of me not to invite you back to my house for supper."

"Oh, Marta, that is very kind of you, but I don't want to put you to any trouble. I'll be fine, really," Alison said.

"But I insist," said Marta. "It may only be a sandwich, or some such, but I would like you to come. Do say that you will." It seemed churlish to turn down an invitation from Marta yet again, so Alison accepted, promising herself that she would not stay long.

It only took a few minutes for them to walk to Marta's house in George Street. The first thing which Alison noticed was that the house was larger than her own, and when she mentioned this, as they took off their coats, Marta informed her that the houses in Saltaire had been built in accordance with the mill's hierarchy, so overlookers had larger houses than ordinary mill-hands, departmental managers had larger houses still, and so on.

"So you lived in this house because your father was a cut above the normal shop-floor workers?" Alison said, and Marta laughed.

"No, no, it wasn't like that when we came to live here," she said. "By then the houses no longer belonged to the mill; anyone was free to buy or rent one. Though you are correct in a sense, because my father was a manager at the mill – oh, not straight away, of course. He spent years working very hard before he got any promotion. He went, at his own expense, to evening classes at Bradford Technical College to learn all he could about the textile industry, and he learned to speak fluent English too, of course, otherwise he would never have made any progress. At first we lived in a much smaller house in Mary Street, then we came here. Saltaire wasn't at all like it is now. All the buildings were soot-blackened and looked dingy. It certainly wasn't viewed as a fashionable place to live, my God no. Nobody considered it to be anything special at all. When the mill closed down there were even plans to demolish everything."

"I'm glad they didn't," Alison said, following Marta into the main part of the house.

In the lounge Alison noted the quality of the furniture – solid, traditional pieces in polished dark wood. She could see that the chairs, carpet and curtains, though old, were expensive and had been carefully chosen. On the walls were several paintings, mainly water colours with one or two oils, nearly all of them landscapes. Everything about the room had an air of genteel good taste, though slightly old-fashioned. And there was also an indefinable Continental feel about it.

"What a lovely room," Alison said.

"Thank you. I thought you would be a person who would appreciate it. Yes, it is very nice now, but it took some time to gather what is here. Many years in fact. My father and I came to England with nothing."

"So, did you live here in Saltaire from the start?" asked Alison, once the two of them were seated. "After you came to England?"

"No, when we first arrived – as refugees – they housed us in a disused army camp near Reading. I can just remember that, but how we got to England, I cannot recall at all. One thing I can remember clearly is my father telling me that we must always tell people that we were Polish… and not what we actually were…"

"So you are not Polish? Originally, I mean," said Alison. Marta did not answer her. Instead she got up and said she would go and prepare the supper. She waved away Alison's offer of assistance, and told her to relax and make herself at home.

Left alone, Alison took the opportunity to look more closely at the pictures on the wall. They were well-executed, and they certainly complemented the room very well. However, Alison thought them somewhat bland; she preferred stronger, more assertive works of art, but she appreciated that such pieces would have been out of place here.

On an oak sideboard, in delicate silver frames, were three photographs. None of them were recent; the first was of a young, and very striking Marta in an academic gown, a diploma held in her hand. There was a college crest at the bottom of the photograph, and a date: 1965. Next to it was another photograph of Marta, standing next to a man whom Alison recognised from the giant photograph in Salts Mill. Here were father and daughter together, he in a dark suit, a flower in his buttonhole, she, very beautiful with her blonde hair cut in the fashion of the mid-1960s. She had a small bouquet in her hand. Was it a wedding photograph? Was Marta the bride? If so, Marta must have married about the same time as she had graduated. Alison wondered where the groom might be.

Alison could feel her curiosity about Marta beginning to grow now. Until now she had regarded her merely as an elderly woman who was a bit lonely, someone in need of company, a nice enough person, but a bit tedious and odd.

Now her feelings towards Marta were subtly changing. Marta was not the kind of person that she and her London friends would ever have bothered with, even if they'd come across her by chance. Ed would laugh out loud, Alison thought, if he could see her now, about to have supper with someone like Marta.

There was a third photograph on the sideboard, a faded and creased black and white shot of three people standing together in a garden. Alison picked it up so that she could study it more closely. Marta's father, though much younger, was nonetheless clearly recognisable, only this time, instead of a dark suit he was wearing some kind of military uniform. There was a little blonde girl who could well have been Marta; yes, you could see by the shape of the face that it was her, the slightly slanting eyes, the intense way in which she was looking directly at the camera. The third person was a young woman, quite pretty in a way, but a bit bovine, thought Alison. She was wearing a plain knee-length dress with a belt, shoes with low stubby heels and ankle socks. Surely this couldn't be Marta's mother, could it? She looked far too young, no more than seventeen at the most. Perhaps it was Marta's elder sister, though she looked nothing like Marta. Still, neither did Marta's father. Alison guessed that, unlike the other two photographs, this one had not been taken in England.

Realising that Marta was re-entering the room, Alison put the photograph down and pretended to be looking at one of the watercolours.

"Here we are," said Marta, and she turned and went back into the kitchen "I'll just go and fetch the rest. Do sit down."

Alison did as she was told, and soon the coffee table in front of her was laden with plates of food – carefully cut smoked ham sandwiches, a tomato salad, a bowl of gherkins and a plate of small chocolate cakes.

"Would you like a glass of wine, perhaps? Or just coffee?"

"Oh, coffee would be fine," Alison said.

For a time they were both silent, occupied with the food and drink, but after an interval, Marta asked, "Were you looking at the photographs when I came in?"

"I was," confessed Alison. "I could recognise you in all three of them. And your father too. Was he in the army at one time? I noticed he was in uniform."

"Something like that," said Marta after a pause, during which Alison was aware again of Marta's direct and intense gaze.

"And the young woman with you and your father. Is that your sister? Surely not your mother," Alison said.

"Oh, that silly old photograph is from ages ago. I'd forgotten all about it until I found it in a drawer. I don't know why I keep it," Marta said irritably. Alison could tell that she was no longer comfortable discussing the photographs. She wanted to brush something away – something which was perhaps more significant than she was going to admit. Quite abruptly she changed the subject. "Now, you tell me something about yourself. That will be much more interesting," she said.

"Well, what would you like to know?" Alison said.

"Well, for example, do you have a husband, or a partner? Any children? Why have you come to live in Saltaire?" Although she was a little disconcerted by Marta's inquisitorial manner, and although she had always viewed herself as a private person, Alison decided it would be all right on this occasion to talk about her personal life. She didn't need to go into all the gory details, such as being brought up by parents who never showed much affection, either to her or to each other.

"Well, let's see. I am thirty-five years old. I was married once, soon after I left university, but it didn't work out, so we separated and divorced after a few years. I have no children (she wasn't going to mention the abortion). I've had several relationships since my divorce, but none which have lasted very long (and some have been downright disastrous, she thought, or just plain idiotic, like her recent episode with Ed). So, right now I'm unattached and I have to say that it suits me fine."

"And is it your job in Leeds that has brought you here?" asked Marta. "I can tell that you are like me; your roots are elsewhere."

"That's right," Alison said. "I was born and brought up in London. In Sutton, a London suburb really. I went to university in London and until this year that's where I lived and worked."

"In Sutton?"

"No, in various places in London. Islington was the last place where I worked."

"So why uproot yourself and come to Yorkshire? Did you lose your job?"

"No, it wasn't like that," said Alison, smiling. "I think it was just that I wanted a change, to see something of the world beyond London. I did consider moving abroad, America maybe, but I decided against it. I think I still need to be reasonably near to London. I'm pretty sure I'll eventually move back there."

"I hope you don't move back too quickly, just when we are becoming friends. Do you like living here?"

"Yes, I think so," Alison said. "Certainly more than I expected to. The job in Leeds is fine, and I like living here in Saltaire, even though it still feels a bit strange. I'm still an outsider, I suppose."

"Aren't we all?" said Marta, and once again she gave Alison that direct and rather disconcerting look. Then, after a few seconds, almost as if she was shaking herself out of a reverie, she became more animated. "Have you had enough to eat? More coffee perhaps?"

"No thank you. More coffee would just keep me awake tonight. And the food was delicious. Thank you very much. Actually, I think I'd better be heading home now. Do you want me to help you clear these things away?"

"Certainly not, I won't hear of it. And if you are really sure that it's time for you to go, I will get your coat."

As she was getting ready to leave Alison said, "You have some very fine pictures. I don't often go for water-colours, but these I do like, especially this one," and she pointed to a small painting of a wide flat meadow, full of colourful spring flowers. "Who is the artist?"

"I painted it myself, many years ago," Marta said softly.

"Really? So are all the paintings…?"

"No, my father bought the oils. That was the medium he particularly liked, though he was never what you would call a connoisseur. I painted the water-colours; that was my particular enthusiasm at one time," Marta said. They walked together to the front door and Marta took Alison's hand. "I do hope we will see each other again soon, Alison."

"So do I. I've had a lovely time. Thank you, Marta."

"No. It is I who should thank you," Marta said.

A few minutes later Alison was walking down George Street, back to her own house in Caroline Street. It had been an interesting day, she thought. She was pleased that she'd sorted out the tricky problem at work; that would be bound to earn her some brownie points. She'd initially been unsure about joining the choir, but it had turned out to be really enjoyable, so there would be no question of not continuing with it. And then there was Marta. Alison had found herself becoming more intrigued by her the longer that the George Street visit had continued. She was certainly looking forward to seeing Marta again.

CHAPTER FIVE

She did not have long to wait. The following Saturday was one of those particularly fine days which sometimes occur in late autumn. There had been a hint of frost in the early morning, but soon after breakfast-time the sun was shining from a clear sky, and there was scarcely a breath of wind. After a cup of coffee and a quick glance at the morning paper, Alison put on her coat, wrapped a woollen scarf around her neck and set off for a walk.

She went over the footbridge at the bottom of Victoria Road and into Roberts Park. Then, following the path which led past the cricket field, she went through a gate and walked across a meadow to reach the riverside at Hirst Weir. There had been a good deal of rain earlier in the week, so the Aire was flowing strongly over the weir, but further on the waters were calmer. Alison followed the path past the rowing club boathouse and entered an area of woodland where oaks and willows fringed the river. Because of the recent rain the path was muddy, but Alison had anticipated this and was wearing her festival wellies, originally bought for Glastonbury a few years earlier.

An elderly man with a liver-coloured dog on a lead passed her and bade her good-morning in a surprisingly posh accent. A minute later, a much younger man in running gear, his legs spattered with mud, overtook her. He said nothing. A boat headed downstream towards the boathouse, the two oarsmen rowing smoothly and efficiently in unison.

The Aire here flows very close to the canal, which is raised on an embankment, and at Dowley Gap, where there is a loop in the river, the canal is carried over it on an aqueduct. Here it was possible for Alison to mount a few steps, cross a stile and gain the canal towpath so that she could walk the half-mile or so back to her house. The woods, the river, the canal and the autumn sunshine made the morning very pleasant and Alison felt exhilarated. And when, after a quarter of an hour, she arrived at Hirst Lock she felt even better, for sitting on a bench next to the lock was Marta Nowakowski, her new friend. Marta had something in her hand – a letter, or some such – which she was perusing quite intently.

It was only when Alison approached her and said, "Hi Marta," that she noticed the rather sad expression on the older woman's face.

"Oh, it's you, Alison," Marta said, her face rapidly brightening now. "How nice to see you. What a lovely day, isn't it?"

"Yes, it is," Alison replied. "Are you all right, Marta?"

"Yes, yes, I'm perfectly fine, thank you."

"Not thinking of chucking yourself into the canal, then? You did look a bit glum just now."

"No, no, I'm not glum. I'm just having a few private thoughts. Nothing important." She stood up from the bench, and Alison noticed that she almost furtively slipped whatever she'd been looking at into her coat pocket. "Have you been for a walk? Are you on your way home?" she said.

"Yes," Alison said, "I've been doing a small circuit, the path along the riverbank, then back home this way, along the towpath. The woods are lovely"

"Yes, this stretch of the towpath is always popular with people, especially if the weather is nice," Marta said, then. "Look out! Be careful!" But Alison had already heard the bicycle bell and she stepped quickly to one side just in time to allow a cyclist, lycra-clad and wearing a helmet, to pedal past. "They should slow down when there are people on foot," Marta said crossly, then, "May I walk back with you?"

"Of course," Alison replied, and they started to walk together. "Is this one of your regular walks, Marta?"

"No, I don't come this way very often at all. Just as far as the lock. This time of year usually…" She broke off. Alison could sense that Marta might have wanted to say more, but for some reason it wasn't easy for her to continue. A minute or so passed before she spoke again, and her voice this time was softer, and it was shaking just a little: "This part of the canal, near the lock, has some… oh, it's silly things. Perhaps sometime, when we know each other better, I will tell you, but not now. Is that rude of me? Impolite?"

"Not at all," Alison said. "You mustn't feel obliged to speak if you don't want to. And, like you say, we are only at the start of our friendship, so hopefully there'll be time enough if you ever want to tell me about…" Alison stopped in mid-sentence because Marta had ceased walking and had turned to face her. She took Alison's hand in a firm grip, and the expression on her face was one that perplexed Alison. Was Marta about to cry? For a moment it looked as if she might.

"Alison," Marta said, after a pause, "I am so pleased that you said that; that you wish to be my friend. That means so much, you can't imagine."

"I do want to be your friend, and to prove it, I'm going to repay a bit of your hospitality," said Alison, trying her best to sound bright and cheerful. "Have you had any breakfast?"

"Just a cup of tea."

"In that case you must let me treat you. We can go to one of the cafes in Victoria Road. I'd ask you back to my place, but I've been in such a rush at work this week, the house is in a mess and I've scarcely anything in the fridge. I'm going to clean and shop later today," Alison said. "So, how about it?"

"How nice! That would be lovely," Marta said, and she beamed at Alison. Then she linked arms with her, and the pair of them walked along the towpath towards Saltaire, all traces of sadness now gone from Marta's face.

They chose a café almost opposite Victoria Hall. In addition to food and drink there was, in the window and on the walls, a selection of paintings for sale by local artists. These were mainly scenes of Saltaire itself, or various other places in Yorkshire. Some were better than others, Alison thought.

"Am I a suspect?"

"You have to understand that in a case like this, we have to talk to everyone that's been connected with the victim in any way. That means workmates, friends, family members, and so on. It's a routine we have to go through." The plain-clothes policeman looked to be in his late twenties, about the same age as the man he was interviewing, but it was clear that he was trying hard to play the part of someone older and tougher – the seasoned, experienced copper who'd seen it all before and had an impressive record of convictions under his belt. Just then a uniformed constable popped his head round the door and completely demolished the illusion.

"Pot of tea if you want one, Gerald," the constable said. He had a slight speech impediment.

"No thanks, I've still got some left here. Maybe later. You might nip out and get me some fags, though. Twenty Players – tipped, not plain. I'll settle up with you later," Gerald said.

"Righto." The constable withdrew and the door was closed.

"Now, where were we?" Gerald asked.

"You were telling me that I wasn't a suspect, or that's what I thought you were saying," said the man on the other side of the interview table. Gerald looked at him carefully before continuing.

"At this stage," he said, "it's important to eliminate from our enquiries…"

"Ah, so I'm helping the police with their enquiries. That's what you call it when you've got a suspect, isn't it?" The man was getting heated, a touch aggressive even, thought Gerald. He decided to change tack.

"Look. A tragedy like this is particularly hard for close relatives, I understand that. And it's bound to be upsetting for you to have to go through an interview with the police so soon, but you've got to understand that if we are going to catch whoever did this to your father-in-law, then there are certain procedures that have to be gone through. Okay?"

"I'm sorry," said the man, less aggressive now. "It's just all so upsetting. We are in shock. My wife is particularly…" He broke off and rubbed both his hands slowly across the top of his head several times, before taking a deep breath in an attempt to compose himself.

"Do you want to take a break?" asked Gerald. "Or I can get you another cup of tea, if that's what you want."

"Is there any chance of another smoke?" said the man, and Gerald pushed the packet of Players towards him, noticing that there were only four cigarettes left. The man took one and Gerald reached across the table to light it for him. "I'll do my best to answer everything you ask," he said, after drawing on the cigarette a few times so as to calm himself.

"Good," Gerald said. "Now Jan, what I've got so far is that the deceased, Petro Semeniuk, was your father-in-law, and that you both lived at the same address in George Street, yes?"

"Yes," Jan said.

"How long have you lived there?"

"My wife and her father have lived there since the late fifties, I believe," Jan replied.

"And you?"

"I moved in after Marta and I got married. That was the summer of 1965, just after she'd finished at college."

"She'd just finished college, I see," Gerald said, making a note of this on the sheet of paper in front of him.

"Yes, she trained as a teacher at the college in Bingley."

"Oh yes? So the three of you lived in the same house?"

"Yes. At first it was meant to be just a stop-gap, till we could afford a place of our own, but it went on longer than we expected," Jan said.

"Nearly five years," Gerald said, consulting his notes. "Why was that, do you think? Not enough money saved up, or what?"

"We'd saved enough. That wasn't why we didn't move out."

"So?" Gerald said.

"Well, I suppose it was Petro, really. He was very protective of Marta. He always had been. They'd come to England after the war, just the two of them. Her mother was dead, so Petro had to be both father and mother to her, I always thought."

"Did he ever say that he didn't want her to move out and set up house with you?" Gerald asked.

"Not as such, but you could tell. It had been the same with her college course. She could have studied fine art at the Royal Acacdemy, or somewhere like that. She had the talent and the qualifications from school –she was at St Joseph's in Bradford – but instead she went to Bingley College, just down the road. That was so she could live at home with her father in George Street. Don't get me wrong, he would have let her leave home if she'd insisted, but she knew that it wasn't what he wanted. He always wanted her to be with him. And she always wanted to please him"

"But he didn't object to her marrying you?"

"Not at all," Jan said.

"And you knew him from Salts Mill?" Gerald said.

"That's right. He'd been there from soon after the war. He started at the bottom and worked his way up the ladder – he was a clever chap in lots of ways. Salts was where I got to know him. I'm a maintenance engineer. I look after the machinery, do repairs if anything breaks down, that kind of thing." He took a drag on his cigarette before continuing. "We got to be friendly through working at Salts together."

"And of course you were both Polish, so that must have helped," Gerald said.

"Well, in fact I was born in England and he wasn't really Polish anyway. He was Ukrainian, but he didn't always let on that he was. He spoke good Polish, but you can tell by his name he is – was – Ukrainian. The English bosses at Salts couldn't care less what he was. He could have been an Eskimo, for all they cared, so long as he did a good job for them. Which he did," Jan said.

"And was it through him that you met your wife?" Gerald asked.

"Yes. Marta told me he'd never approved of her having a boyfriend before, but for some reason it was different with me. He took a shine to me. When I think about it, he was really keen for us to get together. And he was so happy when we said we wanted to get married."

"Bit of a match-maker then, was he?" Gerald said, and he was gratified to see that Jan was now relaxed enough to allow a brief smile to cross his face.

"I suppose he was, yes."

———

Although Alison had gently probed her during their breakfast together at the café in Victoria Road, Marta hadn't given very much away about herself. Using the pictures on the café wall as some kind of way in, Alison had managed, without being too nosey she hoped, to get Marta to talk a bit about her working life. It transpired that she had taught art in local schools, though she had rarely found it as fulfilling as she wanted; she had always felt that she should really have been lecturing at an art college whilst developing her own career as an artist. She had retired from teaching at the turn of the millennium, and at first she had intended to spend her increased leisure time painting, but this had not happened, why she could not say. Other than this, she revealed little, and soon Alison felt ready to depart and do her shopping.

The cafe proprietor, a chatty woman, came to their table for Alison to pay the bill. After the card machine had done its work she began to tell them about a brand new bistro which was due to open on Gordon Terrace. She was acquainted with the owner, who had a good reputation as a chef, and she suggested that Alison and Marta should give it a try. Marta said this puzzled her – why was she putting in a good word for a competitor? But the cafe proprietor said it wasn't like that; hers was a daytime café – breakfasts, soups and sandwiches for lunch, whereas the new bistro, (apparently to be called *Freddy's,* after the owner), would cater more for those who wished to dine in the evenings. The menu, already posted on a website, looked very interesting, she said.

———

The uniformed constable duly delivered a fresh packet of Players tipped, and Gerald immediately ripped off the cellophane, took a cigarette out and lit it. As an afterthought he offered one to Jan, who shook his head.

"So you got on well with your father-in-law?" Gerald said.

"By and large, yes."

"No recent rows?"

"No."

"So everything was hunky-dory at home?" Gerald said and Jan just nodded rather than saying anything. "Can you think of anyone who might have wanted to harm him? Did he have any enemies at all?" Gerald asked, taking care not to blow smoke into Jan's face.

"None that I know of," Jan said, and he shifted about on his chair a little.

"You say that he didn't always let on he was a Ukrainian. Why was that?

"I think it went back to the war," Jan replied.

"Oh yes?" Gerald said, waiting for Jan to say more. Jan asked if he could have a cigarette now, and when it was lit he smoked in silence for half a minute before continuing.

"The Poles and Ukrainians didn't get on. The only people the Ukrainians hated more were the Russians – not counting the Jews, of course; everyone hated them."

"Oh, very nice," Gerald said, sardonically. "And why didn't they get on? The Poles and the Ukrainians, I mean."

"They never had done. Then, in the war, some Ukrainians sided with the Germans."

"Really?" Gerald said. "Well, I never knew that."

He was aware that Jan Nowakowski was not completely at ease with this line of questioning, but he doubted if that meant very much. He decided that there was little point in pursuing the ins and outs of these old tribal feuds. The war had been over for more than twenty years, and Petro Semeniuk had been living in Saltaire for most of that time. If anyone had wanted to do him in just because they didn't like Ukrainians, why wait till now? Jan Nowakowski was not the murderer, Gerald was pretty sure of that. He was a friend of the murdered man and married to his daughter. All of them had apparently lived together in blissful domestic harmony for several years. So what would have been Jan's motive? Gerald couldn't think of one. No, he wasn't the one. No need to pass him on to one of his superiors for a more in-depth interview. All that remained was to make a note of Jan Nowakowski's movements on the night in question, then he would let him go home to comfort his distraught wife. And maybe I can go home too, Gerald thought, and he yawned.

"Just for the record, can you tell me again where you were that night?" he said.

"I was out drinking with a couple of friends," Jan said.

"Drinking where, exactly?" Gerald asked.

"In Bradford. One or two pints in the Royal Standard, then one or two more in the Belle Vue Hotel. One of my mates wanted to see the stripper."

"Oh yes? Any good?" Gerald asked.

"Terrible. I don't really care for that kind of thing anyway," Jan said.

"What time did you come home?"

"My friends dropped me off about ten o'clock. We usually stay out later, but I was ready for bed. They went on to a pub in Bingley, I think"

"And you went straight into the house? You didn't perhaps go for a stroll up the canal?" Gerald said, yawning again.

"At that time of night? You're joking. Anyway, it was raining."

"And your wife, was she still up when you got in?" Gerald asked.

"No, she was asleep in bed. She goes to bed quite early during the week," Jan said. Gerald stubbed his cigarette out in the cheap blue saucer which did duty as an ash tray in the interview room.

Soon afterwards Jan Nowakowski was allowed to go home, and Detective Constable Gerald Cranley got his interview notes together and took them to his desk in the CID room. As the most recently-appointed detective in the Shipley Division of the West Riding Constabulary, he had, of course, inherited the oldest, most battered typewriter in the station, and with this he spent most of the next hour typing up the report of his interview with Jan. He typed quite well for a man, he thought, so long as he didn't try to smoke at the same time.

When he'd finished and checked his work, he sat back and closed his eyes for a minute or two. Interesting the odd things that you learn in this job, he mused. He'd never realised that there had been any animosity between Poles and Ukrainians in the war, or that some of the latter had sided with the Germans. He'd always assumed that the war had been a straightforward ding-dong between Krauts and Japs on one side, and us and the Yanks on the other. That's what you get from reading too many comics and watching old war films, he thought. (*"Donner und Blitzen, … Englander Schweinhund, … Wizard prang, Biggles, old chap …"*)

After he'd deposited the three copies of his report in the appropriate pigeon holes, Gerald went into the cloakroom and opened his locker. It was only when he was getting into his overcoat, and ready for a smoke, that he realised he didn't have his cigarettes. Surely Jan Nowakowski hadn't pinched his packet of Players! No, they must still be in the interview room. He walked down the corridor and through the door. What a relief! The packet of cigarettes was still where they'd been left on the table. Gerald had known all along that Jan Nowakowski was a decent, honest man, and this proved it beyond a doubt. He took a cigarette and lit it, before putting the packet safely into his overcoat pocket. He glanced down at the saucer and noted that it was chock-full of tab-ends. He really must cut down, he told himself.

CHAPTER SIX

The opening night at *Freddy's* went quite well. Fred Nicholson was aware that it was never going to be launched with the same razzmatazz that he might have anticipated had the restaurant been in, say, London. Fred knew that nobody in Yorkshire was going to queue round the block for a table, merely because they had been informed via social media that everyone else was intending to queue round the block for a table. Fred had worked in London. He knew the restaurant scene there. He knew that you could often sell people appallingly bad meals at eye-watering prices, provided that your customers believed they were dining in the latest trend-setting joint.

Here things were different. The pace of life was more measured, and some traditional values still prevailed. So Fred knew that while an attractive décor and an interesting ambience were not to be neglected, his clientele would be more impressed by quality cooking, and service which was efficient and friendly without being too intrusive. He had interviewed the staff with great care and was confident that he had a good team.

He had been very careful with the menu too. There was nothing too exotic – no nonsense with foam or edible soil – rather an emphasis on well-prepared dishes, including some traditional favourites from France and Italy. Fred had some experience of working in restaurants in both of those countries. And there was not so much as a gesture towards the cuisine of the Indian sub-continent. Fred was shrewd enough to realise that, with central Bradford a mere three miles away, it would be foolish to try and compete with the city's numerous well-established Asian restaurants. A review in that weekend's edition of the *Yorkshire Post* had pleased him, especially as the reviewer made favourable comparisons between *Freddy's* and a couple of well-regarded restaurants in Harrogate and Ilkley.

It was a week or so later that Alison first ate at *Freddy's*. She had asked Marta if she wanted to accompany her, but the older woman had declined the invitation, saying that her digestion was not really up to late evening meals in restaurants these days. So, rather than go on her own, Alison had asked a work-colleague, Rachel, to join her. Rachel had only recently broken up with her boyfriend, and consequently she was often at a loose end in the evening. She had readily agreed to go with Alison and see what *Freddy's* had to offer.

Although the restaurant was a pleasant venue and the food was certainly as good as the *Yorkshire Post* review had said it was, Alison found that her choice of company for the evening was something of an error. She soon discovered that Rachel, whom in truth she scarcely knew, only wanted to talk (at great length) about herself, and especially about her recent break-up from a man whom she could now see was nothing other than a sex-obsessed beast who drank too much and took no real interest in her at all. She had grown to hate him and never wanted to see him again. After a while Alison found herself inwardly sympathising with the boyfriend, who had apparently cleared off and gone to live in Scotland. It seemed that the last straw for Rachel had been when, at the height of a particularly heated row, the boyfriend had swept her precious family of fluffy animals off the dressing-table and into a nearby bin; she could never forgive him for that.

Alison was relieved when, at the end of the meal, Rachel summoned a waiter and told him to call her a taxi to take her back to Guiseley. That was where her parents lived, and after the break-up she had moved back in with them. Lucky old parents, Alison thought.

With Rachel gone, Alison poured herself another glass of wine. For the first time that evening she felt comfortable. No need for her to leave just yet. For a second she thought how nice it would be to enjoy a cigarette, but the desire quickly passed. While she was still thinking about the evening and how totally tedious Rachel had been as a dinner companion, Fred Nicholson came over to her table, introduced himself as the owner of the restaurant and asked if she had enjoyed her meal. It was late in the evening by now, and the number of diners in the restaurant was thinning out. Alison had noticed Fred earlier. Sometimes he was working behind the bar, sometimes he was having a brief word with his staff, or he was greeting new customers and leading them to their tables – all done with the kind of unhurried, professional aplomb which Alison could admire.

"Thank you," she said. "The meal was excellent. I enjoyed it very much."

"And your friend? Did she find everything satisfactory?" Fred asked.

"I'm sure she did," Alison said, unable to prevent a wry smile.

"But she had to leave. What a pity!" Fred said. Then after a pause, and because he had seen Alison's ambivalent smile, he added: "Or was it?"

"What makes you say that?" she said.

"Do forgive me if I am speaking out of turn, but I could see that you were not totally happy with your friend's company tonight. Am I right?"

"Perhaps," Alison said, cautiously. "I'd hardly call her a friend. I don't really know her at all. She's someone I work with."

"Ah, so this was business rather than pleasure?"

"No, no. It was meant to be pleasure. It just didn't turn out that way." She took a swig of her wine.

There were two courses of action open to her now; either she could say nothing more, and Fred would be obliged to go and play mine host at another table, or she could add some words of explanation, which would probably mean he would stay and chat some more. Another swig of wine and she had decided.

"If you want to know the truth I've rarely spent an evening with someone who was so totally wrapped up in themselves," she said, shaking her head and smiling, as if to imply that, with Rachel gone, she could now regard it all as

63

an amusing episode. "I'm afraid that it was all me, me, me. I doubt if I said more than a dozen words. All I had to do was to keep on nodding." Alison was aware that the wine was loosening her tongue now. Normally she wouldn't have spoken like this about a companion, not even one as annoying as Rachel, and certainly not to someone working in a restaurant who had simply come to ask whether she had enjoyed her meal.

"I could see that she was doing all the talking, and that you were – how can I say this without being presumptuous?" Fred took a breath before continuing. "Rather bored by it all?" he added, tentatively.

"That's right," Alison said, "but, like I said, the food was excellent and I'll certainly be coming here again, though probably not with the same person." And she smiled again.

"Will you allow me to get you another drink? On the house this time," Fred said, and Alison quickly weighed in her mind whether she wanted to spend a little more time with this man, or just pay the bill and go home. He had now turned away from her to say good night to some customers who were leaving, and this gave her the opportunity to quickly scrutinise him. Rather short and dark, with a shaven head; not really her type, but he seemed pleasant enough, and it was always useful to be friendly with someone who owned a restaurant, she thought.

"Thank you. That would be nice," she said.

"Is Sambuca okay?"

"Perfect," Alison replied. Fred caught the eye of one of his waitresses and within a couple of minutes the girl had carried two glasses of the liqueur over to the table and set them down.

"And may I join you for a moment or two?" Fred asked.

"Of course, but I don't want to keep you from…"

"Don't worry. I have an excellent team here. They can carry on perfectly well without me. They prefer it that way," Fred said, and he sat down opposite her in the chair which had previously been occupied by Rachel. Alison wondered if this was a routine he had whenever a woman was sitting on her own in his restaurant. Perhaps he was merely being friendly, interested in building up a good customer base for his new venture. Or perhaps he found her attractive. Would he have been so attentive if she had been horribly plain? Whatever his motives were, Alison resolved to stay fully in control. So if Fred offered her another drink (or anything else) she decided that she would politely refuse.

Detective Constable Gerald Cranley was viewed as someone who might go far in the police force. Even though his role was mainly that of a fetch-and-carry dogsbody in the investigation into Petro Semeniuk's murder, his superiors sometimes saw fit to give him more responsible tasks. Thus it was that he had carried out a few of the preliminary interviews of people who might have been able to help in the hunt for the murderer. Of course, if he had any doubts or suspicions he was supposed to refer them immediately to senior officers on the team, and he had always to complete a report of all the interviews he undertook. But manpower was stretched; his superiors did not always have the time to read all his reports, so he was often trusted to use his own judgement and discretion.

And Gerald believed that his judgement was sound enough. Jan Nowakowski was soon eliminated as a suspect, he thought, as was Ernest Ingham, who had – almost literally – bumped into Petro while walking his dog along the canal towpath around half-past seven. At the time that Petro was killed, some time after half-past ten, Ernest was playing in an important dominoes match in the Ring o' Bells public house, about a mile from Hirst Lock. His team mates, (and his opponents), had been able to vouch that Ernest and his dog had been with them since about eight o'clock. Gerald felt no need to include the result of the dominoes match in his report.

Petro's body had not been discovered until first light the next day, when two women had spotted it as they walked along the towpath to start their shift at the small cottage hospital in Victoria Road. They worked in the kitchen there. As soon as they had seen the body, floating face-down in the canal about fifty metres from Hirst Lock, the two of them had run back across the lock footbridge and up to the telephone kiosk which in those days stood near the bottom of Hirst Lane. Neither of them knew Petro, although one of them did live in the same road as Katherine Riley, and she thought she'd sometimes noticed a man visiting Mrs Riley, but she'd never taken much notice of what he looked like.

Gerald and a policewoman had accompanied one of the DI's to Katherine Riley's house, once the police had discovered that Petro had visited her that night. Katherine was able to confirm Petro's times of arrival and departure through remembering what television programmes had been on, and which ones they had watched together. She had remained calm and seemingly unemotional throughout the interview, but Gerald and his two colleagues knew that this was just the way that women of her generation and background would behave when dealing with such an event, however shocking it might be.

"Especially round here," the policewoman had said when this was mentioned on their way back to the station.

"Aye, but she'll be a seething mass of upset inside, I'll bet," the DI had commented, lighting a cigarette. He didn't offer one to Gerald.

Alison was the last customer to leave *Freddy's*. She had even accepted a second glass of Sambuca when it was offered, though she insisted that it be put onto her bill; she didn't want to be beholden to Fred – or anyone else, come to that. She did not think him particularly attractive physically; nonetheless she found herself warming to him as they sat together and talked. Fred was interesting company, which was a relief after the earlier endurance test set by Rachel. And they found that they had certain things in common. Both of them had come north after several years of working in London, though whereas Alison had been prepared to move anywhere, within reason, to escape from Ed and his vacuous world, it was different for Fred; it seemed that he had made a deliberate decision to come and open his restaurant in this part of Yorkshire. He was somewhat coy about saying exactly why, throwing up a smokescreen of comments about the time being right, this part of the world being on the cusp of economic regeneration after years in the doldrums, and so on. Alison didn't quite buy it and, perhaps emboldened by the Sambuca, she pressed him.

"Oh, come on," she said. "You're not giving me the full picture, are you? There must be other reasons why you specifically chose here and not somewhere else. Why Saltaire?" Fred didn't answer her straight away. Instead he turned and had a quick word with one of the waitresses who was collecting cutlery from the now deserted tables. It was clear that he was giving himself time to consider his reply.

"Well, maybe there is a particular reason for choosing Saltaire," he said eventually, turning back to face her and swirling the remains of the Sambuca in his glass. "But let me ask you something, if I may?"

"Ask away," Alison said.

"Okay. Do you remember a couple of weeks ago, on the canal towpath, you nearly got knocked down by an idiot on a bike? You had to jump out of the way." he said.

"Yes, I remember that. Why?"

"That idiot was me," he said. He finished the Sambuca and put his glass down on the table with a bang. He grinned at her.

"Really? Well, at least you did ring your bell," Alison said "No harm done. Do you often cycle by the canal?"

"When I have the time, yes. That day I'd been as far as Skipton. Anyway, you were talking to an elderly lady near the lock, is that right?"

"That is right," Alison said. "That was Marta, Marta Nowakowski. She's a friend of mine."

"She's your friend?" Fred said. He suddenly stiffened and stared at her, keeping so perfectly still that after a time she began to feel uncomfortable. Eventually, as if waking from a short trance, he took a deep breath and quickly stood up. His manner had changed, and whereas he'd previously been warm and friendly, now he was almost aloof. Alison felt that it was time to go. She stood up, half expecting him to offer her the formal handshake of a total stranger. "It's been very nice talking to you, Alison," he said.

"And it's been nice talking to you, Fred," she replied, feeling awkward at this inexplicable change of atmosphere. He had become tense and she had no idea why. Was it something she had said? In order to repair things she gushed a little – not something she would normally have done. "My evening has turned out absolutely fine after all, and that's thanks to you," she said. These words seemed to work. She could see that he was regaining his composure now; the stiffness left him, and he began to look more cheerful.

She let him help her on with her coat and they walked together to the door. He opened it for her.

"One more thing," he said. "Is there any chance that maybe we could meet for a drink one Monday? The restaurant is closed on Mondays. It doesn't have to be here in Saltaire. I could meet you in Leeds after you finish work, if that's better for you. What do you say?"

Alison pretended to be considering Fred's invitation, but inwardly she knew she would agree to meet him.

69

Unless she was working late, Monday evening was often a dead patch in her week. A couple of drinks with Fred might make a pleasant change. Anyway, she wanted an opportunity to discover why he'd reacted in such an odd manner when she'd told him that Marta was her friend.

The same team of Gerald, the policewoman and the DI interviewed Petro Semeniuk's daughter, Marta Nowakowski, in the lounge of the house in George Street. Gerald's task was to sit in the background and take notes while his boss, the DI, gently asked Marta a series of questions. Whenever Marta found it difficult to continue with her answers the policewoman, sitting next to her on the sofa, would comfort her by taking her hand.

Back at Shipley police station, the DI summarised what they now knew. Marta had told them that she had been fast asleep when her husband returned home, so she could not say for certain at what time he had come in. Neither had she been aware that her father was absent from the house, until early the next morning when the police had arrived and told her that a body, thought to be her father, had been found in the canal near Hirst Lock. She and Jan formally identified the body the next day.

The DI thought it was just possible, albeit unlikely, that Jan had not gone to bed after he had been dropped off by his friends; he could have walked along the towpath, waited in ambush for Petro, and killed him as he returned from his visit to Katherine Riley. True, Jan had no obvious motive for killing this man who was his friend and father-in-law, but Gerald was reluctantly forced to agree with the

DI that it was indeed possible for him to have committed the murder. He was almost on the point of apologising to the DI for being over-hasty in dismissing Jan as a suspect, but he knew that the DI was a fair man and he wouldn't hold that against Gerald, so he said nothing.

What all this meant was that Jan was interviewed once again, this time by the Detective Superintendent leading the murder hunt. The clothes which Jan had been wearing on the night of the murder were forensically examined. No murder weapon was ever found. There was insufficient evidence to bring a case against Jan Nowakowski, and no new witnesses came forward with fresh information that might shed light on who had murdered Petro Semeniuk and pushed his body into the Leeds and Liverpool Canal. The case was, of course, never formally closed by the police, but as the years passed most people forgot all about it.

Gerald Cranley's career path meant working for police forces in several parts of the country. He retired with the rank of Chief Inspector, and a decent pension, just before the start of the new millennium. Not long after that he was able to persuade his wife, who was originally from Essex, that they should move to Yorkshire, where Gerald had his roots. They relocated to Grassington, but his wife was never really happy living in the north. Just when they were planning to move back to the south, where she would presumably feel more at home, she became ill with breast cancer, and within six months she was dead.

Gerald moved to a small house in Baildon, the village where he had been brought up, and which he had left in the early 1970s. As one might expect, he never forgot the unsolved murder of Petro Semeniuk in 1969, for it had been the first murder case he had been closely involved in. And in particular, he did not forget the interview with Marta Nowakowski in the George Street house. His had only been a minor role that day, and he doubted whether Marta would have remembered him at all. But he would always remember her; her exquisite features and blonde hair made him consider her one of the most strikingly attractive women he had ever seen. And over forty years later he immediately recognised her when he entered Victoria Hall for the inaugural meeting of the Titus Salt Community Choir.

CHAPTER SEVEN

It only took Gerald Cranley ten minutes to drive the short distance from his home in Baildon to Saltaire. He parked his car carefully at the bottom of Victoria Road and walked the short distance up to Victoria Hall. He was pleased to note that the sciatica which had been bothering him all that day seemed to have faded off. The bells of Titus Salt's own church were ringing out, for Wednesday evening was not just the appointed time for the Titus Salt Community Choir to rehearse; it was also when the bell ringing team at the church held their weekly practice.

When he created Saltaire in the 1850s, Titus Salt made sure that the spiritual needs of its inhabitants were well catered for. He provided three non-conformist places of worship, one for the Wesleyan Methodists, one for the Primitive Methodists, and the largest – and most well-appointed – for his own denomination, the Congregationalists, nowadays known as the United Reform Church. Any Anglicans or Roman Catholics living in Saltaire – unlikely at that time – would have had to go further afield to pray. When Salt died in 1876 his body was laid to rest in a grand mausoleum next to his church; not quite on a par with Lenin's tomb in Red Square, or that of St Thomas Becket in Canterbury Cathedral, but evidence nevertheless of the esteem that Titus Salt had enjoyed in the Victorian age, and possibly indicative too of his own high level of self-regard, for nobody could have pioneered an enterprise like Saltaire without a mighty ego, as well as an undoubted zest for philanthropy and Christian charity.

Gerald went up the steps into Victoria Hall and entered the room where the choir always met. This was the third or fourth rehearsal since the choir had been launched that autumn, and Gerald anticipated that much of the evening would be spent practising a rendition of *Hail, Smiling Morn.* The choirmaster was keen that his new choir should do themselves justice when they performed this traditional Yorkshire hymn at the annual carol concert to be held at Bradford's St George's Hall, just before Christmas.

Gerald was glad that he had joined the choir. He liked singing and looked forward to these Wednesday evening sessions. And not just for the singing. Once he had realised that Marta Nowakowski was a fellow-member of the choir there was an added incentive for him. Of course he was much too diffident to approach her out of the blue and introduce himself, and he knew that it would be crassly insensitive for him to remind her of the circumstances in which he had last met her, all those years ago; she'd probably spent the last forty or so years trying to get over the trauma of her father's murder, he thought. The inability of the police to discover the murderer must also have taken an emotional toll.

So Gerald kept his distance. Besides, she was with the sopranos, whilst he was with the bass section of the choir, some distance away, so there was not much opportunity for even a casual chat, except perhaps during the half-time break. Gerald noticed that Marta always spent these breaks with a younger, smartly-dressed woman, and she always left with her when the rehearsals ended. Could they possibly be mother and daughter? Gerald wondered. And what had eventually become of Marta's one-time husband, Jan?

On this occasion Gerald was a little disappointed to see that Marta was absent, and the younger woman was sitting on her own. He took his place with the bass section just as the choir was called to order.

The choirmaster worked everyone quite hard for the next hour, so he felt obliged to grant the singers a little extra break-time. This was Gerald's opportunity. If it was inappropriate for him to try and make any sort of contact with Marta herself, he would do the next best thing; go and talk to her choir companion. He looked to where the woman was standing at the other side of the room. She was sipping water from a plastic cup. Good, Gerald thought, she's on her own, not talking to anyone. What could be more natural than a fellow chorister approaching her in a friendly manner during the break? He wondered why he was feeling nervous as he made his way through the throng of singers. Some people were standing and chatting; others were seated, studying the words and music on their song-sheets. So as not to be too obviously homing in on his target, Gerald made a detour to speak to the choirmaster, who was in consultation with the pianist at the front of the room. After asking a totally banal question about the date of the forthcoming concert at St George's Hall, (there was a poster advertising the event on the wall right in front of him), Gerald turned and, as casually as he could, walked over to Marta's companion, who was still standing alone and a little apart from the rest of the choir personnel.

"Your friend not able to make it tonight?" he said.

"No, she has a bit of a sore throat," Alison said.

"Oh dear," Gerald said, "I hope she'll be better for the concert."

"I'm sure she will. It's nothing serious, but she felt it best not to come tonight. She'll be fine by next week." Gerald noted her accent; not local. Rather posh.

"Good," Gerald said. "By the way, I'm Gerald. I hope you didn't mind me asking about your friend."

"Not at all," Alison said. "I'm Alison." And she held out a hand, rather formally, Gerald thought. He took it and gave it a brief polite shake.

"I've noticed that the two of you always sit together. I thought maybe you were related," Gerald said, unsure if this was the best way to proceed.

"What? Marta and me? No, we're not related," Alison said.

"Well, that's me jumping to conclusions. Sorry about that," Gerald said, and he grinned weakly, hoping that Alison would not dismiss him as just some nosey old fool. But no, she seemed willing to continue the conversation.

"I've only been living here in Saltaire since the summer," she said. "Marta has rather taken me under her wing. Which is nice."

"Yes, that is nice. So you've not known her long?"

"Just a few weeks, really. Do you know her?" Alison asked.

"Not really. I sort of knew her… well… years ago, it was," Gerald said, and he looked away.

"Do you live here in Saltaire?" Alison said.

"No, I live in Baildon. Not far away. Nice enough place, but it doesn't have the same character as Saltaire," he said. "So, are you and Marta neighbours here in Saltaire?"

"Yes. I live just round the corner from her. She has a lovely house in George Street."

"Ah, George Street," Gerald repeated softly, and immediately he was once again a young detective constable, sitting on the edge of an expensive antique chair at the back of the lounge in Petro Semeniuk's George Street house, whilst his boss, the DI (long dead now) gently probed Marta Nowakowski about her husband, Jan, and her father, whose dead body was lying in the morgue after being fished out of the Leeds and Liverpool Canal near Hirst Lock…

"If we can re-assemble now, ladies and gentlemen. Not many shopping days to Christmas. You'll be singing in front of a real live audience before you know it. We might only be doing the one piece at the concert, but it's one that people love to hear, so it's important that we give a good account of ourselves. Now tenors, I think we need to give the last line of the second verse rather more oomph, so can we just have tenors this time? Piano please, Arthur. Eyes on me, tenors. And after four…"

An hour later the rehearsal was over and the choristers began to file out of the room. It was then that Gerald noticed that Alison, rather than leaving with everyone else, had remained in her seat and was now, rather anxiously, rummaging through the contents of her bag. She looked flustered. Gerald went over to her.

"Something wrong?" he said.

"I'm such an idiot," Alison said, still busy delving into her bag and not looking up at him. "It's my keys. I must have left them in my office."

"You're sure you've not lost them?" Gerald said, and he sat down next to her.

"No, I think I can remember where I left them now." She closed her bag and looked at her watch. "I was in such a rush."

"Well, at least they're not lost, so that's all right," Gerald said.

"Not really," Alison said. "My house key was with them. I won't be able to unlock the door. I'm not sure what to do. I suppose I'll have to get a taxi and go back to work. How much do you think a taxi to Leeds will cost?"

"There and back? Could be sixty quid, at least, I'd say. Look, if you like, I can come to your house with you. There'll be a way to get in, I'm sure," Gerald said. Alison looked up and gave him a doubtful smile.

"How will we do that? Are you a burglar in your spare time?"

"No, but I used to be a policeman," Gerald replied. "It's the same thing really." And he stood up.

In less than two minutes Gerald got the Yale lock on Alison's front door to yield. She was mightily impressed.

"I must be out of practice," he said. "I used to be able to do it much quicker."

"That's incredible," Alison said. "I can't tell you how grateful I am. Thank you very much, Gerald." She was pleased that she'd managed to remember his name.

"You need to get a deadlock on this door. A Yale on its own is no good. Just think, if an old retired copper like me can crack it, a young lad out thieving would have no trouble whatsoever."

"I'll see to it as soon as I can," Alison said. "Anyway, let's not stand here in the cold. Come in for a coffee."

"Thanks, but no. I need to be getting back home."

"Somebody waiting for you? You could always phone them."

Gerald was suddenly acutely aware that there was nobody at all waiting for him at his house in Baildon. Moreover, here was a further opportunity, if he wanted to take it, to talk to someone who was a friend of Marta. Marta Nowakowski; Gerald wondered if he was becoming obsessed with her. And if so, was his obsession with the Marta of today, or was it with the Marta of 1969?

"Well?" Alison said. Gerald pulled himself together. He was being silly. It was foolish to think that he was in any way obsessed with Marta – it was more likely that seeing her in the here-and-now had simply triggered some old hidden feelings; feelings about her as a highly attractive young woman, with a father killed by a person or persons unknown; feelings about himself as a young copper, a novice in the CID, a member of a team that had manifestly failed to find the killer. Had he ever thought about Marta and the murder of Petro Semeniuk during the years when he had been living and working hundreds of miles away from Yorkshire? Yes, he had. Frequently.

"Okay, then, just for five minutes," he said, and he followed Alison as she led him into her house.

Gerald felt more confident now that he had accepted Alison's invitation. He could see that her gratitude over the picked lock would make it easier for him to talk to her about Marta, if he wished, although he realised that, as she had only known the older woman for a few weeks, she might not have very much to relate. He was right about that. All she was able to tell him was how she had first met Marta some weeks ago in the 1853 Gallery at Salts Mill, how she'd met her again at the inaugural meeting of the new choir, and how they'd become friendly from then on.

For her part, Alison was curious to know why he wanted to ask her so much about Marta. He had asked her next to nothing about herself, nor had he offered much about himself. She knew only that he was a retired policeman, living in Baildon, keen on choral singing. And good at picking locks.

"Did you say that you'd known Marta at some time in the past?" she asked.

"I did. Over forty years ago now," Gerald said.

"So you've always lived around here?"

"Not always. Originally, yes; I was brought up in Baildon, went to Salt Grammar School, and started as a copper in Shipley and Bingley. But then I moved around a lot. Career moves, you know. I ended up down south and then came back here when I retired."

"So, it was when you were a young man that you knew Marta? Is she an old flame, perhaps?" Alison asked. Gerald smiled at this.

"No, nothing like that," he said. He could sense that Alison expected more, but he hesitated before continuing. "It was a case I was involved in."

"A case?" Alison said, leaning forward, fully alert now. "She's never mentioned anything about involvement with the police."

"Never mentioned her father?" Gerald asked.

"Not much, though I've seen a picture of him."

"A picture?"

"Yes, in Salts Mill. There's a blown-up black and white photo on one of the landings. Near the bookshop."

"Of her dad, Petro?"

"Not just him. It's a picture of workers leaving the mill; early 1950s, I think. Her father is one of the men in the foreground, so she said. I wouldn't have guessed it. He looked nothing like her."

"No, he didn't," Gerald said.

"And you say he was called Petro. You knew him, then?" Alison said.

"Not really, no," Gerald said.

"So, are you going to tell me about this case, or are policemen like priests and doctors, sworn to maintain confidentiality? Even after they retire?" Alison said. Gerald didn't reply, and Alison wondered if she might have offended him. Then he spoke again.

"It's not that," he said. "You could dig it out of the newspaper archives, if you really wanted to know about the case. It only rated a small bit in a couple of the nationals; more in the local press, but not a huge amount even there."

"So was Marta in some kind of trouble? Or was it her father you were after?"

"No, she wasn't in trouble with us. And her dad certainly wasn't." He paused again, then said, "Perhaps you should ask her what it was all about."

"She might not want to tell me," Alison said.

"She probably won't," Gerald agreed. "Anyway, I'll have to be off. Thanks for the coffee." And he got up and started to move towards the door. Then he turned and said, "That was a silly suggestion of mine just now, Alison. Probably best if you don't mention to Marta anything about me being acquainted with her when I was a young copper round here. It's a long time ago now, but she might still find it upsetting to have it all raked up."

"I won't say anything to her, but only on one condition – well, two really," Alison said. Gerald had opened the door by now.

"What are they?"

"If I do go rooting through old newspapers, what date am I looking for?"

"1969. November," Gerald said. "And what's the other condition?"

"If I'm not to talk to Marta about what happened all those years ago, then it's only fair if you fill me in with some of the details about the case, don't you think?"

"We'll see," Gerald said. "Let me have your mobile number. I'm not promising anything, mind. Thanks again for the coffee, and don't forget to get a proper secure lock on this door." And he rapped three times with his knuckle on the door jamb to emphasise the point. "Good night," he said. He shut the door behind him and walked along Caroline Street to where his car was parked at the bottom of Victoria Road. He noticed that the sciatica in his right leg had returned; it was always more bothersome late at night.

Back at her house Alison sat down and picked up her cup, but the coffee was almost cold now, so she put the cup down and sank back into the cushions of the sofa. What was she to make of it all? Clearly something had happened in the past that involved Marta with the police, something important enough to have been reported in the newspapers. Yet Gerald had assured her that neither Marta nor her father had been in trouble with the law. Curiouser and curiouser. So, had they been the victims of crime? Had the George

Street house been burgled, for example? But that would scarcely have merited a mention in the national press. No, it must have been something much more serious than that.

There was so much about Marta that Alison did not know, and while the older woman had been quite open about some aspects of her life – her career as a teacher, her interest in art – she had been reluctant to talk about other matters. She had spoken freely about her father, the man in the Salts Mill photograph, but she had clammed up straight away when Alison had asked her about the other photograph, the one showing her father in a military uniform.

Before she went to bed Alison switched on her laptop and did a little research. She discovered that copies of local newspapers from as far back as 1969 were not available on-line, but hard-copy was kept at a local studies archive in central Bradford. Alison decided that she would visit the archive that coming Saturday. She was unable to find out anything from the usual search-engines, and she had to conclude that she was unsure if she was spelling Marta's name correctly, or indeed whether Nowakowski was also her father's name. Really, all she knew was that his first name was Petro.

After following various potential leads without success she turned the laptop off and closed the lid with a bang. It was frustrating. The problem, she recognised, was that she had no real idea what she was looking for, so as a final throw she had tried entering *Petro and Marta Nowakowski and the police 1969* into a search-engine. Nothing. When she had refined this by adding *Saltaire* (if additions could be termed refinements), all that came up was the Saltaire World Heritage Site website. Time for bed.

But she found that she couldn't get off to sleep. It wasn't the past conversations with Marta that were running through her head and keeping her awake, nor her talk that evening with ex-policeman Gerald. No, for some reason her mind was fixed on Fred Nicholson up at *Freddy's,* and in particular Fred's odd reaction when she had mentioned that Marta was her friend. That had been a few weeks ago now, and Alison had not rushed into accepting Fred's invitation for drinks on some Monday after work. This coming Monday, however, was to be their date, a cocktail bar in central Leeds their rendezvous. By then Alison hoped to know much more about Marta Nowakowski.

CHAPTER EIGHT

The next Saturday morning the weather was fine enough to tempt Alison to take a walk along the towpath towards Hirst Lock. After that she planned to take the train into Bradford and explore the newspaper archives. There were plenty of people about – dog-walkers, cyclists and one group of elderly walkers, dressed as if they were about to tackle a mountain in the Alps, rather than a stretch of English canal towpath and some nearby woods. She passed the football field where groups of small boys (and some girls, she was pleased to note) were being coached by young men in tracksuits. A barge was negotiating the lock, and a number of passers-by were watching the operation. Nearby, a boy aged about twelve, was offering a range of items for sale – second-hand paperbacks, old videos and the like – which he had on display on the flat top of a wall. Alison had noticed him on other weekends, and though she had never purchased any of his tatty wares, she admired his entrepreneurial spirit. Maybe this was how Richard Branson had started, she thought. As always, he called out to her, asking if she wanted to buy a book or a video, and as always, she shook her head.

"No thanks. Not today," she said.

"Something here might interest you," the boy said, and he held something out to her. "Old photo. Yours for ten pence. Or you can have it for nowt, if you buy a book." Partly to humour the boy, and partly out of curiosity, Alison stepped closer to look at the photograph he was holding. It was no longer in its silver frame, but she recognised it immediately as one of the photographs from Marta's sideboard – the old black and white print, with Marta as a child, standing between her father, in his uniform, and the unknown woman. What on earth was it doing here in Richard Branson's scruffy jumble sale? Had the boy stolen it from Marta? Alison was conscious of a sudden lurch in her stomach.

"Where did you get this?" she asked.

"This old lady," the boy replied. "She was sitting on that bench over there, a week or two back. I noticed her looking at the picture a long time. Then she got up and walked off and left the picture on the bench. So I went and picked it up."

"You didn't think to give it back to her, then?" Alison said.

"Course I did," the boy said, affronted that his integrity might be doubted. "I ran after her with it, but she told me to go away. So I thought she mustn't have wanted it anymore. She was nearly crying. I couldn't force her to take it, could I?"

"No, I suppose not," Alison said. "Ten pence, you say? Here." She handed over the coin and took the photograph, now more creased than ever, from the boy's grubby hand.

She put it carefully into her coat pocket and walked away from the lock and the boy towards Saltaire.

What was this all about? On Alison's first visit to Marta's house there'd been a definite awkwardness when she'd asked about the photographs on the sideboard, this one in particular. Marta had made it clear that she didn't want to talk about it. On subsequent visits, usually after the Wednesday evening choir rehearsals, Alison had made a point of neither looking at the photographs, nor even approaching the sideboard, for fear of causing Marta any further embarrassment. In fact she wasn't at all certain if the same photographs were still there in the silver frames. But whether or not she had removed them from the sideboard, surely Marta wouldn't deliberately leave the one that was the most interesting – and the most intriguing – on a public bench for anyone to find. Would she? No, she must have left it there by accident, probably because she was upset for some reason, and she'd not properly understood that the boy was trying to return it to her. But why she was sitting on the bench looking at the photograph "a long time," as the boy had said, was unclear. Alison wasn't fully convinced that the boy was telling her the truth, but she thought that he probably was. Anyway, what was she going to do with the photograph now that she had "rescued" it? Return it to Marta? She would have to think about that.

After lunch, Alison caught the train from Saltaire to Bradford, a journey of less than fifteen minutes. Leaving Forster Square Station, she walked across the centre of the city, past City Hall, its clock tower modelled on that of the Palazzo Vecchio in Florence, and through the adjacent City Park, with its dramatic array of fountains, until she came to the building which housed the local archives. Soon she was examining copies of local newspapers – some on microfiche, others bound in large folders – all of them recording the events of November 1969 and the months following.

POLICE CONFIDENT OF EARLY ARREST
IN CANAL MURDER CASE

A spokesman for the West Riding Police said yesterday that detectives continue to be confident about making an early arrest of the person, or persons, responsible for the murder of Petro Semeniuk, whose body, with severe head injuries, was found in the Leeds and Liverpool Canal, near Saltaire. Mr Semeniuk, aged forty-nine, was a resident of Saltaire and had worked at Salts Mill since the 1950s. A man who has been helping the police with their enquiries was earlier released without charge...   (November 1969)

CID FOLLOWING
"SEVERAL SIGNIFICANT LEADS"

The Detective Superintendent in charge of investigating the murder of Petro Semeniuk today confirmed that the police are following up several significant leads...   (December 1969)

POLICE APPEAL FOR INFORMATION
REGARDING "MOTIVELESS MURDER"

West Riding Police today appealed for people with any information whatsoever, regarding the apparently motiveless murder of Petro Semeniuk, to come forward in confidence… (February 1970)

WHO KILLED PETRO SEMENIUK?

Jan Nowakowski told our crime reporter yesterday that he was "angry and frustrated" by the apparent failure of the police to make any progress regarding the murder of his father-in-law, Petro Semeniuk… (April 1970)

Nowakowski. The same name as Marta's. Her husband? It was some time before Alison felt strong enough to stand up and leave. When she did, she made for a café-bar next to City Park and ordered a measure of Jameson's whisky. A large measure.

The following Monday, after finishing work, Alison had her date with Fred in Leeds. She saw him as soon as she walked through the door of the cocktail lounge. There was an after-work bunch of men talking loudly at the bar, but Fred had managed to secure one of the tables in a quieter corner. He stood up and greeted her with a kiss on the cheek. She couldn't help noticing, once again, that he was at least an inch shorter than her.

"Hi Alison," he said. "So glad you could make it. What would you like to drink?" Although she didn't particularly feel like drinking anything, she knew it would be only polite to go through the customary rituals.

"I'll have whatever you're having."

"Right. Gin okay?"

"Perfect," she said. He got up and went to the bar, returning with two glasses of gin and two small bottles of tonic water.

"So, how has work been today?" he said, after sitting down. She hoped that they weren't going to spend their time exchanging mundane platitudes, though she was unsure how to get round to talking about Marta, which, if she were honest, was her main motivation in agreeing to the date with Fred in the first place. She poured some of the tonic into her gin and took a sip. Relax, she told herself. Just see this as nothing more than a casual drink with an acquaintance. If Marta crops up in the conversation, well and good; if she doesn't, it won't really matter. After all, she'd already got a promise – more or less – from Gerald that he would tell her more about Marta, and now that she'd discovered the shattering information about the murder of Marta's father, would there be anything more that Fred could add anyway? Had she only imagined his strange reaction at *Freddy's* that time, when she'd told him that Marta was her friend? Maybe.

For a time they exchanged pleasantries about the usual things. Fred talked at some length about his new house in Ilkley, and the plans he had to furnish and decorate it. Even though she was a comparative newcomer to Yorkshire, Alison was aware that property prices in the spa town of Ilkley were among the highest in the north of England. Fred must have plenty of money, she thought – and that cannot come just from *Freddy's*. She decided to try out a bit of newly-acquired Yorkshire directness on him.

"*Freddy's* must be doing exceptionally well. Those things you are planning to do with your house won't be cheap, especially in a place like Ilkley," she said. He smiled before he answered.

"At the moment my restaurant hardly covers its costs, Alison, never mind turning a profit. I don't see that happening for at least another twelve months, and maybe not even then."

"Really? So you presumably…"

"Yes," he said, interrupting her. "I have some other money." He paused and looked at her for a moment, before continuing. "I'll let you into a secret. Do you want to hear it?"

"Yes please. I like secrets," Alison said.

"Let me get us some more drinks before I tell you," he said. He stood up and crossed to the bar, manoeuvring himself around the crowd of drinkers, who were still occupying most of the space. A few minutes later he was back with fresh drinks. Alison didn't bother to protest that it had been her turn to buy them.

"Okay," he said, after he had resumed his seat. "My father died when I was quite young, eight years old to be exact. I was brought up by my mother. When I was eighteen, in 1998, I got the money that my dad had left me in his will. It had been in a trust up until then. I'd known about the trust, but I'd always assumed that it would produce no more than a couple of thousand pounds at the most – perhaps enough to buy a second-hand car, or something like that. But – big shock – it was considerably more than

I ever expected. I wasn't sure at the time how my dad had managed to acquire so much. But to tell you the truth, I wasn't particularly bothered about where it had come from, just that there was a lot of it. And it was all mine!" he said, before pausing to take a drink. "But then it turned out that there were some things my dad wanted me to do, if at all possible. They were there in the will. Nothing major, or so I thought, but it did mean me travelling about a bit, including coming up here to Yorkshire. I didn't have to do any of it straight away; I could do it in my own time. Anyway, I'd got into the restaurant trade by that time, and the money I'd inherited helped me to get some good training and experience as a chef. Then I opened my own restaurant. After a time I sold it on and opened another; that's become the pattern. Some have been more successful than others and *Freddy's* is the latest one. Oh, and I did buy a car."

"Not an old banger, though, I'm sure," Alison said.

"That's right. It was one for a boy-racer, and I stupidly wrote it off not long after I'd bought it. But I was very young. Young and foolish," he said. There was a pause. Alison took a hefty swig of her gin and tonic, almost emptying the glass. She wanted some Dutch courage. Here goes, she thought.

"And where does Marta come into the story?" she asked, putting the glass down on the table.

"Who?"

"My friend Marta Nowakowski, the old lady who was with me that time you and your bike nearly knocked me into the canal."

"Oh, her," said Fred. "I'm not sure that she does come into it, does she? Why do you ask that?" There was an expression of puzzled innocence on his face now, but Alison was not to be fooled. She wondered if he'd prepared himself to feign ignorance about Marta, if her name came up. Was she going to let him get away with that? Definitely not; fuelled by the gin she went ahead.

"That time in your restaurant, when we were having a drink together, I mentioned that Marta was my friend,"

"I think I can remember," he said, cautiously.

"I'm sure that you can. Your reaction was very curious, almost as if I'd given you a shock," Alison said.

"Really? I don't recollect…"

"Fred, I'm not an idiot. Either you know Marta, or you know something about her," Alison said. She had rather surprised herself with this blunt approach, though she was not at all sure if it was producing the desired effect. Up to that point Fred had been friendly and rather gracious. Now he had become silent, surly almost, staring down at the table top, avoiding looking at her. What if he stormed out? Had she blown her chance of finding out more? But eventually – it seemed like ages – he sighed, looked up and spoke.

"All right, Alison, you are right; it was a bit of a shock, I can't deny it," he said, speaking so softly now that his words were almost drowned by a volley of raucous guffaws from the gang of men standing at the bar.

"But why?" Alison asked. "She's just an old lady who lives round the corner from me. Is there some reason why I shouldn't be friends with her?"

"No, no, it's not that all," he said, and he flapped his hand in front of his face, as if he were getting rid of some troublesome insect. "But there are certain things you don't know, and it's not really the time to tell you about them. I've already told you one of my secrets. Not a big one, I'll admit, but let it be enough for the time being. Now, shall we have just one more for the road?"

A little later Alison was heading down Park Row towards the railway station. Although it was not yet December, the streets of central Leeds were already decorated with Christmas illuminations. As she walked she went over what Fred had said; how there were certain things that she didn't know. Perhaps, but she knew more than Fred realised. For a start he didn't know about the photograph in her bag, nor about the ream of scribbled notes concerning an unsolved murder which had taken place in Saltaire, years before she and Fred were born.

———————

"You said earlier that you were born in England?"

"That's right," Jan replied.

"But your parents were Polish?"

"My father was in the Polish air force when the war started. After Poland was carved up by the Germans and Russians he managed to get to England. As I'm sure you know many Polish airmen joined the RAF at that time. My father served in 300 Squadron. That was a really famous Polish outfit in the RAF," Jan said.

"Indeed it was. And your mother?"

"Before the war she'd been a clerk with the Polish air force. She worked at the base where my dad was stationed. That's how they met. When he came to England, she was able to come with him," Jan said.

"It was fortunate that they both managed to get away, wasn't it?"

"Yes, I reckon it was. And she may well have been pregnant with me before they got here. They weren't married till after I was born, I do know that."

"And when and where were you born?"

"Bonfire Night 1940, at the maternity hospital in Lincoln. My father was stationed at East Kirkby."

"And after the war the family moved to Bradford?"

"That's right," Jan said.

"And, growing up in Bradford, did you consider yourself to be Polish or English?"

"Both really, I suppose."

"What language did you speak."

"We usually spoke Polish at home and English outside the house. My parents encouraged me to go to Polish Saturday school. You know what that's like. We were meant to learn about Polish traditions and culture, but I must say I found it so boring – all that folk-singing and dancing – that I refused to go after a while. I went to a normal school during the week, a Catholic one, you'll be pleased to hear, Father Benedykt. Obviously I spoke English there," Jan said.

"And after you left school you became an apprentice. You trained as a maintenance engineer, is that so?"

"Yes," Jan said.

"And you were working at Salts Mill when you met Petro Semeniuk, who was to become your father-in-law?" the priest asked.

"Yes."

"What do you know about his past history?"

"How do you mean?"

"Well, you know about how and why your own parents came to England. What about Petro Semeniuk? What's his story?"

"He's never really spoken about his past. All I know is that he and Marta came to England as refugees at the end of the war. I think for a time they were in some kind of refugee camp, before they came up to Yorkshire. Marta can sort of remember it," Jan said.

"Checkendon."

"What?"

"Checkendon. It was a resettlement camp for Poles, set up after the war. It was in Oxfordshire, not far from Reading."

"I've never heard of it," Jan said.

"Your father-in-law has never spoken about it?"

"No. Like I said, Marta told me that she could just about remember being in a camp when she was a child, but she's never given it a name," Jan said.

"Your father-in-law is Ukrainian, but he's sometimes pretended to be Polish, isn't that so?"

"Yes, I believe so."

"He even had a Polish identity card with another name, at one time. Did you know that?"

"No, I didn't, but it doesn't surprise me."

"Doesn't it? Why do you think he pretended to be Polish?"

"I suppose he thought it might have made things easier, especially straight after the war," Jan said. "The Poles had been Britain's gallant allies. My dad said that during the war Polish airmen were always very popular in England, especially with the girls. He always said that a Polish pilot could have as many English girls as he wanted, even if he looked like a monkey and smelled like a pig. But the Ukrainians? Well, that was a different kettle of fish. For a start, they'd not been Britain's allies during the war; they didn't come to Britain until afterwards. Maybe they had to keep a low profile. Some of them had even been on Hitler's side."

"Did that include your father-in-law? Do you think Petro Semeniuk was on Hitler's side in the war?"

"I'm sure he wasn't. That's a ridiculous thing to say. He is a kind man, always friendly to me, and very loving towards his daughter," Jan said. He was getting heated now.

"They say that Hitler was always kind and friendly to his female staff. And very loving towards his dog, of course," the man sitting next to the priest said.

"Yes, I've heard that, but I thought we were talking about Petro Semeniuk, not Hitler and his bloody dog," Jan said.

When Alison got back home to Saltaire she looked once more at the notes she had made concerning Petro Semeniuk's murder. Then she took from her bag the old black and white photograph of Petro, Marta and the unknown woman. This she placed next to her laptop. Using a scanner, she saved the image onto her computer. Soon she was comparing Marta's photo with pictures illustrating the various uniforms worn by Polish soldiers and police personnel during the war. Some of these looked quite similar to the uniform Petro was wearing, but nothing really tallied.

Then Alison remembered a curious remark that Marta had made on that very first occasion they'd had supper together, after the inaugural choir rehearsal: "...I can remember clearly my father telling me that we must always tell people we were Polish... and not what we actually were..." When Alison had asked Marta to explain, she'd gone to prepare supper in the kitchen instead of answering. So, if Marta and her father were not Polish, what were they?

Alison got to work on her laptop and searched through more illustrations: Latvian gendarmerie, Estonian reservists – even Romanian mountain troops – until, well past her usual weekday bedtime, she found what she was looking for; a picture of a man wearing the uniform of the Ukrainian Auxiliary Police. That was definitely the uniform that Petro was wearing in Marta's old photograph.

But it was not so much this, nor the glasses of gin imbibed earlier that evening, which caused Alison to start feeling queasy. It was the paragraph of writing which accompanied the illustration. From this, Alison learned that the Ukrainian Auxiliary Police had been established by the invading Germans to keep order in the occupied territories of Eastern Europe, and one of their main roles had been that of guards, under the auspices of the SS, in the Nazi concentration camps.

CHAPTER NINE

Later that week Ed phoned her from London. As usual a good deal of his talk concerned a lifestyle, and was couched in a language, which Alison had all but forgotten. He was very keen to tell her how he'd managed to get tickets for a must-see gig at the O2 Arena, featuring a band which, according to anyone who really knew about music, occupied a space in the stratosphere somewhere between Pink Floyd and Jesus Christ. Because he knew the right people, he'd only paid £400 for his ticket – cheap really, as they had been like gold dust, and had sold out within milliseconds of becoming available online. Like everyone else at the concert, he had, of course, videoed the entire performance on his phone. He was sure that Alison would want to see the result, so he would send it to her. Would she like it now? Alison thanked him and said that she was probably too busy to watch it just at the moment. She heard him snort with derision at this.

Then he surprised her by asking her if she had any Christmas plans. Before she could think of a reply he suggested that the two of them should get together for a couple of days. For five terror-filled seconds Alison thought that Ed was about to invite himself to come and stay with her in Saltaire. Please, God, no! Then the panic subsided.

She realised that he would be more likely to spend his Christmas helping to feed slum dwellers in Calcutta than miss out on exciting things happening in London. No, his invitation was, of course, for her to come to him in Hoxton. He told her that, given their current status, she could avail herself of the spare bed in his flat, if that would make things easier. What on earth would be the fucking point of her spending the Christmas holiday up in the dull wastes of the frozen north, (he made Yorkshire sound like the Yukon), when all the manifold delights of London, himself included, were just waiting for her?

As soon as she could get a word in Alison thanked him for the invitation, and said that she'd have to think about it. Then she ended the call. Afterwards she spent some time debating with herself about whether to take Ed up on his invitation. A Christmas spent away from London might not work for her. It was still the place which drew her. Here in Yorkshire she knew very few people, and was unsure what there would be to occupy her. And although her relationship with Ed was, in her eyes, definitely over, a small part of her recognised that a couple of nights in his bed, rather than the spare one, might – just might – be what she required right now. After all, she reasoned, she was a woman who had her needs, and since coming to live in Saltaire that side of her life had been in cold storage. Ed was physically attractive, and whilst, like many men, he was nowhere near as competent a lover as he imagined himself to be, nevertheless sex with him, given the right conditions, could be rather satisfying. The problem was that the right conditions were largely to do with ensuring she didn't have to suffer hour after hour of his inane, self-aggrandising blather.

Five minutes later she'd dismissed the idea of accepting Ed's invitation. Not wanting to have to listen to him any more, she sent him a polite text message, stating that she already had some firm arrangements for Christmas, so she would have to decline his kind invitation. He didn't reply.

Of course, Alison had no firm arrangements at all, but while she'd been texting Ed an idea had begun to form. She knew that *Freddy's* would be open for a special festive lunch on Christmas day. What if she were to invite Marta to join her there? It wouldn't be cheap, but so what? Another thought came into her head. Why not invite Gerald too? He would leap at the chance, wouldn't he? If, as it seemed, he had rather a thing about Marta, this would be like a date for him. Alison smiled to herself. Here she was, trying to match-make for a couple of pensioners, while her own love life currently amounted to nil. She'd even turned down a dead certainty with Ed. And quite right too, she thought.

"If I were you I wouldn't spend any time feeling pity for Petro Semeniuk."

"Why do you say that? He has been a good friend to me, as well as being my wife's father," Jan said.

"He's a Ukrainian."

"I know that," Jan said.

"And you know what the Ukrainians did? In the war?"

103

"I know what some of them did, yes."

"Lots of them."

"Not him," Jan said.

"How can you be so sure?"

"I know him."

"What if there is proof, testimony from people who witnessed things or suffered themselves because of him?"

"I've heard the rumours that go round. Bigoted people with grudges; people who've resented him because he's made something of himself, climbed up the ladder. Of course, nobody ever says anything to his face," Jan said, drawing heavily on his cigarette and blowing the smoke out towards the two men sitting opposite him, the one man in his ordinary working clothes, the other in clerical garb – his working clothes too, Jan suddenly thought.

"Your own people suffered."

"I know they did, Father Benedykt. But not because of him. Not because of Petro," Jan said.

"Maybe," the priest said.

Hail smiling morn, smiling morn

That tips the hills with gold, that tips the hills with gold,

Whose rosy fingers ope the gates of day,

Ope the gates, the gates of day,

Hail! Hail! Hail! Hail!

Who the gay face of nature doth unfold

Who the gay face of nature doth unfold

At whose bright presence darkness flies away, flies away,

At whose bright presence darkness, flies away, flies away,

Hail! Hail! Hail! Hail!

Hail! Hail! Hail Hail!

"Much, much better," said the choirmaster, and he gave them a short burst of applause to show how he pleased he was with their performance. "What did you think of that, Arthur? Good, eh?" he said, turning to the pianist. Arthur beamed and nodded his approval from the piano stool.

Alison had never heard this Christmas carol before she'd come to live in Saltaire, but through joining the choir she'd learned that it had a long tradition of being sung at Christmas throughout Yorkshire; in particular in Sheffield, Huddersfield and Bradford of course, where the choir was soon to perform. She had grown to like the rousing tune and the words even more so. As a non-believer she'd warmed to the fact that there was no mention at all of God in the carol, and certainly no references to virgins giving birth to saviours in cowsheds, surrounded by doting shepherds and peripatetic wise men.

Some years before she had unwisely accepted an invitation to attend a children's nativity play with a distant cousin whose small daughter had been cast as an angel. What Alison remembered was not so much the mawkish lines of dialogue mangled by the cast of six-year olds, nor the costumes created from redundant dressing-gowns and old tea-towels; no, it had been the endless snuffling of parents, overcome with emotion at witnessing their progeny performing the traditional Christmas story, no matter how ineptly, on a school stage. As the audience departed after the performance she had noticed that a nearby wastepaper basket was quite full of Kleenex tissues. Her cousin had contributed several, but Alison herself had remained dry-eyed and unmoved. Did this, she asked herself later, mean that she was a cold-blooded person – cynical and unfeeling? Was she Scrooge reincarnated? Bah! Humbug! Or was it rather that, from an early age, she had resolutely refused to be taken in by the excess of sentimental schmaltz which always accompanied Christmas – the same ghastly recycled Xmas songs in shopping centres, and the tiresome exhortations from television advertisers to go out and spend, spend, spend? Now, in her mid-thirties, she had concluded that any religious or fluffy Disneyesque aspects of Christmas were definitely not for her, but she was certainly not averse to a certain amount of yuletide feasting and drinking, provided that she could choose her companions. She was rather relieved to discover that the firm where she worked did not go in for an elaborate office party; just a few lunchtime drinks on Christmas Eve at Whitelocks, the famous old pub in the middle of Leeds. Then people would slope off home to sleep it off. Perfect.

"Who was that old man you smiled at earlier?" Marta asked, as she unscrewed the top of her bottle of spring water at the start of that evening's break.

"Which man would that be, Marta?" Alison replied, amused by the epithet "old man," uttered by Marta, a woman of more than seventy years. She was impressed too by Marta's hawk-like vision. Here is a woman who doesn't miss anything, she thought.

"That man over there, in the bass section, the one looking over here now. He's staring at us," Marta said.

"Well, you'd better not stare back, then," Alison said.

"Why not?"

"It would be rude," Alison said.

"Would it?" Marta said. "Anyway, who is he? Do you know him?"

"Only from the choir. I was chatting to him a bit at that rehearsal you missed. Oh, and he helped me break into my house. I forgot to tell you that," Alison said.

"What do you mean? Helped you to break..."

"I'd left my keys at work. He came back to my house and we broke in. He used to be a pol..." Here Alison stopped.

"Used to be a what?" Marta asked, but Alison didn't have to answer her. The choirmaster was calling everyone to order, keen to commence the second hour of the rehearsal.

After the rehearsal Marta and Alison walked the short distance from Victoria Hall to Marta's house in George Street. Supper at Marta's had now become their weekly ritual. When Alison had suggested that they should take it in turns to provide hospitality, Marta had been adamant. She would provide the supper because she had the time to prepare it, whereas Alison was a busy career woman, working hard all day, so to operate on a *quid pro quo* basis would be unfair to her. After making a couple of token protests, Alison was content to go along with this.

By now she was beginning to understand Marta a little better. She knew, for example, that on this particular evening she would want to return to their earlier conversation – it certainly wouldn't have been forgotten. And, sure enough, as they finished supper, Marta spoke.

"So, Alison, you were telling me about that man," she said. "Something about him helping you to break into your house? How very strange."

"I'm very glad that he did help me," Alison said. "Otherwise I'd have had to spend hours, and God knows how many pounds on a taxi, going back to Leeds to get my house keys from the office. That would have been a nightmare."

"Oh, Alison, you should have come and stayed the night here. Then you could have retrieved your keys the next day," Marta said, shaking her head at what she clearly deemed to be Alison's foolishness.

"But you were ill," Alison said. "It would have been too much of an imposition, especially at that time of night."

"It was only a sore throat. I wasn't in bed. I never go before midnight anyway. It would have been fine," Marta said.

"That is a kind offer, Marta, but I didn't need to trouble you, as it turned out."

"No, you let a strange man into your house instead. What if he was up to no good?" Marta said. Alison hid a smile by holding her cup up to her face and pretending to take a long drink of coffee. Then she replied.

"Oh, I think I would have been safe enough, Marta. As you said earlier, he's an old man. Besides, I don't think any of our fellow choristers would…"

"You can never tell," Marta said, interrupting her. "You can go along thinking the best about people, thinking that you know them inside out. Then, out of the blue, they do something terrible and shocking," she said with a sudden burst of passion. There was a pause before Alison spoke.

"You don't know him yourself, then?" she said.

"Know who?" Marta said.

"That man, the one in the choir who helped me." Alison looked steadily at Marta's face, ready to note any sign of the older woman being economical with the truth. But Marta started to busy herself with the crockery on the coffee table, gathering plates and cups onto a tray. Then she stood up and began to move towards the kitchen with the tray in her hands. Her back was towards Alison when she eventually replied.

"No, I don't recall ever seeing him before," she said.

"Are you sure?" Alison said. "You must have seen him at choir rehearsal."

"Maybe I have. I don't notice everything and everybody, you know," Marta said, calling from the kitchen. Fibber, thought Alison.

Marta returned from the kitchen and sat down on her chair. Her hands were folded neatly on her lap; lovely hands still, with only a few faint liver spots. And those rings she wore! They were quite splendid, Alison thought. Now was the time.

"Oh, by the way," she said, trying to sound as casual as possible. "I came across this a few days ago. It was on the canal towpath." She took the old photograph from her bag and held it out for Marta to see. Marta took it from her and looked at it in silence for a while. She showed no emotion whatsoever.

"Ah yes, that old photograph," she said slowly. Then looking up at Alison, and with a calmness in her voice that Alison found herself almost admiring she said, "And where did you say that you found it? By the canal? Strange."

"Yes," Alison said. "You must have dropped it." She wasn't going to mention anything about the boy and his rummage sale, unless Marta asked for more details. But, to her surprise, Marta held out the photograph to her, as if to return it. This was done with something of a bored air, like when snapshots of a recent holiday or a new baby are passed around to people who are not really all that interested.

"I'm not sure I want it anymore. You can have it, if you wish," she said, putting on a marvellous act of indifference, thought Alison, an act that was betrayed only by the tiny pulse that could be seen beating quite rapidly in her temple.

"But I thought you would want it. I thought it was important – a memento of your childhood," she said.

"Well, yes, I suppose it is," Marta said, looking at the photograph again. "Yes, you are probably right. On second thoughts, perhaps I should keep it." And she rose and went out of the room, the photograph in her hand. Soon Alison could hear her moving about upstairs. She returned a few minutes later. "There," she said, as she sat down. "It's safe and sound now." And I have a copy safe and sound on my computer, Alison thought to herself.

"Now, Jan, have you ever heard of Henry Borynski?"

"Of course I have. Every Pole in Bradford has heard of him; probably every Pole in England, come to that," Jan said.

"And what have you heard about him?"

"That he disappeared. He was a Polish priest here in Bradford. It happened when I was a boy. I can remember all the fuss. I don't know that I grasped all the details, though," Jan said.

"Well, let me refresh your memory. Like you said, Henry Borynski was the chaplain to the Polish community here in Bradford. One evening, without any warning, he walked out of his lodgings in Little Horton Lane and disappeared into thin air. That was in July 1953, and no trace of him has ever been found."

"People disappear all the time," Jan said, stubbing out his cigarette and pretending to stifle a yawn. "Maybe he got tired of living in Bradford and wanted a change."

"Doubtful. The police strongly suspected that Father Borynski had not just wandered off, looking for a change of scenery. They believed that he had been abducted and murdered."

"I remember that now. And wasn't there a rumour that the Church was somehow involved?" Jan said, nodding and smiling pointedly at the priest. The priest noticed this, and he sighed before he answered.

"Some foolish people said Canon Martynellis was wrapped up in it," the priest said wearily. "He was Father Borynski's predecessor. But if that's true, he can only have been an innocent dupe, manipulated by others outside the Church. He died of a heart attack soon after Father Borynski vanished, so we'll never know for certain if he was involved at all. But the Church was certainly innocent. Cardinal Heenan himself said that the Church was in no way implicated…"

"Just wait a minute," Jan said, interrupting him. "What has all this got to do with me and Petro Semeniuk?"

"If you wait a minute you'll perhaps see." The priest sat back in his chair and folded his hands across his stomach before he went on. "The thing is that Father Borynski was vehemently anti-communist, so the theory was that he was eliminated by agents of the new Polish regime; the communists."

"Why would the communists do that?" Jan asked, reaching for another cigarette. The man sitting next to the priest leaned across and lit it for him.

"There were agents here in Bradford trying to persuade people to return to Poland. Borynski's view was that nobody should go back there to live under communism. Being the local chaplain, his views counted for a lot. So, he had to be got rid of. That's the usual theory that's trotted out," the priest said.

"I'm still waiting to hear why you are telling me all this," Jan said.

"We have a rather different interpretation of the affair," the priest said.

"Oh yes?" Jan said.

"Yes, we believe that the theory is essentially accurate, but that one important detail is missing."

"Which is?" Jan said.

"The identity of the person who carried out the actual abduction and murder."

"And?" Jan said. He knew what was coming, and he could feel himself getting hot and angry, even before the priest spoke.

"We believe that person was Petro Semeniuk."

"What? That's absolute rubbish!" Jan said, his voice raised. He stood up from his chair and then abruptly sat down again.

"Listen to me, Jan. The man was in the SS during the war. He worked for the Germans. He killed Poles for the Nazis, maybe even some members of your own family, who knows?" the priest said, speaking more forcefully now.

"I can't believe I'm hearing this… this nonsense," Jan said. The other man spoke. Up to now he had remained largely silent, letting the priest do most of the talking.

"He'd been a killer," he said. "That was his job in the war, so when the Polish communists came along, wanting someone to get rid of a troublesome priest, here he was, ready, willing and able. And living in Bradford." Now the priest spoke again.

"The police got a tip-off that Borynski's body might be buried on Ilkley Moor," he said, leaning forward close enough for Jan to smell the alcohol on his breath. "And here's the cunning part. Semeniuk actually joined with volunteers from the Polish community to help the police search for the body up on the moors. Nothing was ever found, but what a good way to divert any suspicion, eh?"

"I don't believe a word of it. Petro Semeniuk has lived among Polish people all his life, back in the old country and over here…"

"And he even pretended to be Polish for a while," said the priest. "Probably to cover his tracks."

"He is a kind and gentle man, Father Benedykt, not a killer," Jan said angrily, and he rose from the table and began to walk towards the door.

"You'll see," said the priest, turning his head to call after Jan, who slammed the door as he went out of the room. The empty glasses on the table rattled.

When Alison got home she switched on her laptop and looked once more at the picture. That young woman standing with Marta and her father, who was she? Now that Marta was pretending indifference to the whole issue of the photograph, there could be little harm in asking her, perhaps the next time they met. Alison enlarged the image on the computer screen and looked closely at it to see what else might be there. The three people, Petro, Marta and the unknown woman, were standing in a garden. In the background you could clearly see shrubs growing against a low fence, and there was a small mound of earth topped with what looked like a small wooden cross. A miniature grave? Beyond the fence there was a long single-storey building which Alison could just make out, if she peered closely at the computer screen.

It reminded her of the community hall-cum-Scout hut that had stood in a village in Sussex, the destination of tight-lipped family outings when she was a child. Her parents had stopped loving each other by then, but they maintained a charade of family life, so they all had to endure regular trips to the country. Alison was never certain if her parents really loved her.

That building in Sussex had been a reclaimed army hut; Alison surmised that the one in the picture was something similar. Perhaps it was the barracks where Marta's uniformed father worked. Perhaps the three of them lived in an army camp. Or some other kind of camp.

CHAPTER TEN

"You know what we were talking about at your house?"

"Go on."

"About the old police investigation involving your friend and her father?"

"What about it?"

"I said that another time I'd try and give you a few more details."

"Yes, you did."

"I have to come down to Saltaire anyway, so I thought maybe I could pop in to see you for an hour."

"You mean tonight?"

"That's what I was thinking, yes."

"What time?"

"Would eight o'clock be okay for you? You'll be at home?"

"Yes, I'll be home by then. I'm on the train right now. We're just leaving Shipley station."

"Should I come later, then? Or perhaps another day?"

"No, no. Tonight at eight is fine, Gerald."

"Righto, I'll see you then."

"I'll look forward to it," Alison said. She wondered, as she put her phone back into her bag, if any of the other passengers in the carriage had been listening to her conversation with Gerald, but then she concluded that it didn't really matter if they were. Besides, nearly all of them, she noted, were either updating social media, or they were listening to music, oblivious to anything occurring in the real world.

Alison stood up and joined the short queue of people who were moving towards the carriage door, ready to get off at Saltaire station, just two minutes' travel time from Shipley. It had stopped raining when she got off the train, but the cobbled street between the station and Victoria Road was still wet and shiny under the light of the street lamps.

At home she took a lettuce and tomato salad from the fridge, and some slices of smoked duck which Marta had presented to her earlier in the week. Alison rarely left Marta's house without a small gift, usually some foodstuff which Marta had bought especially for her, perhaps a jar of olives, or a packet of small Polish honey cakes, covered in chocolate and icing sugar; food parcels donated to a poor refugee from London. Alison finished most of the salad, then sliced a peach and mixed it with some Greek yoghurt in a bowl. She ate about half of it.

After she had eaten and placed things in the dish-washer, she took a bottle of Fleurie from her small wine rack and laid a corkscrew next to it. Just in case Gerald didn't want a drink, (she suddenly realised that she was dying for one herself), on account of driving, she took a packet of Italian coffee from the cupboard and filled the kettle. It was now a quarter to eight. Alison waited with impatience, willing herself to stay calm, valiantly resisting any temptation to open the bottle of wine and fill a glass for herself. At 7.59pm, there was a knock at the door.

Gerald came into the house, and Alison took his coat and hung it up near the door. He accepted her offer of wine, and she uncorked the bottle. A few minutes later they were ready to start.

"Did you manage to find anything in the newspaper archives?" Gerald asked.

"Yes, I did."

"So, what did you find out?"

"There was not a huge amount of detail, but enough to tell me what had happened," Alison said.

"Were you shocked?" Gerald said.

"I felt upset reading about it," Alison said. "Even though it happened all those years ago."

"It doesn't seem like years ago to me," Gerald said. "I can remember it as clear as day. I must have investigated dozens of murders up and down the country since then, but none of them stands out like the murder of Petro Semeniuk. Odd, isn't it?"

"Is that because it was your first?" Alison asked.

"It was my first murder case, yes. I was just a junior member of the investigating team, new to CID, still wet behind the ears. Before that I'd been in uniform, out on the beat, telling folk what time it was, and helping old ladies to cross the road." He paused, hoping that Alison might react to his self-deprecating little joke, but she didn't. In a quieter, more serious tone, he continued: "And of course we never cracked the case." He paused again, and Alison knew that he was thinking about events that had happened years before. She waited. Then Gerald put down his glass, scratched his head, and returned to the present. "So, what if you tell me what you found out from the old press archives, and I'll fill in what I can for you," he said.

· "All right," Alison said. The notes she had taken were close at hand, but she didn't need them. "Well, what I found out was that Marta's father, Petro Semeniuk, was murdered in November 1969. It sounds quite horrible. He was hit over the head and pushed into the canal near to Hirst Lock. The police – your team, I suppose it must have been – never found the murderer. You did have a suspect at one point, but he was released without being charged. The police appealed for witnesses after a time – probably getting a bit desperate, I thought. Then, a few months later, a man called Jan Nowakowski complained that the police were dragging their feet. This Jan fellow was described as Petro's son-in-law, so I guess he and Marta were married. Nowakowski is her surname. Was he her husband?"

"That's right," Gerald said.

"Marta has never mentioned him to me," Alison said.

"But you knew that she'd been married," Gerald said.

"I've always assumed that she was a widow, but she's never talked about who she was married to. She does have a photo on her sideboard that looks as if it was taken on her wedding day, but there's no bridegroom on it, just Marta and her father. So what became of this man, this Jan?" she said.

"Marta and Jan separated not long after the murder. Jan moved away, somewhere down south, I believe. I was on the move myself by that time, so I pretty well lost touch with it all," Gerald said.

"Did they have any children?"

"Not to my knowledge," Gerald said.

"What about the suspect who was later released? The newspapers mentioned that. Who was he?"

"Well, that was Jan again, Jan Nowakowski," Gerald said. Alison recoiled and nearly spilled the wine from the glass she was holding. She realised too that it wasn't just in story-books that people's jaws dropped open in surprise. She had to take a large gulp of wine to help her get back to normal.

"What? You mean Marta's husband was a suspect?" she said, when she was able once more to speak in a reasonably calm tone.

"Yes. We had him in for questioning more than once. In fact, I did the first interview myself. I was dead certain that he wasn't our man, but my gaffer was less sure, so we brought him in again, and this time the superintendent in charge of the case had a go. His clothes went to the forensic lab, but there was nothing found that was suspicious. DNA profiling wasn't available then; it only came in after 1985, though it wouldn't have helped in a case like this one anyway."

"Why not?"

"Well, in a sex case you might get something from a semen stain, or a saliva trace, but it would be nigh on impossible to get anything from a victim who'd simply been banged over the head and dumped in a canal. Okay?"

"I see."

"Oddly enough though, there was another murder on the canal towpath which was solved because of DNA profiling," Gerald said.

"Another murder by the canal? God! What kind of a place is this?"

"Do you want to hear about it?"

"Of course I do," Alison said. She was listening intently.

"It was in the late 1970s, probably 1977. A woman called Mary Gregson lived in one of those small cottages on the canal bank on the far side of Salts Mill, going towards Shipley. Do you know where I mean?" Alison nodded. Gerald continued: "She worked at Salts Mill. It was only a five-minute walk from her house. She was attacked, sexually assaulted and murdered on the towpath one afternoon on her way to work. The case was reopened years later and DNA profiling identified a chap called Lowther. He confessed and got a life sentence. There was a twenty-three year gap between that poor woman being killed and the murderer being convicted."

"Twenty-three years! So could there be a chance that Petro's case might be reopened?" Alison asked.

"Well, the file won't have been closed, but it's unlikely that there'll be any further investigation. With the Gregson case, it was precisely because a DNA match became possible that the ball started rolling again. With Petro it's just not the same. We knew that Jan had the opportunity to kill Petro. He'd been out drinking in Bradford with some mates, and they'd dropped him off at home. He could have walked along the towpath, instead of going straight into the house, and he could have waited for Petro to come past, then clobbered him. Of course, that pre-supposes that he knew Petro was visiting his lady-friend near Hirst Lock that night, and that he'd walk back to George Street along the towpath, rather than on the road. But we couldn't work out any motive he might have had. Jan and Petro were close friends, as far as we could tell, and Jan and Marta were a loving young couple, apparently. What did he have to gain by killing his father-in-law? So, in the end we had to let him go, because we had no evidence, though the Super gave him a proper grilling. For hours. Like a dog with a bone, he was. Aiming for a confession, but no joy."

"And are you still certain today, after all these years, that it wasn't him?" Alison asked. At this Gerald inhaled deeply and held the breath for a few seconds before releasing it.

"More or less, I am. You can never be 100% sure. In a murder case you usually pull in the nearest and dearest for a chat, and nine times out of ten you find that it's a family member that's done the deed. But not in this case. I've never really believed that Jan was guilty."

"So was Marta ever a suspect?"

"We talked to her, obviously, but we didn't consider that she could have done it."

"Why not?" Alison asked.

"We just didn't. You've got to remember that this was years ago, before women's lib and all that. In those days nobody would have thought for a second that a woman would have been capable of clubbing a grown man over the head and tossing him into a canal. It wasn't what a woman would do. Arsenic and old lace maybe, but not blood and guts," Gerald said.

"So, who do you think did it?"

"I don't know, but almost definitely not Jan, and certainly not Marta."

"So who?" Alison said, more insistently this time.

"Well…" Gerald began, then he stopped again.

"Go on," Alison said, coaxing him.

"It's only my own little pet theory. I have no proof at all," Gerald said.

"I'd like to hear it anyway," Alison said, and she waited for him to divulge something which she surmised he'd revealed to few, if any, other people. He sat forward in his chair, with his shoulders hunched and looked at her.

"Okay," he said. "You've no doubt heard of the Yorkshire Ripper." For a few seconds Alison looked at him in utter bewilderment. Then she almost laughed. Surely Gerald wasn't going to suggest that Peter Sutcliffe was Petro's murderer. That seemed preposterous; about as likely as Dr Crippen or Billy the Kid being the guilty person. Was Gerald being serious?

"But I thought all the Ripper murders happened later. And he only murdered women," she said, still trying with some difficulty not to laugh, and very conscious that hilarity was hardly an appropriate reaction when talking about a series of horrific killings, most of which had been committed only a few miles from where she and Gerald were now sitting.

"That's what everyone thought at the time. The usual line is that Sutcliffe's first definite victim was a young lass, a fourteen-year old from Silsden. Tracey Browne she was called. This was in the summer of 1975. He hit her on the head right outside the farm where she lived with her parents. He didn't actually kill her, though he fractured her skull very badly. In fact Tracey gave the police a very accurate description of the man who'd attacked her. If they'd taken more notice of that, the silly buggers, it could have saved the lives of all the women Sutcliffe killed later on," Gerald said.

"But that was nearly six years after Petro's murder," Alison said.

"I know, but more recently there's been a suggestion that Sutcliffe's first murder was actually as early as 1966. And the victim was a man."

"Go on," Alison said. The giggling fit had passed; she was listening closely to Gerald now.

"There was a bookmaker who had a place in Bingley, in Wellington Street, near the railway station. He was called Fred Craven. He was clubbed to death in his office. That murder has never been solved. I was a uniformed constable at that time. I wasn't directly involved, but I can remember all about it."

"And you think that this chap, Fred whatever, was a victim of the Ripper?"

"I don't know for definite, obviously, but it's a thought," Gerald said. "There are certainly some people who've always believed Fred Craven was murdered by Sutcliffe."

"And you think he might also have killed Petro?"

"It's a possibility. Striking the victim on the head from behind was how Sutcliffe attacked his victims. In Petro's case no weapon was ever found. That might be because Sutcliffe used to carry it with him. He used a hammer. He kept it in the boot of his car between murders."

"How gruesome!" Alison said. "Have you ever told anyone else about your theory?"

"No," Gerald replied. "I don't think anyone would go along with it. They'd just laugh, like you did, wouldn't they?"

"I'm sorry about that," Alison said. "I didn't mean to."

"Don't worry, I'm not offended," he reassured her. "These things all happened a long time ago. Before you were even born."

"But it's all still crystal clear to you," Alison said. "And very important to you."

"I suppose it is, yes," Gerald said.

Alison waited a short while before she spoke, then she said: "And I think that Marta is important to you too."

"Why do you say that?"

"When you were here before, that time you picked the lock for me, you were very keen to talk about her," Alison said.

"Was it so obvious?"

"Pretty much, yes."

Gerald didn't reply. Instead, he drank some of his wine and remained silent, deep in his own thoughts. Alison was certain that he had a thing about Marta. Perhaps he'd had it all the time that he'd been married. He'd said very little about his erstwhile wife; just that she had died from breast cancer, and he'd come to live as a widower in Baildon. Alison wondered what it must be like to be quite happily married to one person for years, yet all the time continuing to have deeper feelings for someone else. Would you confess to your spouse and try and make light of it? Or would you keep it to yourself? The latter, probably, Alison thought.

"Thank you very much for talking to me about all this, Gerald. I'm grateful. I've become fond of Marta since coming to live here, and I've wanted to get to know her better, but she doesn't necessarily give much away," she said.

"I understand," Gerald said. "I've never thought it was just idle nosiness on your part. And I've kept my side of the bargain, so I hope you'll keep yours. No telling Marta that I was a young copper on the case when her father was murdered, agreed?"

"Agreed. But let me show you something. Come over here." He rose from his chair and followed her to a desk at the rear of the room. Her laptop and a printer were neatly arranged, side by side. Alison switched the laptop on and soon the copy of Marta's old photograph came up on the screen. The three people, a blonde child, a teenage girl and a young man in uniform, stared at them out of the past.

"Who are these people?" Gerald asked, adjusting his spectacles.

"Who do you think?" Alison said. Gerald studied the image carefully for some time, then he looked up and frowned.

"There is something familiar about the man," he said, and then he shook his head. "Do you know them?"

"I don't know who the young woman is, but the man in the uniform is Petro Semeniuk…"

"Good God! So it is. And, don't tell me, the little girl is Marta," Gerald said, looking closely at the picture once again.

"That's right. She must be about four, I would think," Alison said.

127

"How come this is on your computer?" Gerald asked.

"Marta has the original photograph in her house. She let me have it for a couple of days, and I scanned it into my computer." This wasn't strictly true, but it would do for the time being, Alison thought. "Any idea where the photograph was taken?"

"Well, not in this country, I'd say. If they were Polish, I suppose it would be somewhere in Poland, wouldn't it?"

"I suppose it would," Alison said. "What about the uniform that Petro's wearing? He looks very smart, doesn't he?"

"Yes he does. He must have been in the army. Mind you, it could just as well be a station-master's get-up, or even a postman's. Do you know what it is?" Gerald said, turning to look at her.

"I think I do. I think he's wearing the uniform of the Ukrainian Auxiliary Police."

"Oh, so they're not in Poland, then?"

"Probably Poland, yes."

"So who were they, these Ukrainian auxiliary policemen? And what were they doing in Poland, if they were Ukrainians?"

"Working for the Germans. Collaborating."

"Really? So, are we talking about the war? I guess we are," Gerald said, leaning forward again to study the computer image. Then he stood back from the table quite abruptly, and Alison could tell that something had struck him; something of importance. "Wait a minute… wait a minute," he said, more to himself than to Alison.

"What is it?"

"I'm remembering that I already knew something about Ukrainians collaborating with the Germans in the war. Now, how would I know that? Who would have told me?"

"Maybe you learned about it at school," Alison said. "Hitler and the Nazis were all we ever did in our history lessons, that and the Tudors."

"All we did in my day was the Kings and Queens of England and the Repeal of the Corn Laws. God, that was boring. No, it wasn't at school. Somebody told me about it later on. Who was it?" He looked up at the ceiling for inspiration. Then: "I know."

"Well?" Alison said.

"It was Jan Nowakowski who told me, when I was interviewing him at Shipley police station after Petro had been murdered. Yes, that's right. He told me that Petro was a Ukrainian, not a Pole, but he'd not always advertised it once he came to England, because there had been bad blood between Poles and Ukrainians going back a long way. It was made worse because some Ukrainians had sided with the Germans in the war. Yes, it's all coming back to me now. So, if Petro was in this Ukrainian police outfit, that means he must have been a collaborator," Gerald said. He paused before going on. "I wonder what the Germans had him doing?"

"Not directing the traffic, that's for sure," Alison said.

"What then?"

"I've looked into it a bit. The Nazis used the Ukrainian Auxiliary Police to do a lot of their dirty work."

"Such as?"

"Oh, just the usual stuff – massacring Jews, shooting Russian POWs, persecuting Poles…"

"God, Alison…"

"Now the good news is that not all Ukrainians were like that. Apparently there were some who sheltered Jews, looked after Poles and were generally heroic and good eggs. The bad news is that Petro is in that uniform." Here she pointed at Petro on the screen. "So presumably he wasn't one of the good guys. Let's sit down and have another drink, shall we?" she said.

"I think I need one, Gerald said.

They went back to their seats and drank their wine in silence for a time, before Gerald said that it was getting late and he would have to be going.

"Before you go, I have a proposition for you," Alison said. "No need to give me a definite answer straight away, but I want to invite you for lunch on Christmas Day."

"What, lunch here?" Gerald said.

"No, up at *Freddy's,* the new bistro that's opened on Gordon Terrace. I've got to know Fred – he's the proprietor – and he's putting on a special Christmas lunch. I've eaten there. The food is superb; Fred really knows what he's doing. And he's a very nice chap."

"I'm not sure, Alison" Gerald said cautiously.

"Well, you might have other plans, I realise that," Alison said.

"No, I don't, as a matter of fact. In the past couple years I've had Christmas dinner with a very nice couple who live a few doors from me, but I know that this year they're going to spend Christmas with their daughter in Harrogate. I hadn't made up my mind what I was going to do this time."

"Well, there you are, then. Have a Christmas lunch with me at *Freddy's.*"

"I don't know…"

"Oh, come on, Gerald. Stop looking a gift horse in the mouth. You've just been asked out for lunch by a talented and beautiful woman – no, make that two talented and beautiful women."

"Who's the other one?"

"Marta, of course."

"Marta? You've asked Marta?" Gerald said, his eyes widening. It was difficult to tell from his facial expression and his tone of voice if the prospect filled him with great joy or abject terror. "God, Alison, I'm not sure if that makes it better or worse."

"Why should it be a problem?"

"Because of all the things we've been talking about tonight. All the stuff we've both discovered, that's why. What if one of us has too much to drink and blurts something out that we shouldn't. 'Oh, by the way, Marta, I understand that your father was a Nazi war criminal.' Something really tactful like that." Alison couldn't stop herself laughing at this, especially as Gerald had substituted his local accent for a very poor imitation of hers. Then Gerald joined in the laughter, and Alison was relieved, because she knew now that he'd accept the invitation and come to the lunch.

"So you'll do it, then?" she said

"I'm still not sure."

"Of course, it'll be my treat. I'll be paying."

"Will you?" His face lit up. "Oh, in that case it would be rude of me to refuse, wouldn't it?" He walked to the door and reached for his coat. As he left the house he winked at her.

After Gerald had gone Alison helped herself to another glass of wine and thought about the evening. It wasn't the hair-raising revelations about Marta's husband, nor Gerald's weird theory that Petro might have been an early victim of the Yorkshire Ripper that immediately occupied her mind. Instead, bizarrely, she was thinking about accents, and Gerald's hopeless attempt at imitating hers. She squirmed when she remembered that her mother had made a very conscious – and very noticeable – effort to emulate the speech of her idol, Margaret Thatcher. Alison wondered who she herself sounded like – or more precisely, who she sounded like to these alien Yorkshire people; to someone like Gerald, or her work colleagues, or her neighbours in Saltaire. Possibly a polished yet bland BBC news presenter – it could be any one of them, for they all sounded the same – or perhaps the Duchess of Cambridge, though she couldn't recall ever hearing her speak. Her eyes began to close. It was time for bed.

CHAPTER ELEVEN

The Saturday afternoon before Christmas Alison and Marta travelled together by train to Bradford for the carol concert at St George's Hall. Alison had already invited Marta to the proposed Christmas lunch at *Freddy's*. She had been rather surprised at the alacrity with which Marta had agreed to come, even when informed that "that man from the choir," as Marta referred to Gerald, would be joining them. You could never tell how Marta was going to react, Alison thought. Sometimes she would dig her heels in over something that seemed to Alison to be essentially trivial. For instance, she refused point-blank ever to wear a certain particularly beautiful silk scarf, on the grounds that it had been a birthday gift from a neighbour and one-time close friend (Mrs Ball, long since dead), with whom she had subsequently fallen out over that lady's cat sometimes using Marta's small garden as a lavatory. Yet here she was, positively glowing at the prospect of Gerald's company at the meal – Gerald, whom she had initially demonised as someone who could potentially have done something terrible to Alison on that evening when he had helped her to gain entry to her house. And when, at a subsequent choir rehearsal, Alison had screwed her courage to the sticking place and introduced Marta to Gerald – fully expecting

Marta to be quite frosty, or even downright rude – she had been all sweetness and light, smiling graciously and even flirting with Gerald. And how Gerald had enjoyed that! No wonder he had drawn Alison aside after the rehearsal to thank her again for the invitation, and to say how much he was looking forward to the Christmas lunch.

"Listen to this," Marta said.

"What's that you are reading?" Alison asked, as the train left Shipley Station for the short journey to central Bradford.

"It's a local guide book. This is what it says about St George's Hall, the place where we're singing:

Often cited as Britain's oldest still functioning concert hall, (she read aloud to Alison), *St George's Hall is reputed to possess the very finest acoustics, a feature noted by Charles Dickens, no less. In 1854, Dickens read extracts from A Christmas Carol to a packed, appreciative audience. He received the then princely sum of £100 for his performance. Churchill spoke at a political rally in the hall in 1910. Instead of being applauded, like Dickens, he was attacked by suffragettes, and forced to seek refuge under the stage."*

"Well," Alison said. "Let's hope that the Titus Salt Community Choir emulates Dickens rather than Churchill."

"Indeed, yes," Marta replied, chuckling over the thought of Churchill's ignominious retreat. She closed the guide book and placed it back in her bag.

They got off the train at Forster Square Station and walked through light rain past a could-be-anywhere modern shopping centre, and then past the glorious Victorian building on Market Street which used to be the Wool Exchange. A few minutes later they were entering the stage-door of St George's Hall.

Whilst bills and junk-mail did, of course, come through his letter-box with depressing regularity, it was unusual, in these modern times of electronic communication, for Fred to receive a personal letter through the post. Not long out of bed, and still wearing his dressing-gown, he sat down in the kitchen of his Ilkley home, poured himself a cup of coffee, and opened the envelope. He could guess from the stamp and the postmark who had sent the letter to him.

Berlin
10th December 2015

My Dear Fred (he read)

I trust that you are well and that your new restaurant venture is meeting with success. I note with interest that there is a direct flight from Düsseldorf to Leeds/Bradford airport, so I am hoping that soon I can pay you a visit and partake of your undoubted excellent cuisine.

And now to business. As you requested, I have continued with the investigations since you left here, and I believe I have come up with some added details which may help us to further the completion of this complex jigsaw puzzle.

I have discovered that, almost for certain, the man you are interested in and the child who was later to become your father's first wife, did indeed live in Berlin for a short period during the highly confused months after the war ended in May 1945. This man made himself out to be a Pole, and even had Polish identity papers, giving him the name of Tomasz Grabowski, but he was in fact a Ukrainian, called Petro Semeniuk. Already that you may know, but this next may be new to you. His maternal grandmother was an ethnic German, and, although she resided for many years with the Semeniuk family in Ukraine, she had distant relatives living here in Berlin. These relatives were allocated an apartment in Meinekestrasse in the suburb of Charlottenburg, quite near to Zoo Station. That apartment had previously been owned by a Jewish family, which was deported by the Nazi regime. In fact there is a small brass memorial plate in the sidewalk outside the apartment building which refers to this crime. There were several Jewish families in the immediate neighbourhood, all suffering the same fate. Meinekestrasse was fortunate to escape any damage from the severe Allied bombing of Berlin. The apartment still exists and it is where Semeniuk-Grabowski and his daughter found shelter with these distant relatives, until they could make arrangements to move to a camp for displaced persons. That may possibly have been a camp in the British occupation sector near Osnabruck, I am unsure. At this moment I have been unable to discover much more, but using his Polish identity of Grabowski, Semeniuk and his daughter do seem to have moved to England quite soon afterwards, possibly as early as 1946, more likely 1947or even 1948.

That is all I have. If we can make a piece of it with what we have already found, (and what I hope to find) I am confident that we will come to the full wartime story of Petro Semeniuk and his daughter Marta, who was your father's first wife.

I wish you a happy Christmas.

Bis bald

Ulrich Fassbinder (Dr)

PS: Also, I have found a reference to a person, Elsa Muller, who may have been in Berlin with Semeniuk and his daughter, but there is nothing so far in later records about her. I will try and find out her destiny.

"Oh, Uli, what a long-winded, old Prussian fart you are! But bloody well done!" Fred said to himself. He wasn't sure how much the letter advanced things, but he was nevertheless grateful to the corpulent academic, with his bottle-bottom spectacles, for being so thorough – so quintessentially German – in his research. And there was no mention of him requiring any fee for all this painstaking work! Just an opportunity to come to visit Fred in England and dine at his restaurant. *Kein Problem!*

"Okay, guys, it's a full house out there, and that's not a problem, it's a plus-factor," the choirmaster said in his best stage-whisper. "Now, you'll notice also that we're sharing the stage with a brass band. Don't worry about that. All they will do is a few bars of introduction, then I'll bring you in, and we're off – no Arthur on the piano this time – just you giving it your all *a cappella,* exactly like we've rehearsed it. You know the words by now, so the key thing is to keep your heads up, keep your eyes on me all the time and, most important, look as if you're really enjoying it. Anything to add, Arthur?" Arthur had nothing to add. "Right, we are on straight after the children's choir, so once all the little pests have vacated the stage, it's our turn. And make sure you go on stage in the right order – we don't want basses mixed up with sopranos, or anything like that. That will never do…"

Indeed, that will never do, thought Alison, glancing first at Gerald, lining up with the bass section, then at Marta, just in front of her with the other sopranos. A few butterflies in the stomach now as they waited in line, like teams in the stadium tunnel before an important match. Suddenly, loud applause came from above; the children's choir had done its bit, and very soon a crowd of small bodies tumbled into the backstage room. Two matronly women, their fingers on their lips, ushered the children into the far corner and out of the way, so that the members of the Titus Salt Community Choir could now ascend the stairs leading to the wings and thence proceed in an orderly fashion onto the hallowed stage for their first public performance.

Fred read Dr Ulrich Fassbinder's letter through several times. That Petro Semeniuk had lived in Berlin for a brief period seemed less important than the revelation that Petro was partly German. Fred's visit to Krakow had not uncovered that, nor the name of the young woman who had accompanied Petro. Elsa Muller. Fred surmised, from the name, that she too was German. What became of her, he wondered? Did she make it to England with Petro and Marta? It didn't sound like it.

Still clad in his dressing gown, Fred rose from the kitchen table and carried the letter into an adjacent room, which served as an office. He took a box file from a shelf, opened it and carefully placed Ulrich's letter on top of a pile of other documents and notes of various sizes. Later he would go through the entire file again. In the meantime he needed to get dressed, drive to Saltaire and open up his restaurant. He had a business to run, and Christmas was a busy time.

As is frequently the way with these occasions, it was all over very quickly, and the members of the Titus Salt Community Choir were backstage again almost before they knew it. There was an interval in the concert programme now, so there was no longer any need for silence. The performance had gone well. The choirmaster entered the room and was effusive in his congratulations. The choristers themselves were euphoric, everyone speaking at once, like players on a winning team after a match. Even the normally taciturn Arthur said: "Well done!"

There were seats available right at the back of the upper gallery for those choir members who wanted to see the second half of the concert. Gerald, rather diffidently, asked Alison and Marta if they wanted to join him there, and he smiled happily when the two women accepted his invitation.

A long-established and renowned Bradford choir now took the stage. The whole of the second half of the concert consisted of this august group of singers leading the audience in a series of traditional Christmas carols, which alternated with less familiar sacred pieces sung by the choir alone. The finale was the choir's rendition of "Unto Us a Child is Born" from Handel's *Messiah,* sung with such skill and beauty that Alison, non-believer though she was, felt deeply moved. When the audience stood and applauded at the end of this piece, Alison glanced at her two companions; Gerald looked as if he were blinking back his tears, but Marta was dry-eyed, looking towards the stage with an inscrutable expression on her face.

Later, seated in the concert hall's comfortable bar with Marta and Gerald, a large glass of mulled wine in her hand, Alison felt more content than she had felt for some time. Until her phone rang. Out of long-established habit she took it quickly from her bag and looked at the screen; it was Ed, and the screen indicated that there had also been a missed call from him earlier that afternoon.

"Shouldn't you answer that, dear?" Marta said.

"No, I know who it is. It's not important." Alison replied, and she let the phone ring. A few more rings and then it stopped. The screen on her phone informed her that a voicemail message had been left.

A little later, alone in the ladies' cloakroom, she listened to Ed's message.

"Hi Ali. Too busy to answer, eh? Can't imagine how that can be, wherever it is you're withering away right now. Still, what the fuck? Just to update you, there's a party at Mike and Nikki's place on Christmas Eve. Should be good. They always have good shit. Couple of hot names I'm keen to meet will be there. Got to keep on networking, even if it is Christmas, hee, hee. Give me a call if you want to go. Love ya."

Alison deleted the voicemail and returned to her glass of mulled wine and her two elderly companions. Ah, London, she thought. The city where it's so important to be in the know; and if you're not, you must pretend, quite furiously and desperately, that you are. Was she missing it? Up to a point, yes, she had to confess that she was.

"Alison! Good to see you. I trust you're not wanting a table straight away, are you? Very busy right now, but maybe I can fix you up with something later."

"No, no, Fred, I just popped in to confirm my booking for Christmas Day lunch."

"Right, but I'm sure that it's in the book."

"Yes, but there will be three of us now, not two."

"That's fine. I'll make a note," Fred said.

"Excellent."

"So, am I allowed to ask who number three is?"

"Gerald, a friend from the choir. I've been in Bradford with him and my friend Marta this afternoon."

"Of course, it was your carol concert. How did it go?"

"I think we acquitted ourselves rather well," Alison said.

"I'm sure you did. Time for a drink? Or are you in a rush?"

"I thought you were busy," Alison said

"Always got time for you, Alison," Fred said, and he started to lead her by the hand towards the small bar.

"I'm full of mulled wine. Marta insisted on proposing about ten toasts in the bar after the concert – to the choir, to Titus Salt, even the Queen crept in there somewhere," Alison said, arriving now at the bar where one of Fred's staff had set up two glasses and was filling them with Prosecco.

"Well, that's the Poles for you," Fred said.

"If that's in fact what she is."

"Indeed," Fred said, and he looked away. Alison took a drink of the fizzy wine. "I'm looking forward to meeting your friend Marta. She sounds very interesting," Fred continued, after taking a drink himself.

"I'm sure you'll like meeting her," Alison replied. "And she is very interesting, there's no doubt about that." She watched him. He knew he'd made a little blunder and she was interested to see how he was going to wriggle out of it. "So how do you know that she's Polish?" she asked. He shrugged and took another drink.

"You told me, didn't you?"

"No."

"Oh, but I think you did."

"I would have remembered if I had," she said.

"It was when we had a drink together in Leeds."

"I talked about her a bit, but I never said what country she was from, just that she was my friend."

"Well then, it must be the name, Marta; not English, is it? Maybe I just presumed she was Polish with a name like that. Lucky guess, eh?" he said. Alison gave him no more than four out of ten on the scale of plausible excuses for this bit of wriggling.

"You know a lot more about Marta than you're prepared to admit; I've known that from the very first time her name cropped up," Alison said and Fred sighed a giant sigh.

"You're a shrewd woman, Alison." he said

"I know I am."

"Believe me, very soon I'll be able to tell you the lot, but I can't tell you just yet. Can you accept that?"

"If you say so."

"And will you make me a promise? Two promises, in fact."

"Go on."

"Will you promise not to tell Marta that I know anything about her?"

"Of course I promise," Alison said. "What do you think I'm going to do? Do you think that I'll introduce her to you, then blurt out that you have a head full of secrets, some of them concerning her?"

"No, I don't think that," he said. He smiled and just briefly laid his hand on top of hers.

"And what's the other one?"

"Other what?"

"The other promise you want me to make?"

"Oh, right. Well, I was just wondering if we could perhaps have another drink together some time, just the two of us. If I ask you, will you promise to turn up?"

"I never break promises."

"So you'll come?"

"Yes," she said.

"Good," Fred said. He turned from the bar now and surveyed his domain. Every table was full, and the atmosphere in the restaurant was suitably convivial. "You'll have to let me go now. I'd better start setting a good example to the staff."

Soon Alison was walking away from *Freddy's*. It was still raining a little, but despite that, everything about the day was acting like a tonic, lifting her spirits: the excitement of the performance at St George's Hall; the enjoyable time spent with Gerald and Marta, drinking mulled wine in the bar afterwards; her resolute snubbing of that fatuous idiot, Ed; the quick drink with the enigmatic Fred.

At the end of Gordon Terrace she was about to turn and walk down Victoria Road towards her house in Caroline Street. Gerald stood on the corner, an umbrella over his head.

"Hello Gerald, no home to go to?"

"Oh, hello, Alison. I've just phoned for a taxi. Thought I'd wait here for it. Been having a drink over there with an old friend," he said, and he nodded in the direction of a pub further up the main road.

"I've just called into *Freddy's* to confirm our booking for Christmas Day," Alison said.

"I know you have," Gerald said.

"Do you? How do you know?" Alison asked.

"I was passing, and I saw you through the window. Was that Fred himself that you were talking to?"

"That's right, it was. So, Gerald, spying through the window, eh?"

"Well, always the copper, I suppose," he said, and he shrugged in a way which made him look almost French for a moment. Would he be Inspector Maigret or Inspector Clouseau, Alison wondered. Then he dropped his voice and continued: "I'll tell you what, though."

"What?" asked Alison, mimicking his lowered voice.

"Fred's the spitting image of someone we've recently been talking about," Gerald said.

"Who might that be?"

"Who do you think?"

"I don't know. You'll have to tell me."

"I know it's years ago, but I never forget a face – copper's training maybe – and that Fred chap looks just like him."

"Who are we talking about, Gerald?"

"Jan Nowakowski. Fred looks just like Jan Nowakowski looked forty-odd years ago."

Now Alison could see all kinds of dilemmas. If Gerald was right, was it just a coincidence that Fred and Jan looked alike? Surely they couldn't be related. Or could they? More to the point, what if Marta saw straight away that Fred was a carbon-copy of her former husband? How would she react? There was still time to abort the Christmas lunch.

Alison could say that there had been a mix-up with the booking, and they didn't have a table after all. Or was she worrying too much? After all, as far as Marta was concerned, Alison knew nothing at all about Jan; not even that he'd existed; and certainly not that he'd once been suspected of murdering Marta's father. Indeed, Alison only knew about the murder because... Oh, what the hell, she thought. No point in worrying. Certainly no point in second guessing how Marta might behave when she met her ex-husband's look-alike. And anyway Gerald didn't seem too worried about it. So, let's go ahead with the lunch.

Gerald's taxi drew up. He wished her good night and she gave him a quick peck on the cheek. She watched the cab drive away towards Baildon. It had stopped raining, she noticed.

CHAPTER TWELVE

December 2015 was particularly wet, especially in the north of England. Not a week seemed to go by without reports of some place or another suffering severe flooding. First it was Carlisle, then it was various towns in the Lake District and east Cumbria; Kendal, Keswick and Appleby. Over the Christmas holiday period it was the turn of Lancashire and Yorkshire. The media, of course, loved it. Rainfall was described as being, "unprecedented" or, "of biblical proportions," whatever that might mean. Every newspaper and television news broadcast featured images of soldiers carrying sandbags and wading knee-deep through flooded streets, and there were plenty of pictures of emergency services personnel rescuing people from their devastated houses in rubber boats. Should the Government be doing more? Is this all to do with global warming? The experts and pundits took a break from their Christmas dinners and gathered in television studios to ponder these imponderables in excited tones.

Saltaire escaped the worst – almost. The River Aire burst its banks and Roberts Park and the sports fields, which Titus Salt had so thoughtfully provided for the recreation of his workers, were under water for a day or two. A few reporters from the national media turned up to have a look. Then the waters receded, and the television crews departed to re-assemble in the city of York, parts of which were particularly badly affected. Pretty young women, clad in expensive anoraks and wearing pastel-shaded Wellington boots faced the cameras, microphones in hand, and earnestly informed the TV audience that York was flooded, something which scarcely needed to be said, for the television pictures of the devastation were perfectly clear.

None of this affected Alison's planned Christmas lunch at *Freddy's,* although it offered a suitable topic of conversation with which to break the ice when the trio took their seats at a table near the window, soon after 1:00pm.

"Just imagine," Gerald said. "Your house gets flooded, and then the Prime Minister comes along to commiserate with you. I believe that's what they call a double-whammy."

The food arrived, and it was excellent. Alison watched her companions closely. Marta was on very good form, offering lively conversation throughout the meal, without ever becoming self-centred or tedious – so unlike Alison's dining experience with Rachel earlier that autumn. And Gerald, quite in awe of Marta (or so it seemed to Alison anyway) behaved impeccably. The only thing which was puzzling was the absence of Fred himself. Where was he? Between courses Alison excused herself and made as if to visit the ladies' cloakroom. The cloakroom was close to the double swing-doors which led to the kitchen, and when a waiter emerged Alison stopped him and asked where Fred was.

"Working in the kitchen today. Keen that we get everything just right," the waiter said, attempting to move round Alison and head towards a table where diners were eagerly anticipating the several plates of food which he was skilfully balancing. Just then one of the kitchen doors opened a little way, and Fred stuck his head out.

"Come on," he said, beckoning to her, and when she hesitated, looking over her shoulder to see if her two companions were watching, Fred came out, took her by the arm, and steered her into the kitchen. They squeezed past people and equipment and headed towards a back door. Out in the alley the cool air contrasted with the over-heated atmosphere of the small, crowded kitchen. And the rain seemed to have stopped for once. Taking Alison by the hand, Fred led her along the alley, round the end of the terrace and past the short sandstone obelisk on the corner, informing people that Saltaire was a UNESCO World Heritage Site. A few seconds more and they were standing on the pavement outside the entrance to *Freddy's.* Fred made sure that they took up a position where it was unlikely that they would be spotted by anyone on the inside of the restaurant, and through the window they could clearly see the table where Gerald and Marta were sitting. They seemed to be so absorbed, so deep in conversation, that Alison wondered if they'd even noticed her absence. Eyes only for each other, she thought, and that made her smile.

"Do you normally spy on the customers like this, Fred?" she asked.

"What?" he replied, not paying her much attention.

"What are we doing? It's starting to rain again."

"Sorry. I just wanted to get a really good look at her."

"I could introduce you, if you like," Alison said. "I thought that's what you wanted."

"No, no… I'm not quite ready for that," he said.

"Why ever not?" Alison said. "Look, I'm getting wet. I'm going back inside." She could see now that he was in something of an emotional state, shivering a bit and breathing rapidly. Had he been knocking it back in the kitchen? Then he stopped staring through the plate glass window and turned to face her. He took both of her hands.

"I'm being ridiculous. Sorry," he said.

"You'll have to tell me what all this is about. Not now, obviously…"

"Yes, yes, I will. That's a promise," he said, releasing her hands and backing away from her. "You go back inside, before you get soaked." He turned and started to jog-trot along the pavement. Clearly he was going to use the back door again. Just before he turned the corner into the alley he called out: "I'll phone you, Alison. We'll go for a drink."

Alison watched him disappear round the corner, then she went back into the restaurant through the front door and sat down with Marta and Gerald. If her two companions were in any way puzzled by her leaving their table in one direction, then coming back to it via the front door, slightly damp, they didn't show it.

"Brandy or a liqueur, Alison?" Gerald asked her.

"Where are you taking us? My brother is very weak."

"Listen, you must do exactly as I say. It is your only hope – our only hope. Do you understand?"

"Those others, we left them."

"I'm sorry, I cannot help everyone."

"Why should we trust you?"

"You have no choice."

"You could be leading us into more danger. It could be some kind of trap."

"Look, this young woman is my… wife, and this little girl is our daughter. They will be with us all the time. Surely you can see…"

"But why are you taking us away from the camp? What is happening there?"

"They are evacuating the camp. It is terrible to say it, but those who are too feeble to walk are being shot, probably right now as we speak."

"But some of us can walk fine. We wouldn't be shot. Maybe we would be safer in the camp."

"No, you wouldn't, believe me. They will compel those who can walk to march to the west, under guard, away from here. A forced march."

"So maybe we should be on that march. Maybe we will reach a safe place."

"There are no safe places now. And how many do you think are going to survive a forced march? In this weather? In the condition that most of you are in? Tell me that."

"How do you know all this? How do you know what their plans are?"

"I know because I work for them."

─────────────

Fred didn't come out of the kitchen again that afternoon, but this seemed of no consequence at all to Marta and Gerald, who never remarked upon his absence. And why should they? They were clearly having such a good time in each other's company that now and then Alison almost felt like an interloper; "playing gooseberry" would have been her mother's quaint expression.

"Thank you for organising this, Alison," Gerald said at the end of the meal. "I'd almost forgotten how really nice Christmas can be, even when you're no longer a child. When you're a kid it's the most exciting time of the year, isn't it?"

"Yes, it is," Alison said, trying not to think of the sterile Christmases of her own childhood. "Do you have children, Gerald?"

"Two, a son in Vancouver and a daughter in Christchurch, New Zealand. Both grown up, of course. Five grandchildren between them at the last count."

"That must be nice," Alison said, "even though they live a long way away."

"I know. Thank God for Skype, I say. What about you Marta? Any children?" Gerald asked, all innocence. They both looked at Marta, waiting for an answer. Once again Alison noticed the tiny pulse beating in Marta's temple.

"So what is this Skype?" she said, frowning and fiddling with her glass of Cointreau. Neatly side-stepped, Marta, thought Alison. And for the next few minutes Gerald delivered a short lecture on the intricate wonders of modern on-line communication. It was what blokes of his age did, Alison thought. Her father would have been just the same. Surreptitiously she glanced down at her watch; Marta, hawk-eyed as ever, saw her do it.

"This has been lovely," she said. "Thank you a thousand times, Alison. I think that perhaps it is time for us to go now. A pity that it continues to rain." She stood up and looked out of the window onto what was normally a busy road, but on this Christmas Day afternoon the traffic was light. At intervals, cars swished past through the rain, as the brief winter daylight faded and night came on.

Alison and Marta shared an umbrella on the short walk from *Freddy's*. Gerald had departed from the restaurant by taxi, having declined Alison's invitation to have one more drink at her house. With arms linked the two of them, like mother and daughter, walked down Victoria Road, past the row of single-storey alms-houses which Titus Salt had built for those of his workers who, because of their diligence, loyalty and sobriety, were deemed worthy of a home once they had retired from employment at his mill.

"Have you enjoyed yourself today, Marta," Alison asked.

"Immensely, my dear," Marta replied. "The food and the company too."

"So what do you make of Gerald? I think that he's a very nice chap."

"Indeed he is," Marta said. "Of course, I have met him before. I mean, before you introduced me to him at the choir."

"Really?" Alison said. "So when was that, Marta? A long time ago? "

"I'm not sure when it was."

"Interesting," Alison said, more to herself than to her companion.

"Fred too, the man who owns the restaurant," Marta said as they waited at the pedestrian crossing on Saltaire Road. "I have seen him."

"What? Today?" Alison was taken by surprise and her arm twitched. Marta, arm-in-arm with her would have noticed.

"No, no, I don't think he was in the restaurant today, was he? Unless perhaps in the kitchen," Marta said, and Alison was aware of a certain emphasis on the final phrase, and an accompanying sidelong glance. Had Marta seen her with Fred? Had they been clocked staring through the restaurant window, like a pair of waifs out in the cold and wet? Alison hoped not. It would seem such a dishonest and shabby piece of behaviour on her part, even though it was scarcely of her making. The light turned to green and they crossed the road. Marta spoke again, once they had gained the far pavement: "I saw him last week in that delicatessen near his restaurant. He was buying stuffed figs, I believe."

"How did you know it was him?" Alison asked. By now they were approaching the brightly illuminated Victoria Hall.

"I heard him talking to Mario. Mario was asking him how the restaurant was doing. He called him Fred. I was listening." Of course you were, thought Alison.

"Did he see you?"

"Perhaps he did, perhaps he didn't," Marta said. "The shop was rather full."

———————

The front door had never been properly secured after the explosion, so he had little trouble in getting it to open. All it took was a bit of brute force. He stepped over the threshold and into what had once been the reception area. This part of the building had been single-storey. Most of the roof had gone and he could see the night sky above him. Every now and then the sky was illuminated by a weak flash of light, and he could hear a muffled roar from afar, so that one might have innocently thought that, despite it being winter, a thunderstorm was in the offing. But he knew different; he knew that these rumbles and flashes signified that a different kind of storm was on the way. The Russians were approaching. How long before they arrived? Would it be tomorrow? Or later in the week? And what would become of them all then?

"Where are we going? I am sorry but my brother cannot possibly go on."

"Listen. There is a cellar here. It was used for storage. We are going to go down into the cellar and wait. Those are the Russian guns that you can hear. Maybe the Russians will find us, maybe they will just go past us, I don't know. But for the time being we will have shelter, and we can rest a little. Perhaps I can find some food…

"But what is this place?

"Follow Elsa. She knows the way to the cellar. Follow her."

"Please answer me. What is this place? Why do you and this woman know it?"

"Elsa and I used to work here. Before a Russian plane dropped a bomb on it, this was a hotel, the Hotel Lew."

———————

Gerald sat in the back of the taxi and thought about his afternoon. About Marta. He had had a great time at *Freddy's,* and he felt that she had enjoyed his company too. He wondered if she would allow him to take her out one evening. Just for a drink perhaps. Or maybe for lunch? Would she come up and visit him at his house in Baildon? Probably out of the question at this stage, but who could tell what the future might hold? It wasn't just young people who became – what was the expression? – "an item." People of his and Marta's age did too. Couples even in their nineties got married; you read about it sometimes in the newspaper. And he and Marta were nowhere near as old as that. Of course they'd have to come to some suitable agreement about the physical side of things. He smiled to himself. My God! He was almost at the point of mentally undressing her, like some spotty adolescent drooling over… stop it now!

Anyway, talking of matters physical, he noticed that his sciatica was beginning to give him some discomfort down his right leg. That's what comes of sitting in one position for a long time in the restaurant, he told himself. And it often troubled him when he was a passenger in a car, but rarely when he was driving; funny, that. Oh, and if he did start to see more of her – develop a relationship, or whatever – he'd have to make damn sure never to mention his involvement in her dad's murder case. Should he even tell her that he'd been a policeman? Neither he nor Alison (bless her) had let that slip yet, but he would probably have to tell her eventually. He wondered, not for the first time, what had become of her husband, Jan…

"This is the street you said, sir. Which house is it you want?"

"The one over there, the one with no lights on."

Meanwhile, back in Caroline Street, Alison and Marta were making themselves comfortable. Alison decided that coffee rather than more alcohol was what she wanted, but Marta, it seemed, was still in festive spirit, and she wanted more wine, so Alison was obliged to take a bottle of Vouvray out of her fridge and open that. Marta was keen to chat, and for a time they spoke once more about the successful meal, the poor weather and other Christmas trivia. Then, part way through her second glass of wine, Marta turned to more serious – and far more interesting – matters.

"You know, some time ago, when we were first becoming friends, I said I would tell you certain things, but not just then," she said. "When we were at Hirst Lock that time. Do you remember?"

"Yes, I do," Alison said. "You were concerned that I might think you... impolite, I think was the word you used. And I said that it was really up to you what you chose to tell me, and when, especially as we didn't really know each other very well at that time."

"And what do you think now? Do you know me better?" Marta said.

"I think we know each other much better now," Alison said. "I think we have become good friends."

"I agree. We are friends. And that is why I want to tell you something. Is that all right with you?"

"Of course it is," Alison said. "Go ahead."

"You remember the picture of my father, the one I showed you displayed in Salts Mill?"

"Yes," said Alison, not at all sure what Marta was going to tell her.

"My father and I were very close. I believe I told you that. He worked at Salts Mill for many years. And I think I told you that I became a teacher; I taught art."

"Yes, you've mentioned that," Alison said, patiently waiting for what might come.

"What I haven't told you is that my father had a dreadful accident."

"At Salts Mill?" Alison asked, still very unsure where Marta's story was leading.

"No, no. Not at Salts. He fell into the canal, near to Hirst Lock," Marta said. She paused, as if for dramatic effect. "He drowned." She said this quite calmly, rather matter-of-fact, then took another sip of her wine.

"How awful!" Alison said. This was the best reaction she could offer to Marta's almost comic statement.

"It was an awful tragedy, yes. He was such a good man; such a loving father. But what I wanted to tell you was this. When you saw me at Hirst Lock that time, when I seemed rather sad, that was because it was the anniversary of his accident. I go there each November, to the lock, and I also put some flowers on his memorial stone in Nab Wood Cemetery. He was cremated there. That's what I wanted you to know." She fell silent. After a suitably tactful pause Alison spoke.

"Thank you for sharing that with me, Marta. I think I should apologise to you. I can remember that morning when I bumped into you. I made a silly joke about you looking so down that perhaps you were going to jump into the canal. A bit tactless of me, given the circumstances." To Alison's surprise Marta laughed quite loudly at this, before she spoke again.

"No, no, no, you mustn't blame yourself for that, Alison. How were you to know why I was there? No need for apologies." And she emptied her glass.

A little later Marta decided that it was time to go home. Alison offered to walk her round the corner to her house, but Marta wouldn't hear of it. "Not worth putting your coat on," she said, as she let Alison help her into hers. When she had gone, Alison put the unfinished bottle of Vouvray back into her fridge and made herself another cup of coffee.

So, that was Marta's version of the death of her father, was it? How peculiar. Not a murder at all, eh? Well, perhaps Marta really did believe that her father's death had been a horrible accident – his being murdered might be far too difficult for her to live with, so she had constructed an alternative story, and now that was the one that she sincerely held to. It was so very plausible, wasn't it?

No, it wasn't. Alison stopped herself right there. There was too much psychobabble in all that. It was just the kind of trashy nonsense you might get from a self-help book ("This book will change your life. Over ten million copies sold.") Or in a glossy magazine you read while you were waiting to see the dentist. There had been no accident, and Marta knew it. In November 1969 Petro Semeniuk, had been murdered, and the police, including a young detective called Gerald Cranley, had been unable to catch the killer. Alison knew Marta well enough by now. There was a hard edge to her which would scorn any self-deluding, any notion of avoiding the realities of life, no matter how painful they were. No, this version – that Petro had suffered a terrible accident – was intended solely for Alison's consumption. But why Marta had felt the need to spin such a tale was not clear at all.

Fifteen minutes later Alison was in bed, but she was fully awake. Marta was still on her mind, and so were the two men who seemed so fascinated by her. One of them,

Gerald, she could understand; he'd clearly carried a torch for Marta for years. But what was there about Marta that had got Fred so intrigued – and so palpably anxious, if today was anything to go by? And what about Jan? Marta had never mentioned him at all. She'd never dropped the slightest hint that she'd once been married to him. So where was Jan Nowakowski in all this?

Tomorrow, she would go and find Petro's memorial in Nab Wood Cemetery.

CHAPTER THIRTEEN

Nab Wood Cemetery and Crematorium is on the main road which runs between Bradford and Keighley; it is quite close to Saltaire. Alison spent part of the next morning looking at a website which gave details of how to locate who was where in the cemetery. She learned about the graves of two noteworthy persons. One was that of a sailor who had won the VC in the Second World War for his part in attacking a Japanese cruiser in a miniature submarine. The other was that of an actor who had featured in a long-running television soap opera. He had apparently been a native of Shipley. Alison had never heard of him.

The rain stopped in the early afternoon, and Alison walked to the cemetery. It took her about half an hour, then a further half-hour to locate Petro's memorial, a small stone monument in the Garden of Remembrance. Despite Marta's assertion that she had placed flowers there only the previous month, there were none to be seen. Indeed the area around Petro's memorial stone was quite overgrown and unkempt. The inscription on the stone simply said:

PETRO SEMENIUK

Born Ukraine 1920
Died Saltaire 1969

That was it; no further information, no clues. Alison felt let down. Depressed too. It was Boxing Day and she imagined that all her London friends, Ed included, would be out on the town, partying as if there were no tomorrow, whereas she was hanging about in a gloomy Yorkshire cemetery, like some character from a gothic horror story. It was beginning to get dark now, and a bit creepy, especially as there was nobody else about. Trying not to think too much about ghosts, vampires and mortality, she made her way back to the main road.

————————

Petro counted them again, just to make sure they'd not left anybody behind in the snow. There were five women and five men, plus Elsa, Marta and himself. The men all looked utterly exhausted; the one who had been semi-carried by his sister wouldn't survive long, he could see that. He was more confident about the women; they would be more resilient. Women always were. Elsa had managed to find some candles in a cupboard at the back of the cellar, and the light from one of these threw shadows onto the whitewashed walls. There were no seats, but Elsa had gathered some dusty sacks, which had probably once held potatoes. Marta helped her to spread the sacks on the floor, so that the escapees had somewhere to rest.

Petro was full of admiration for Elsa. It was she who had suggested that they try and give these people refuge in the Hotel Lew's cellar. She had even managed to gather some bits of food in a haversack. Crucially, she had urged Petro to discard his uniform and put on some civilian clothes – not his best suit, naturally, but something which would give the impression that the three of them were just a local family who had somehow been caught up in the confusion. Whatever else, they must not be seen as having had anything to do with the running of the camp.

The camp itself had been like a scene from Dante's *Inferno*. The German commander – the one who had conscripted Petro several months earlier – had driven off in his Mercedes-Benz staff-car, leaving instructions for his underlings to follow. All records were to be burned, that was the number one priority; those prisoners who were too weak or sick to walk were to be disposed of; those capable of walking were to be marched westwards towards the complex of camps beyond Krakow. As much of the camp as possible was to be destroyed.

Of course, these instructions were dutifully carried out. Groups of guards went methodically from hut to hut and murdered the sick, the halt and the lame. Others rounded up the remainder, those deemed capable of walking. This crowd of shuffling humanity was driven out through the main gate of the camp and escorted down the road like a herd of semi-starved cattle. A third group of guards set fire to the prisoners' huts, incinerating the bodies of the dying and those who were already dead.

Petro's instructions had been to make a bonfire of all the documents from the administration block. This he had done. By then most of the SS overlords had fled. Realising that any vestige of order and control in the camp was rapidly disappearing, Petro had come to a decision. He would try his best to help at least a few people to escape.

After making sure that his bonfire was well alight, Petro had walked the short distance beyond the perimeter of the camp to his quarters. Elsa had been waiting for him there with Marta, and he had told them of his intention. Elsa had then suggested that they might use the nearby ruined hotel as a refuge.

It had been easy enough to organise the escape. Close to the perimeter fence there was a prisoners' hut which he knew had not yet been visited by the killing squads, nor had it been set on fire. As he had expected, the door of the hut was not locked and he had gone in. The stench had made him nauseous with disgust, and he had been obliged to cover his nose and mouth with a handkerchief. Although no longer in uniform, his authority was not challenged, and those inmates who were able to walk had lined up by the door, in response to his instructions. There had been only a handful of them. The rest – the sick, the dying, and those already dead – lay quite passively in tiers of wooden bunks, jammed together. There had been nothing that Petro could do for them.

Once outside the hut he had shepherded his small flock through the camp towards a side-gate, beyond which lay the guards' barracks. A short distance beyond the barracks was the abandoned, bombed-out ruin of the Hotel Lew. Many of the camp's buildings had been on fire by then, and there had been the sound of pistol shots coming from some of the huts on the far side of the camp. Orders were being obeyed. But that part of the camp through which his small group had passed seemed uncannily devoid of people, and the watch-towers which rose high above the perimeter fence were unmanned. Soon the camp had been left behind. So far, nobody had noticed their departure.

In the Lew's cellar Petro looked at his new companions. They were all ethnic Poles. Any Jews would have been killed months ago, transported to the camps near Lublin, or the huge complex of camps on the other side of Krakow. Nobody knew for certain what happened to them there, but the rumour was that they were all slaughtered – "sent up the chimney" was the light-hearted euphemism he'd heard used by some of the guards when they'd talked about the cremations which were said to take place round the clock.

But this camp where Petro had been employed for the past few months was on a much smaller scale. It was essentially a holding resource for non-Aryan *untermenschen* who had been rounded up prior to being transferred to various parts of the Reich to work as slave-labour. It was a dreadful place. Food and medical supplies for inmates, never adequate at any time, had become even scarcer since the late autumn of 1944. Many prisoners had died from malnutrition, or from a variety of diseases. Petro knew all about this because his principal job, since he had been conscripted into the Ukrainian Auxiliary Police, had been to keep the prisoners' personal records in good Teutonic order. He had, in his office, files for new arrivals, files for current inmates, files for those who had been transferred, and (a large category, this) files for those who had died whilst resident in the camp. Or, to be strictly accurate, he'd had all these various files until that morning. Now most of them were just a heap of smouldering ashes on the path outside the camp's empty administration block.

———————

A few days after Boxing Day Alison was in Bradford, looking through the old newspaper archives again. This time she was searching for a notification of Petro's funeral in the Family Notices section of the local newspaper. It didn't take her long to find it:

SEMENIUK
Petro

On November 6th 1969,
his life tragically cut short, Petro
aged 49, of Saltaire. The
loving father of Marta and a
dear father-in-law to Jan…

There was no need for her to read the details of the funeral service and the cremation at Nab Wood Cemetery. The important point was the confirmation that Marta had been married to Jan Nowakowski, just as Gerald had said. But why had Marta never mentioned this husband? Had she deliberately erased him from her memory? Was that why there were no photographs of him on her sideboard? Could it be that she suspected – or even knew for certain – that he had murdered her father? Gerald had told her that the two of them, Marta and Jan, had separated soon after the murder, and Jan had possibly gone to live in the south of England. Why had they separated? Surely, Alison thought, a horrible tragedy like the murder of a parent, would bring the surviving members of a family closer together, but clearly not in this case. There was nothing else to be gleaned from these old newspapers, so Alison went and caught the train back to Saltaire.

———————

While it was still dark Petro, moving with extreme caution, returned to the barrack blocks, just outside the perimeter of the camp. It had not snowed for a number of days now, and the sky above him was clear and full of stars. The cold – and some fear – caused him to shiver as he approached the single-storey mess hall. He was ready to turn and run if anyone appeared; nobody did. The mess hall door was open and he stepped tentatively into the pitch-black interior. Although the darkness might offer some protection, if needed, it also hindered his progress as he tried to make his way towards the kitchen. Once he banged against a table, quite violently, and the pain that shot through his shin was, for a moment, sharp enough to make him cry out. He had matches, but he knew it would be foolish to strike one, at least until he'd reached the larder which adjoined the kitchen.

Once inside the larder, and with the door closed, he struck a match and held it up above his head like a little lantern. There was some food here. The kitchen staff had clearly been in such a hurry to leave with the rest of the camp personnel that everything had just been abandoned. True, the few loaves of bread that he found were stale, but what did that matter? He discovered a small box of apples, some potatoes and several pieces of smoked salami – even a half-empty bottle of schnapps. He stuffed as much as he could into his haversack and his coat pockets.

He paused, a potato in his hand. It struck him, not for the first time, that the staff of the camp – he and his small family included – had always had sufficient to eat, whereas the prisoners had been forced to make do with the most meagre of rations. His job in the administration block had normally kept him apart from the prisoners; he scarcely ever saw any of them. He'd kept his head down, concentrating his attention on the impersonal files in his office. Now, renewed feelings of guilt convinced him even more that helping some prisoners to escape was the right thing to do; it was his attempt at atonement. Thinking on this, he made his way back through the darkness of the mess hall and out into the starlit night.

Over in the camp he could see that smoke was still rising from the burned-out ruins of two of the prisoners' huts. In the distance, to the east, flashes lit the horizon, but the sound of gunfire seemed fainter than it had been. Did that mean that the Russians were no longer approaching? It was impossible to say. Taking care not to drop any of his booty, and ever watchful for signs of anyone lurking nearby, he followed his own footprints in the snow and returned to the sanctuary of the Hotel Lew's cellar.

The woman – the strong one who had helped her brother to walk from the camp to the Hotel Lew – now volunteered to accompany Petro back to the mess hall to collect more food. The brother lay quite still on the ground, and she did not wake him when Elsa, helped by Marta, distributed bits of food to the group. Petro ate a little of the stale bread, then took a slug of the schnapps, hoping that it would keep out some of the cold, and give him the courage for a second expedition to the barracks. He offered the bottle to the woman, but she shook her head.

The two of them made just one foraging trip to the mess hall that night, hoping to bring back whatever bits of food they could carry. They encountered nobody at all until they were returning to the hotel. By now it was starting to get light. As they came around the corner of the Hotel Lew, intending to go through the remains of the front door, they saw that a military truck was parked in what used to be the hotel's forecourt. Their immediate instinct was to turn and run back the way they had come, but it was too late. Two Russian soldiers, dressed in long greatcoats and wearing fur hats, appeared and pointed their rifles at them. Petro and the woman stopped and held up their hands. Items of food dropped onto the snow. Petro felt no fear, just a mild surprise that the Russians had arrived so quickly. He had started to think that they might be moving away from the vicinity.

More Russian soldiers came out of the Hotel Lew, ushering the prisoners. Elsa came out too, carrying Marta in her arms. A young man who was clearly the officer in charge followed them out and spoke to the two soldiers who lowered their rifles. The officer made a gesture, indicating that Petro and the woman could lower their hands, then he turned away to speak to a soldier – scarcely more than a boy – who was trying to lower the tailgate of the truck. The woman took the opportunity to move closer to Petro and press something into his hands.

"What are you giving me?" Petro asked.

"My brother's identity papers. You may need them," the woman said.

"But won't he need them?"

"No, he won't. He died a few hours ago, before I went with you back to the barracks. You thought he was sleeping. Don't say anything. He is at peace now," she said, and, as she stepped away from him: "His name was Grabowski, Tomasz Grabowski."

The Russian officer turned to face them again. He beckoned and they followed him into the hotel's ruined reception area. It was daybreak now and a weak sun shone on the snow, making it sparkle in those places where it had not been disturbed and dirtied by footprints and tyre tracks. Two soldiers came out of the hotel's interior carrying a chair and a small table, which they placed near the front doorway. The Russian officer sat down at the table, and the two soldiers pushed Petro and the woman forward until they were standing opposite him. He removed his fur hat and placed it on the table. Then he spoke to them in Russian.

"I see that you have been scavenging for food. Have you been to the camp?" he said.

"Just to the barracks, this side of the camp," Petro replied in Russian.

"And is the camp still occupied?" the officer asked.

"Not as far as we could tell," Petro said.

"You are a prisoner in the camp, that I can see," the officer said to the woman, looking at her striped prison garb, parts of which were grimed and matted with dirt.

"Yes, that is so," the woman replied, also in Russian. The officer turned to address Petro again.

"But you are not a prisoner," he said.

"No."

"Maybe you work in the camp?"

"No," Petro said.

"He has nothing to do with the camp, comrade. I would know if he did," the woman said. "He has helped us to escape and brought us here to hide. We have him to thank for saving our lives."

"Really?" the Russian officer said, studying Petro closely. "And do you have anything, any papers that may say who you are?" Petro handed over the crumpled papers which the woman had passed to him only minutes before. The Russian officer examined them closely before speaking again.

"So, you are Tomasz Grabowski. And you are Polish?" he said, still holding the papers. Petro had initially wondered if the Russian would understand what was written on the papers, or if he would just put on an act in order to show that he was the person in charge. "And you have been helping these people. Sheltering them here in the hotel cellar. Hiding like mice. Is that so?"

"Yes," Petro replied.

"Why have you been helping them?"

"It seemed the right thing to do," Petro said in a quiet voice, looking down at the dust-covered floor.

"What did you say? Speak up, man," the officer said. Petro raised his head and looked directly into the officer's eyes.

"I said that it seemed the right thing to do," he said, slowly and clearly. The officer laid the identity papers on the table next to his fur hat.

"And if you are not a prisoner, Tomasz Grabowski, and you are not connected with the camp in any way, how did you become a Good Samaritan for these people? Please tell me that," the officer said.

Petro had never considered himself much good at lying, or even embellishing the truth, but he knew that a plausible story was now required, and he had his story ready. If the Russians discovered – or even suspected – that he was a member of the Ukrainian Auxiliary Police, and that he had worked for the Nazis in the camp, even in a clerical capacity, he would almost certainly be taken out into the hotel forecourt and shot. And Elsa and Marta would no doubt see it happen. He took a deep breath and began.

"My wife and I – that's her outside, with our little girl – were sent by the German authorities to a farm not far from here. We had no choice in the matter. Some Jews used to own the farm, I believe, but they'd been… replaced by a family of *Volkdeutsch* who had been encouraged to settle in this area. I worked on the farm as a labourer, and my wife was a domestic servant in the house. Because she was blonde and fair-skinned our little girl was supposed to be adopted by the family and brought up as an Aryan German. That's part of the German's racial policy, but it never really happened in our case. Then, when your army

174

was starting to get closer, the farmer and his family suddenly left. Overnight, they just disappeared. I don't know where they went. A few days later most of the farm buildings were burned down and the livestock driven off. Perhaps it was some German soldiers retreating, perhaps the partisans, I don't know," Petro said, inwardly praying that this wholly fictional account would be sufficiently convincing.

"Or perhaps it was our army," the officer said softly. Petro gave a slight shrug and remained silent. "Do go on," the officer said.

"We hid in the woods, but we needed food, so we came down here, hoping to find something. I wandered into the camp by accident. They were shooting some of the prisoners, but nobody bothered me. Most of the guards had gone. I found one hut with prisoners still in it, so those who could walk I brought here for shelter. I couldn't think what else to do." He was aware that his heart was beating very fast as he waited for some reaction to his story. The officer was silent for a while.

"You worked as a farm labourer, you say," the officer said at last. Petro nodded. He could guess what was coming next, and all his hopes began to fade. "Show me your hands," the officer commanded sharply, and Petro offered them to him for examination. Of course they showed no evidence of manual labour at all. For what seemed like an age the Russian scrutinised Petro's hands, then his face. Then he said: "Go and stand over there. I wish to talk privately to your companion." One of the soldiers took Petro by the arm and pushed him roughly into a corner of the room, far enough away from the table to prevent him

175

from overhearing what was being said. The woman leaned forward and put her clenched fists on the table, so that her face was level with that of the Russian. Petro watched closely. For the next few minutes she seemed to do most of the talking, while the Russian officer listened. Now and again he would look across at Petro.

Eventually the woman and the Russian officer ended their conversation, and a rifle butt to the small of the back indicated that Petro was required to return to the table to re-join them. He had no idea what his fate was going to be.

"Well, Tomasz Grabowski, you seem to be in luck today. You are no farm labourer, that I do know, and whether you are even Polish may be open to debate." At this, he offered the crumpled identity papers to Petro, who took them back. The officer went on: "But no matter. Do you know who your companion is?" he asked, nodding towards the woman, who was allowing herself the faintest of smiles.

"No," Petro replied. "We only met yesterday." Yesterday! It seemed like a hundred years ago, at least.

The Russian officer's tone had changed. Up until this point he had sounded like an ordinary human being, but now he clearly felt it more appropriate to adopt the air of a loyal Party *apparatchik*: "This is Comrade Krystyna Voynich, secretary of the Lublin branch of the Polish Workers' Party. Of course, the Fascists did not know who she was, otherwise she would certainly not be alive and here with us this morning," he said. "Sometimes it is necessary to have another identity." Indeed it is, Petro thought to himself. The Russian officer went on: "Comrade Voynich has told me all about your valour in rescuing her and her companions and sheltering them here in this abandoned hotel." To Petro's utter astonishment the Russian officer then came from behind his table and, grasping his upper arms, planted noisy kisses on both of Petro's cheeks, while Comrade Voynich offered a brief round of appreciative applause.

"Thank you," was all that Petro felt able to say.

"You and your family are free to go. We will not detain you any longer," the Russian officer said.

"What will happen to the prisoners?" Petro asked.

"These former prisoners of the Fascist beasts will be properly cared for, you have no cause to worry about that," the Russian said. "Sadly, one of those you helped has died. My men will have to cremate his body. The earth is too hard to dig a grave." And he turned and led them out into the sunlit forecourt of the Hotel Lew.

The former prisoners were already sitting in the back of the truck. Elsa and Marta were standing nearby. Beyond them, under a line of birch trees which, in happier times would no doubt have formed part of a pretty view from the hotel terrace, two Russian soldiers were dousing the prone corpse of Comrade Voynich's brother (if that was indeed who he was), in petrol from a jerrycan. The two stepped back and one of them threw a lighted match at the body. It went out before it landed. The other soldier grabbed the matches irritably and struck one. He held it for a time to make sure that it was well alight, then tossed it towards the corpse. This time there was a "whump" as the petrol ignited and the body immediately started to burn. Petro knew that before long there would be the unmistakable sickly-sweet odour of burning human flesh drifting through the morning air.

A second truck was now in the forecourt, and it was into the back of this one that the two Russian soldiers climbed, their duties as crematorium attendants now at an end. The engine came to life and the truck was driven away, followed by the other, which carried the former prisoners. Marta, standing with Elsa, waved farewell to the departing vehicles. Nobody returned her wave.

CHAPTER FOURTEEN

Alison saw Fred waving to her from the other side of Victoria Road. She stopped and waited for him to cross over and join her. She hadn't seen him since the Christmas lunch, and with the elapse of two weeks she had concluded that his promise to phone her had been little more than an empty gesture. It was disappointing, but she knew what men could be like. She hadn't been holding her breath.

"Hello, Alison. Look, I must apologise for not phoning. I know I said I would, but so many things have got in the way," he said, once he had given her the customary peck on the cheek. She looked at him without smiling. Although he was looking suitably guilty, Alison wasn't going to let him off too easily.

"A busy time at the restaurant, I suppose" she said, with enough frostiness to let him know that his broken promise had been noted. "Anyway, why aren't you there now? You're not normally closed on a Friday."

"I know, but we've had to close until Monday."

"Why is that?"

"We've got a problem in one of the cellars."

"A burst pipe?" she asked.

"No. Mice. We found droppings. It looks as if a whole tribe of them have been squatting there, probably seeking shelter from the lousy weather. I've had to get the pest control people; they're going to gas them, I think. Fortunately it's not a food store. I've just been in to make sure we'll be okay to open next week. It's a bloody nuisance, it really is," he said. She looked at him. He looked tired out. Alison relented. She decided that she'd forgive him for not phoning. "Anyway, shouldn't you be at work?"

"I've been working from home today," Alison said. "I do that some of the time."

"Darling, how very modern!" Fred said, adopting a silly affected voice. Then, he added grimly: "I wish I could work from home, especially on days like today." He relaxed a little then and gave her a rueful smile. It was hard not to like him. "So, does working from home involve wandering the streets as well? Or is this a late lunch break?"

"Just be careful," Alison said, and she playfully poked his chest with her forefinger. "Listen, I was emailing and phoning overseas clients late last night and first thing this morning. I've been hard at it for hours, but I've finished now."

"Good for you," Fred said. "Anyway, have you had any lunch?"

"No," she replied. She thought for a while. She would try and make amends for her earlier brusqueness. "If you like, we can go back to my place for a bite to eat. No point in us going up to your restaurant, if you're overrun with mice."

"It's hardly that. But thanks, that would be nice. Are you sure you have enough food for two? I've not eaten today. I'm starving."

"Perhaps we could get something over there and take it back with us," she said. There was a sandwich shop on the opposite side of the road.

"Good idea, let's do that," Fred said.

Their lunch of shop-bought sandwiches was hardly gourmet standard, but it was adequate. When they had eaten Alison took the plates into the kitchen and placed them in the sink. Fred followed her.

"Would you like me to help you wash up?" he said. She was conscious that he was standing very close to her.

"No, it's all right. I'll do it later," she said.

"Right. Anything else?" he asked. She was unsure what he meant by this.

"Such as?" she replied. Instead of answering her, he moved his face towards hers and kissed her briefly on the cheek, then, rather clumsily, on her mouth. More out of a sense of politeness than any overwhelming feelings of passion, she allowed him to do this. The kiss went on for longer than she had expected – or indeed wanted – and although she felt a slight frisson of pleasure when his hand moved lightly over her breast, it was not sufficient to make her want to continue. Quite gently she pushed him away. His breath smelled a bit of Branston pickle.

"Fred, I'm not sure this is really the best way to round off lunch," she said. "I'll put the kettle on and make some coffee." She turned to face him, and saw that his expression was one of disappointment mixed with a touch of sheepishness. Poor Fred, she thought.

"Sorry. Forgive me, Alison. I got carried away," he murmured, looking down at the plates in the sink.

"No harm done," she said, attempting to sound reassuringly cheerful. Then she added: "You can take the coffee into the lounge, but try not to get too carried away. We don't want you spilling anything on the carpet, do we?" This was intended to lighten the atmosphere, but when she looked at his still crestfallen face she realised that it hadn't worked, and she wished she'd not said it.

"I do find you attractive, you know, but I suppose lots of men will have said that to you," Fred said, glumly aware that he was spouting the usual clapped-out clichés. He watched her pouring hot water from the kettle into two cups.

"Oh, there must have been hundreds," Alison said airily, trying for some self-mockery, but not really succeeding. It was true she'd had her share of men, but that didn't mean her love-life had been a catalogue of thrills and happiness. If she allowed herself to think about some of the men she'd been involved with – especially those who'd cheated on their wives, and just as glibly lied to her – she could easily start to feel depressed. She was astute enough to realise that Fred was probably an all-round nicer fellow than many of her former sexual partners, but that wasn't enough for her. He just didn't press the right buttons. It was a pity really.

She led the way back into the lounge and Fred, as instructed, followed her, carrying the cups of coffee. He still looked miserable and embarrassed, sitting there on her sofa, so she went and stood behind him. She massaged his shoulders for a few seconds, then planted a kiss on the top of his head.

"You're a good man, Fred Nicholson, and I like you a lot," she said, as she came and sat down opposite him. He smiled at her, just a little wistfully. "And now," she went on, "as I've given you your lunch you can tell me a bit more about your interest in my friend Marta."

"What do you want to know?" he said, warily.

"I want to know everything. You promised me."

"I know I did," he said with a sigh. "Maybe we can make a deal."

"You mean you'll tell me, provided I …?" Alison said, rolling her eyes.

"No, that's not what I meant at all. Stop teasing me. The deal is I will tell you, so long as you forget about me making an idiot of myself in the kitchen just now. Okay?"

"I've forgotten it already," Alison said. "So you can start to spill the beans straight away. I want to hear the lot."

"You'll have to remind me. What do you already know?" Fred said. More than you think, Alison thought to herself. She would have to tread carefully now. All she was supposed to know was what Fred had told her in the bar in Leeds. Nothing more.

"Okay," she began. "I know that you inherited money from your dad, quite a tidy sum, and that meant you were able to train as a chef and later open some restaurants. *Freddy's* is the latest one. You opened it in Saltaire because you believed this area was on the way up, so it made sense from a business angle. But I managed to wheedle out of you that there was another motive. You'd also come to Saltaire because of something to do with Marta. There'd been some part of your dad's will that requested you to… do some things? (Fred nodded at this)… including coming up here. I'm guessing that the 'up here' bit was where Marta comes in. You wanted to meet her, and you had an opportunity at the Christmas lunch, but you lost your bottle for some reason that I can't yet fathom. And that's it," she concluded.

"Yes, that's it, more or less," Fred said. "Could I possibly have a glass of water?"

"I'll get it for you." Alison rose and went into the kitchen, returning with a tumbler of water, some of which Fred drank before he started to speak.

"I suppose the easiest way to explain things is to say that I've been doing some research into my family's history, a bit like, *Who Do You Think You Are?* Do you know it?"

"I think I may have seen it once," Alison said.

"Right. I knew nothing about my family tree before my father died. In his will he didn't just leave me a pile of cash, there were various documents and letters. And some things he wanted me to do. He'd been looking into the past, but he'd only got so far. He asked me to finish off what he'd started."

"And where does Marta come in?" Alison asked, aware that this was not the first time she'd made this enquiry of Fred. "Is she part of your family?" Fred shuffled about on the sofa and took another swig of the water. He was struggling to find the right words, she could tell.

"Not exactly, no," he said at last.

"What does that mean?" Alison asked. Fred shifted awkwardly some more.

"She's not directly a member of my family, but at the same time… oh God, I suppose I'd better tell you. You see Marta was…"

Here he was interrupted by someone knocking at the door. Alison got up and went to see who it was. It wasn't the postman. It was Gerald Cranley.

———————

Two letters arrived in the post. One had a Shipley postmark and he knew it was from Marta. The other looked as if it had been redirected several times. He opened the one from Marta first. It was in English.

George Street

Saltaire

20ᵗʰ June 1980

Dear Jan

I hope that you do not object to me writing to you, but I thought you would want to know that I have recently had a visit from the police. It seems that every so often they go over old unsolved cases.

It was ten years last November that my father was killed. They wanted to talk to me about it. I was unable to tell them anything new. They asked if I knew your current address, but I do not see why I should help them so I said I did not know it.

I realise that it may be of no interest to you but my health has slowly improved and I am working again, part-time in a local primary school. It has taken me many years to recover from my father's death and the miscarriage which came so soon afterwards. Losing a child is just as painful as losing a father.

I shall not write or try to contact you again, unless you wish me to.

Marta

This was the first direct contact he had had from Marta in almost ten years; he didn't count the letters from her solicitor pertaining to the divorce. It was possible that the police might take the trouble to trace him to Reading and interview him. Then again, they might not be all that bothered. Petro's murder was a cold case from more than ten years ago. If they did come he would, like Marta, have nothing new to tell them.

He put Marta's letter into his jacket pocket and opened the one with the Polish stamps on the envelope. This one was undated, but its contents were of the same ilk as others he had received down the years. Nevertheless he read it. It was in Polish.

Esteemed Sir!

I have been asked to write to you by a parish priest living in England who contacted me through a relative of his. The subject of my letter is a man called Petro Semeniuk. I believe I knew this man during the war when I was living near Lublin. He was a Ukrainian who worked for the Germans and he had a terrible reputation for cruelty and also killing. I believe he was the man who I saw with my own eyes beat a man to death in our village square when he came one day in September 1941 with the Germans, seeking out the Jews…

There was no need for Jan to read any further. The person referred to was not his former father-in-law, he knew that. According to other letters sent to him, Petro Semeniuk had been variously identified as a senior guard in Treblinka, a squad-leader in the Waffen SS Galicia Division, a member of an *Einsatzgruppe*, murdering Poles and Jews in the Radom District, and so on. He popped up all over the place. It was as if every Ukrainian who had collaborated with the Nazis bore his name. The more of these "authenticated testimonies" Jan received – and there had been dozens – the harder it had become to pin down who Petro Semeniuk actually was and what monstrous crimes, if any, he had committed against his fellow men during the terrible years of the Nazi occupation of eastern Europe.

Jan replaced the letter in its envelope. He would put it with the rest in the drawer in his bedroom. There were two piles in there, both secured with rubber bands. One consisted of letters like this one. Most of them had been sent to him years before at the behest of the ultra-nationalist group in Bradford. Time and again they had managed to locate individuals who would send him letters claiming they had witnessed Petro Semeniuk committing all manner of terrible atrocities. Initially this was intended to turn him against his father-in-law and incite him to take a patriotic and justifiable retribution for the crimes against Polish people which Petro was supposed to have perpetrated. Later, when Petro had been killed, the letters were intended to justify his summary execution and offer gratitude.

The other pile was smaller and constituted his largely unsuccessful attempts to find out the truth about Petro, and about Marta, who had been the wife he had thought he loved.

He went into the bedroom where his new wife, Dorothy, was still asleep. It had been another difficult night for her. Frederick had woken several times, and eventually Dorothy had felt it necessary to bring him into their double bed so that she could, with luck, snatch just one or two hours of rest before morning. Frederick, not quite six months old, was snuggled against her, fast asleep now. For a full minute Jan looked down at the two of them, mother and child. Then, as quietly as he could, he turned and went to the drawer which contained his cache of letters. The letter from Poland went on one pile; the letter from Marta went on the other.

———————

Fred didn't linger. After exchanging the usual ritualistic pleasantries with Gerald, who was full of praise for the excellent Christmas lunch served at *Freddy's*, he said he'd better get back to see how things were progressing up at the restaurant. And off he went. Gerald said that he too could only stay a short while. He'd been passing and he thought he'd just pop in for a minute to wish Alison a belated Happy New Year. No, he wouldn't take his coat off. A cup of coffee? Oh, go on then.

Although she knew he was in no way to blame, Alison felt annoyed and frustrated because of Gerald's unexpected arrival. Did people up here never use the telephone? Then she smiled to herself when she considered what Gerald might have blundered into if she'd not put a damper on Fred's ardour. What a picture that would have made! She and Fred naked on her lounge carpet, while Gerald rattled the door and shouted his New Year greetings through the letterbox. At least he would have congratulated her on fitting a more effective lock on the door.

"What are you smiling at?" Gerald asked.

"Oh, nothing important," she said. Then, to change the subject she added: "Have you seen Marta since our Christmas lunch?"

"No. Have you?"

"No, but I have something to tell you."

"Have you?" he said, and he unbuttoned his overcoat and removed his scarf.

"Marta and I came back here after the meal and had a good old chinwag. I think she was a bit tiddly, to tell the truth. Anyway, she started to talk about her father and about his death."

"Really?" Gerald said, keen to hear more. "So, what did she say?"

"She said that Petro's death was a tragic accident. He'd fallen in the canal and drowned."

"Rubbish!" Gerald said with a snort which had him reaching for his handkerchief to wipe his nose.

"I suppose it definitely was a murder? There couldn't have been some kind of mistake, could there?" Alison said. Gerald put the handkerchief back in his pocket.

"No," he said. "You've seen the newspaper reports, and you've heard my account. The fact that it was a murder was the only thing that was clear. Who did it and why were the real mysteries. An accident? She's kidding herself."

"Or kidding me," Alison said, "but I can't work out why she should want to do that. Can you think of a reason?"

"Maybe she thought you were getting too close. You were interested in the photo of her dad in his uniform. Perhaps it's tied up with that."

"Perhaps," Alison said, not convinced.

"You didn't tell her that you knew for certain it wasn't an accident, did you?"

"Of course not," Alison said, rather affronted by his presumption that she wouldn't have kept her mouth shut. Gerald saw that he'd said the wrong thing.

"Sorry," he said, apologetically. Then, after a pause: "Did she tell you anything else?"

"Just that she thought she'd met you a long time ago, but she couldn't remember the circumstances."

"Bloody hell!" Gerald said, almost to himself. "Do you think she'll have recognised me from all those years back, when I was on her dad's case?"

"I don't know," said Alison, "but you can't rule it out. One thing I have learned about Marta is that she usually knows more than you realise, and much more than she lets on. She's a very sharp, intelligent woman."

"I know. Sharper than me, that's for sure," Gerald said, once again more to himself than to Alison.

"Oh, and she said that she'd seen Fred before too, even though he wasn't in the restaurant on Christmas Day."

"Really? So where had she seen him?" Gerald asked

"She said she'd seen him buying food in the deli. Stuffed figs, I think she said. She was behind him in the queue."

"And what else did she say?"

"Nothing really, just that the deli-chap called him Fred and asked how the restaurant was doing. That's how she knew who it was."

"Well, that's very interesting, Alison, and I'll tell you why," Gerald said, adopting a portentous tone, typical of old men, Alison thought. It amused her, but she was keen to hear what he was going to say, nonetheless.

"Go on. I'm on tenterhooks," she said, a bit too flippantly. Gerald ignored it.

"Just now I got a better look at Fred myself, even though he cleared off almost as soon as I walked in. And now, I'm more convinced than ever," he said.

"Convinced about what?" Alison asked.

191

"That Fred's a close relative of Jan Nowakowski. The likeness is uncanny."

"How close?" Alison asked.

"Probably his son. I'd be prepared to put money on it"

CHAPTER FIFTEEN

The following week, out of the blue, Alison received an offer of a job. It was from her old London firm, which was wanting to expand. Would she be interested in coming back to work for them? They had always considered her work to be first-class, they said, and they knew from the industry grapevine that she had been doing some impressive things in Leeds – "whilst in exile up north," was how they expressed it. They did not require an immediate response; the position would not become available much before the summer. The remuneration package would be an attractive one. Would she give it some thought?

Alison drank her breakfast coffee and gave it some thought – not so much to the job offer itself, more to the notion of her self-imposed exile. Was that really her current status? If she took up the offer she would have spent a full year in Yorkshire. That made it sound like a stint of voluntary work in foreign parts; a gap-year, undertaken before returning to real life in the only place that counted – London.

As it was a Saturday she decided she would go for a walk after breakfast and do some more thinking. Saltaire was getting back to normal after the Christmas floods. Scores of volunteers had filled hundreds of bags with detritus of all kinds which the swollen Aire had deposited along its banks. The branches of all the trees in the flooded area had been festooned with ragged strips of plastic, hanging like hideous catkins. Most of that had been cleared up too. So many people had turned out to help restore the flooded boathouse at Hirst Weir that the organisers had been obliged to send many of them back home. Hirst Weir itself had been breached, but it was now being repaired; rowing would recommence before too long. The Scouts had done such sterling work up and down the river banks that they had received a commendation from the Chief Scout himself. The pub which stood on the Aire at the bottom of Victoria Road would be closed for months, but Alison noticed that the nearby tennis courts, which had been badly damaged by floodwater, were already being resurfaced. Titus Salt (or at least his statue) no longer had to survey a miserable vista of water-ruined chaos; instead he could look out over a Roberts Park, which was beginning to be spruced up, ready to greet the spring.

Alison walked along the canal towpath until she came to Hirst Lock. Ever since she had learned about Petro Semeniuk's murder she had experienced a mixture of fascination and repulsion whenever she approached the spot. Today, benefiting from a sliver of February sunshine, it all seemed so pleasant and peaceful that it was difficult to appreciate someone had carried out a brutal killing close to where she was walking. Who had killed Petro? Why did Marta tell her it had been an accident? Did Jan kill Petro? And was Fred Jan's son, as Gerald had suggested?

She sat down on a bench next to the lock and tried to think about London rather than vicious unsolved murders. The job offer was certainly tempting. At one time she would have accepted it without hesitation. She would have believed that only an idiot would pass up such an opportunity, for living in London surely meant being right at the heart of things, enjoying a lifestyle which everyone knew to be the best there was. Why should she stay up here in this alien land? Its paradoxes were still confusing for her; landscapes and towns which were beautiful and imposing one minute, barren and threadbare the next; a people friendly and hospitable for the most part, but given to sudden outbursts of hostile aggression. Gerald, who fancied himself as something of a local historian, had told her that the dour bluntness and chip-on-the-shoulder mentality came from Yorkshire's Viking heritage. He maintained that up here Alfred the Great was not viewed as a national saviour, but as a dastardly predator; the first in a long line of southern-based oppressors of the people of God's Own Country. It had taken a while for Alison to realise that Gerald was not joking; he actually believed this ridiculous nonsense.

A picture came into her head of Gerald in the prow of a Viking long ship He was wearing his policeman's helmet adorned with a Norse warrior's horns. She took a small pad from her bag and drew a quick cartoon sketch of him, truncheon in one hand, battleaxe in the other. Up above, Alison drew the face of God emerging from the clouds. He was wearing a flat cap. This skill of rapidly transmitting ideas from her imagination onto paper had been something of which Alison had always been justifiably proud.

She was about to add a suitably rude caption to her cartoon when the tinkling sound of a cycle bell interrupted her. She looked up and saw Fred, standing astride his bicycle and grinning at her from the towpath. She wondered why almost every cyclist in England wore a helmet and specialised cycling apparel. Fred looked faintly ridiculous in his. She'd visited Amsterdam often. Everyone rode bikes there; none of them wore helmets. And people wore their normal clothes too, so nobody looked any sillier than usual. With just a few strokes of her pen she added Fred and his bicycle to her picture. Instead of the helmet she drew Fred in a tall chef's hat.

"Hi Alison, out sketching the view?" Fred said as he trundled his bike up the short, steep bank to her bench. "Going to show me?"

"No," she replied, and she put the pad back into her bag. "I was only doodling." He sat down next to her on the bench. The sun had gone in now, but the clouds were high; there was little chance of any rain. "I'm glad I've bumped into you. I think you've been avoiding me," she said. "I popped into the restaurant earlier in the week, but they told me you were out. Were you?"

"I saw you come in and I dodged into the back. Sorry." He had that sheepish look on his face again.

"So you were avoiding me," Alison said.

"Sort of. I felt a bit embarrassed after…"

"Oh, come on," she interrupted him quite sharply. "That's all forgotten. I told you that at the time."

"You could have phoned me," he said.

"I could, but I didn't," she said.

"Well, I'm here now."

"Yes. And that's good, because I want to ask you something."

"Ask away," he said, as if everything about him was totally transparent; his life an open book. If this was his mood, she thought, there was no need to prevaricate. She would get straight to the point.

"Tell me, Fred, was your dad, by any chance Jan Nowakowski?"

"Why do you ask?" he replied, speaking quite softly now. He showed not the slightest hint of surprise at her question. It made Alison wonder if he'd been expecting it, and all of a sudden she felt like an interfering busybody; it wasn't a comfortable feeling. After all, who was she to pry into other people's lives? What gave her the right to burrow through the archives, or to pore over someone else's old family photos? Why was she doing it? Was all this amateur sleuthing just a way of passing the time in a strange place – a place where she didn't really belong? She should be minding her own business. At that moment she felt the pull of London becoming stronger; the big city with its crowds of people who would be more like her, sharing her values, and none of them giving a damn what anybody else did with their lives.

"Sorry, don't answer if you'd rather not," she said. Her voice was much weaker than she wanted it to be. She felt peculiarly feeble.

"No, no, don't apologise. You've asked a straight question; it deserves a straight answer," Fred said. "And the answer is yes, Jan Nowakowski was my dad. I was born Frederick Nowakowski in Reading to Jan and Dorothy Nowakowski." He spoke in such a deadpan tone that he might have been reading words from an instruction leaflet. "She was English; Nicholson was her maiden name. I adopted it when I started up my first restaurant because I thought it would be better for business if I had an English name. Sometimes it is necessary to have another identity. That's what I remember my dad once saying."

He stopped speaking. Alison couldn't think of anything to say in reply. Fred stood up and took hold of his bicycle.

"Someone has been talking to you, Alison. Stop pretending you don't know anything about all… this." He gestured towards the canal and the lock. Then, without saying another word, he pushed his bike towards the towpath, mounted it and rode off towards Saltaire. Alison watched him go. He was upset, that was clear. The only sound which broke the silence was that of water from the canal flowing down through the lock's overflow sluice.

———————

They felt as if they had been walking for ever. Sometimes Marta would walk resolutely beside them; at other times they had to take it in turns to carry the child. Most of the time they stuck to the roads. If it seemed that there might be soldiers about – stragglers from the defeated German army, or the vanguard of the advancing Russians – they would leave the road and hide in the woods, until they judged that the danger had passed. They avoided the towns and villages, but they found that there were sometimes scraps of food to be found in those abandoned farms which had not been destroyed. They were, nevertheless, becoming increasingly tired and weak, and Petro began to wonder how much longer they could go on.

Then, after several days, they had a piece of good fortune. Searching a barn close to a deserted farmhouse, Petro came across two exhausted boys asleep on the ground. He guessed straight away that they were deserters from the German army, for although they had abandoned their uniforms in favour of ragged civilian clothes, they had quite sensibly kept their army-issue boots. They were unarmed. Petro held his pocket knife to the throat of one and roused him by shaking his arm roughly. The boy jerked awake and was terrified when he saw Petro crouching over him with the knife in his hand. Speaking in Polish he begged Petro not to kill him; he told him that he and his companion (now also awake and equally frightened) were cousins who had been forcibly dragooned into a hastily assembled German infantry unit only a few weeks previously. This rag-tag regiment was largely made up of Polish conscripts. It had been supposed to help mount a last-ditch counter-attack against the Russians, but instead of going into action the press-ganged Poles had killed their German officers in the night and run away into the woods. The two cousins were heading for their grandfather's farm. It wasn't far away, they said; it was off the beaten track. They might all find a safe refuge there.

Alison remained seated for a while longer. It occurred to her that this must be the bench where Marta – either by accident or quite deliberately – had left the old photograph, and where the scruffy boy had found it. That was only a few months ago, but it seemed much longer. Alison hadn't known about the murder and all its surrounding mysteries then.

She sighed and got to her feet. As she began to walk back along the towpath towards Saltaire, an elderly man passed her. He smiled and made some friendly comment about the pleasant weather before he continued his walk towards Bingley. Alison had read somewhere that some survivors of the Yorkshire Ripper had reported that he had engaged them in friendly conversation just before attempting to kill them. Had that happened to Petro, she wondered? Although she knew it was laughable she felt compelled to turn round to check that the old man was not sneaking up behind her, intent on murder. Of course he wasn't; he was plodding along in the opposite direction. For the second time that morning she felt foolish and embarrassed.

Ten minutes later she had left the towpath and was starting to walk up Victoria Road. Fred and his bicycle were waiting at the end of the cobbled street that led down to Saltaire Station.

"I'm just going to open the restaurant," he said. "Look, after the lunchtime crowd has gone there's usually a bit of a lull. If you'd like to come up, say about three-thirty, I may have something to show you."

―――――

The camp at Checkendon had closed some years earlier, but there were still plenty of Poles living in and around Reading who had happy memories of it. Even though it was nothing more than a disused army camp with Nissen huts for accommodation, it had seemed like paradise in comparison with what people had suffered after September 1939. Poles from the west of the country had been systematically tyrannised and often arbitrarily killed by the Nazi invaders; many from the east had been deported to Kazakhstan or Siberia by the Soviets.

Jan and his co-workers produced thousands of biscuits every day at the giant Huntley and Palmers factory in Kings Road. It had been easy enough for him to get a job there in the maintenance department. It had been just as easy to find lodgings with Mrs Nicholson, whose house was not far from the factory. She had an unmarried daughter, Dorothy, living with her. After a few weeks Jan started to take Dorothy out to the cinema; a short time later he was sleeping with her. Soon Dorothy and her mother were making wedding plans.

Jan would always seek out and talk with those people at the factory who had been housed in the camp at Checkendon. He found a few who thought they could recall a pretty blonde girl called Marta, but nobody could remember much, if anything, about her father. It was as if Petro had kept such a low profile that he had been almost invisible. If Jan cautiously enquired whether any of the Checkendon residents might have been Ukrainians rather than Poles, he was met with puzzled looks and occasionally with angry assertions that such a thing was completely impossible. The vehemence of the denials made him speculate that maybe Petro and Marta had not been the only ones at Checkendon masquerading as Poles.

One day, a man called Franek approached him in the factory canteen.

"You've been asking about a girl called Marta, I think?" he said.

"That's right," Jan said. "Do you remember her? At Checkendon?"

"I think so, yes. She was in the same school class as my daughter. She was a very pretty little girl. Blonde hair. Bright too. She liked to draw and paint."

"That could be her," Jan said. "Do you remember her father? A man called Petro?"

"I don't remember anyone called Petro. Tomasz Grabowski was the name of her father, not Petro," Franek said. "He was a quiet chap. He kept himself to himself. He didn't join in much."

"Do you know what became of them?" Jan asked.

"I believe they moved up north," Franek said. Then he went to the counter to get himself another cup of tea.

Dear Frederick

I have instructed the solicitor to make this letter available to you on your eighteenth birthday, together with the money which has been held in trust for you, in accordance with the terms of my will. First of all, it is important that you understand that for you to receive the money you do not have to accede to any of the requests contained in this letter. You may decide to ignore them. That will be your choice.

Next I want to tell you something about my life before you were born. Your mother knows very little of this, and I want that to remain so. Please respect that wish.

Your mother was my second wife. I was previously married to a woman called Marta Semeniuk. We were married in 1965. That was when I was living and working in a place called Saltaire, near Bradford, where I was brought up. In 1969 Marta's father, a man called Petro Semeniuk was murdered. I was a suspect for a time, but the police had insufficient evidence to put me on trial. However, some people believed that I was the man responsible and a few tried to persuade me that Petro Semeniuk was a war criminal and deserved to die. They even gave me money. The pressure of it all became too much for me and soon afterwards I came to live in Reading, where I met your mother. I married her soon after Marta Semeniuk and I were divorced. I have three requests:

1) That you try to find out Petro Semeniuk's war record. I myself have tried, but I have only made a little progress. Notes on what I have found, with some relevant documents, are attached to this letter.

2) That once you know for sure what her father did in the war, you contact Marta Semeniuk, if she is still alive, and inform her. It is best for her that she knows the truth, however painful.

3) That you use the money wisely, but without feeling any guilt.

I hope that you will find it in yourself to carry out these requests.

Your loving father Jan Nowakowski

Dated and witnessed: 31ˢᵗ August 1984.

(Confidential to my son, Frederick Nowakowski , to whom it should not be given until he attains the age of eighteen years.)

Alison read the letter twice to make sure that she had taken it all in. She and Fred were sitting at an empty table in *Freddy's*. The last of the lunchtime diners had departed and the staff had cleared the tables. There were occasional noises from the kitchen, but the dining room itself was empty and quiet.

"What do you make of it?" Fred asked.

"What am I supposed to make of it?" Alison replied.

"I think you already knew there had been a murder."

"Yes," Alison said.

"Did Marta tell you?"

"No, she didn't. It doesn't really matter how I found out." She picked up the letter again. She wasn't going to reveal what Gerald had told her, nor what she'd unearthed in the newspaper archives. She shifted the focus. "But I can begin to see now why you've been on your quest, and why it was important for you to come up here to Saltaire, though I must say I think opening a restaurant as some kind of cover is going a bit far – why not just tell Marta and have done with it?"

"How could I? I didn't know if her father was a war criminal or not. I'm not at all sure if I know now. That's why I keep holding off. I'm just not sure." He was no longer upset and annoyed with her, she could tell, so she felt she could move things on a little.

"And what about your own father?" she said, quite gently and aware that she was still stepping on all manner of eggshells.

"You're asking me, did he – my father – murder Petro?" Fred shook his head. "Who knows? This letter doesn't tell us. He doesn't confess to murder, yet he doesn't he's innocent either."

"And the reference to you not feeling guilty about the money? I'm not sure…" she began, and he interrupted her, as she expected he would.

"I think it can only mean one thing; most of the money coming to me was a reward he got for supposedly carrying out the killing. Blood money," Fred said.

"But surely he wouldn't have accepted it if…" She left it hanging.

"I know, I know. 'You've given it to the wrong man, but I'll keep it anyway because I'm a bit short at the moment. Many thanks.' Don't ask me why he kept it, Alison. Maybe giving it to me, the beloved son – which I was – somehow let him off the hook, I don't know." He looked downcast. "I feel as if I'm at a dead end right now. I have all kinds of letters and stuff – I'll show you them – but none of them will tell you whether Petro was a Nazi butcher or not, let alone whether my dad killed him as retribution. And my own feelings are so mixed up anyway. What I mean is this: if Petro did murder shedloads of people in the war – Poles, Jews, or whatever – maybe my dad was right to bump him off. Petro was a monster that didn't deserve to live. And even if he was innocent, but my dad sincerely believed that he was guil…" Here Alison held up her hand, like a policeman on point duty.

"No Fred, if Jan killed Petro just on the say-so of others; if he believed what he was told to believe, without having any real proof," Alison said, "then it can never be justified. And neither can taking the law into his own hands, even if there was definite proof Petro was a war criminal. I think you know that." Fred looked at her, sighed heavily, and nodded his agreement.

"You're right, I suppose. Oh, God! It's all so complicated." He looked up at the ceiling, as if for guidance, and his body rocked to and fro for a while before he spoke again. "Anyway, as to opening a restaurant up here, I might have done that, even if Marta wasn't around. It wasn't just a cover; it made good business sense." Then he added: "And it's where my dad's English roots were. I feel as if I owe it to him."

CHAPTER SIXTEEN

As the New Year got well under way, so did the Titus Salt Community Choir. Weekly rehearsals re-commenced at Victoria Hall in preparation for the choir's participation in a concert to be held at Bradford Cathedral during Easter Week. This time the choir was scheduled to perform two pieces from Bach's Easter Oratorio, *Preis und Dank,* followed by a short chorale. The choristers were initially uncertain if they were up to Bach, but felt reassured when they recognised the chorale was just an early version of *All People That on Earth do Dwell.* True, the other piece would be trickier for such an inexperienced group, but the choirmaster was confident they could pull it off. And Arthur, seated at the piano, sagely nodded his agreement.

Wednesday evening rehearsals, of course, meant supper with Marta at her George Street house. As before, these meals consisted of beautifully prepared salads, smoked meats and unfamiliar cheeses from central and Eastern Europe. Wine was always available, but Alison would only drink one glass, if that. Conversation was usually confined to the choir and music, interspersed with those bits of everyday chit-chat that are normal between friends. Alison was wary of attempting too much probing about the questions and issues which really interested her.

Then, after perhaps the third of these late winter suppers, Marta suddenly said: "Ah, I have something I want to show you," and without waiting for any response from Alison she hurried out of the room. A little later Alison could hear her moving about upstairs. When Marta came down and re-entered the lounge she was holding a photograph which she thrust at Alison. "There," she said. "You are always showing interest in my paintings and photographs. I thought you would like to see this one. I came across it again the other day. I had mislaid it, you see."

Alison looked at it closely. It was a black and white snap of the same vintage as the one she'd scanned onto her computer. Indeed, it had probably been taken at the same time, as it again showed Marta as a young child standing in the same garden next to the same unknown young woman. All that was missing was Petro in his dubious uniform.

"What a pretty child you were, Marta," Alison said. Then, as casually as possible she added: "And who is the woman with you. She looks very nice."

"Oh, she was," Marta said. "She was what you might term my guardian. I called her Aunt Elsa. She looked after me." She paused, and then added: "When my father was working."

"Not a relative, then?"

"No, no, not a relative," Marta said quickly.

"And did she come to England with you and your father?" Alison said cautiously, knowing that Marta was quite likely to suddenly clam up if she thought she was being interrogated, or switch to a mundane topic like the weather or that evening's choir rehearsal.

"I don't know what became of her, I'm sorry to say. You know, these days I can hardly remember anything about those times before we came to England. It must be my age; perhaps I'm getting senile," she said, and she giggled, quite girlishly.

"You're not senile," Alison said. "You're as sharp as a pin, I'd say. And I bet you remember Aunt Elsa well enough."

"Oh yes, I do. She was such a kind person, not just to me, but to other people too, especially if they were in difficulties…" Her voice trailed off and she stretched out the fingers of one hand and closely studied her rings. Then she clapped her hands and was full of life again. "But I'm forgetting. Of course you've seen this photograph before. I told you I was getting senile."

"No, I haven't seen this one before," Alison said.

"Yes, you have," she insisted. "It's the one you found by the canal. The one I must have dropped. You returned it to me, a little before Christmas. Don't you remember?"

"That was a different photograph. Your father was on that one, next to you and Aunt Elsa."

"My father?" Marta said. Her face had a puzzled expression, as if Alison was making no sense whatsoever. "I have a photograph of my father on the sideboard over there," She pointed towards it. "He's standing beside me on my wedding day." Then, in a hushed mock-conspiratorial tone she said: "What a disaster of a marriage that was; better not to mention it." And she gave another little giggle, before resuming her slightly perplexed air. "But I don't think I have any others of him. Of course there is the large one I showed you, near the bookshop in Salts Mill."

Alison didn't press the point. Trying to get the information she wanted from Marta was rather like fishing. If you didn't play the fish with a sufficient amount of delicate skill, it would let go of the bait and swim off.

Later, back in her own house, Alison went over the evening's events. Marta was attempting to create a smokescreen, that was obvious; hence her desire for the picture of Petro in his uniform to be somehow airbrushed from Alison's memory. May Day parades in Moscow came to mind; pictures of Trotsky standing with Stalin one minute, then obliterated the next – now you see him; now you don't. But why had Marta displayed the incriminating picture on her sideboard in the first place? Had she never had other curious visitors? Nobody as nosey as Alison, wanting to know why there was a photograph of a man wearing the uniform of a Nazi collaborator? Had Jan seen it when he lived in the house with Marta? If he had, perhaps he'd never realised its significance, until he'd had it pointed out to him by the people seeking to use him as their avenging angel....

"Hello, Gerald."

"Hello, Alison. Good to hear from you."

"I thought I'd get in touch. I've not seen you at choir practice. Been bunking off?"

"I've had difficulty walking, with sciatica playing up in one leg and gout in my other foot. It's been like toothache,

I can tell you, but I'm feeling a lot better today, I'm pleased to say."

"Gout, eh? Sounds like too many beers and sticky puddings to me. And we'll need a note from your mum for missing choir practice three weeks in a row."

"Has Marta been going?"

"She has. You haven't been in touch with her, then?"

"I was going to phone her, but I lost my nerve at the last minute."

"And you used to be a big tough copper!"

"I know. It's shameful, isn't it? Anyway, how is she?"

"She's fine. I was at her house last night after choir practice. That's why I'm phoning, really. And to check that you were still alive."

"Which I am. Just. So what do you want to tell me?"

"It's all rather strange. You remember the photo I showed you? Of her as a child, with the unknown woman and her father in uniform?"

"Yes, of course I remember. It was on your computer."

"Well, last night she showed me another photo, clearly taken at the same time, but with just herself and the young woman. No dad in uniform."

"And so?"

"So then she tried to tell me that I'd seen the photo before, which I hadn't, and that it was the one I'd found by the canal…"

"Found by the canal? Wait a minute, Alison, I'm not sure I'm with you. What do you mean?"

"Right, I think I may have not told you the whole story about the photo on my computer, the one with her father…"

"…in his uniform, yes, yes. I know the one you mean. I've got that bit straight. At least I think I have."

"Marta didn't actually lend it to me. To cut a long story short, I found it on the canal towpath. She must have dropped it. I copied it before I gave it back to her. The important thing is that last night she denied that such a photograph existed. She claimed the one I'd found was the one with just her and the young woman, and that was the only one there was."

"Really?"

"Aunt Elsa was the name of the young woman, by the way. Not a relative, just someone who looked after her when she was small. When her father was… at work."

"At work, eh? Does she know you have a copy? Of the one with her father, I mean."

"No. And I'm not sure that I'm going to tell her. It'd be tantamount to calling her a liar, and I don't want to do that. She is my…. Oh, and the other thing is that I asked Fred straight out if Jan Nowakowski was his father, and you were right. He was his dad. So, what do you think is going on, Gerald?" There was a pause.

"I could be wrong, but I think I can see what Marta is trying to do," Gerald said at last.

"Go on."

"Letting you see the photograph of her father in his uniform was a mistake. She realises that now, so she's trying to cover her tracks by having you believe there isn't such a photo. Likewise, the yarn that her father's death was an accident, not a murder; that's another attempt at a cover-up."

"But why is she trying to cover these things up? And so ham-fistedly?"

"No, it's not very subtle, is it? Still, I'd say she's doing it because she really wants you to think that there's nothing untoward about her, no skeletons in the family cupboard. If you discover dark deeds from the past, a father who might have been in cahoots with the Nazis, a former husband who might have murdered him to avenge the entire Polish nation, well…"

"Well what?"

"You might run a mile. That's the last thing she needs. She's a lonely woman. She just wants you to be her friend. Don't you see?"

A little later Ed phoned. At first Alison wasn't going to answer, but she reasoned that a conversation with Ed was always so one-sided that she wouldn't be required to speak anyway. With this in mind, she simply greeted him and then let him burble on. Which he did.

"Whoa, news travels fast and a few little birds have told me that you may soon be coming to join the rest of us again in the promised land of the really living. Fucking excellent! I guess you must be getting your head together at last. Which reminds me that the bash at Nikki's last weekend was fucking mind-blowing. And I mean mind-blowing. It must have been Tuesday before I returned to planet earth…"

And so it went on. Perhaps he had been to an amazing party at Nikki's (whoever he or she was), but it was just as likely that he'd spent the weekend watching television, or gaming on his Xbox, or even visiting his mum and dad in Dunstable. You could never tell with Ed. His desire to impress with tales of a fabulous lifestyle, spent in the company of ahead-of-the-curve trendsetters, was so strong that self-aggrandising fantasy was never far away. At thirty-something he was still a child.

But Alison was somewhat annoyed that Ed seemed to know all about the job offer she had received. Gossip was the common currency of the world she would be re-entering in London, she knew that; no need for thumbscrews to prise information and opinion from people; Twitter would do it for you. So different with Marta.

———

The winter had been hard in every respect; spring was late that year. At first the old man at the farm had been reluctant to shelter them at all, but the two cousins – his grandsons – had persuaded him. They told him that they were grateful to Petro for helping them; what they really meant was that they were fearful Petro would denounce them as deserters, if shelter was denied. So the old man grudgingly let them stay.

Still, he demanded a price for his hospitality. Petro's wristwatch and Elsa's necklace and bracelet were quickly surrendered. After that, Petro paid the old man with labour. There was plenty for him to do. The old man had lived alone since his wife had died, and the farm had become a mess, so Petro spent several weeks repairing the outbuildings and the small farmhouse. Other than one goat, kept for milk, there were no animals left, but there was a barrel of salted cabbage and some cured hams in the cellar under the farmhouse. Salted cabbage, ham and goat's milk became their diet; it could have been worse.

The two cousins pretended to help Petro around the farm, but they were both quite feckless; they would have been useless as soldiers, Petro thought. Elsa did her best to keep the farmhouse clean and tidy. She kept Marta close to her, rarely letting her play outside for fear that someone or other might come to the farm and demand to know who they were. Nobody did come. As the cousins had said, the farm was remote and well off the beaten track, although there was apparently a small town about fifteen kilometres away. In happier times the old man had regularly taken his farm produce to the market there. Now he didn't know if the market still existed; or even the town. He lived the life of a hermit. When his wife had died in the winter of 1943 he had buried her body next to the barn.

Marta suddenly became quite ill with fever, and for a time Petro and Elsa feared that she would die. They had no medicines, and consulting a doctor was, of course, out of the question. Elsa gradually nursed the little girl back to health, but it took several weeks. And Elsa herself was not in good health at that time. She had developed a hacking cough and once Petro saw her cough blood into the rag she was using as a handkerchief, despite her attempt to hide it from him. He feared that she had the beginnings of tuberculosis. Perhaps she would start to improve with the arrival of warmer spring weather.

Then, one day in early May a jeep was driven up the rutted track to the farm. The two cousins immediately ran into the woods behind the farmhouse to hide, but Petro did not follow them; he wasn't going to abandon Elsa and Marta. Anyway, at first he was quite elated – a jeep! It's the Americans! And he waited outside the farmhouse to meet them. But instead of a gum-chewing GI, it was a young Red Army officer who climbed out of the jeep, followed by a man in civilian clothes. It was only much later that Petro learned that the Americans had equipped their gallant Soviet allies with all manner of military equipment, including jeeps, for the final onslaught against the Nazis.

The civilian, who, judging by his armband with the bright red star, was some kind of newly-appointed Polish official, greeted him with the news that Adolf Hitler had committed suicide, the German armies had surrendered unconditionally, and the war was therefore over. Petro felt no boundless joy, no heartfelt relief; just a monumental indifference. So, that's that, was all he thought.

The Russian officer now approached. He had been leaning against the bonnet of the jeep whilst his companion told Petro the good news. Petro turned to face him, and for a few seconds the pair of them looked at each other in silence. Then, as recognition dawned, the Russian officer spoke.

"Greetings, Comrade Grabowski," he said, "and how are your wife and daughter?"

_____

"Me again. I've been thinking about what you said. About Marta being lonely. I think you are right. I know that you would like to see more of her, so why not…?"

"Why not make my play, you mean?"

"If you want to put it like that, yes."

"I've thought about it. I even had the phone in my hand."

"So what's stopping you, Gerald?"

"Fear of rejection, I suppose. Ever since I first set eyes on Marta, all those years ago, I've thought of her as – let's say – out of my league. And I'm a shy bloke anyway."

"I think you should go for it."

"Really, do you?"

"Yes, ask her out for a drink. Something like that. I'm sure she'd accept."

"I might ring her. But not while I've got this sciatica and gout problem. She won't fancy going out with a bloody cripple."

"And I think you're wrong about her being out of your league. You say Fred looks very like Jan. If that's true it shows she was hardly married to a tall, handsome heartthrob. Jan was just a chap who mended machines in a mill. He probably wore a boiler suit and smelled of Swarfega…"

"What a snob you are!"

"I'm just trying to be helpful; rubbishing the opposition to give you a bit of encouragement. I know you've got strong feelings for her."

"That's true."

"In fact, all three of us, you, me and Fred, have all got some kind of a stake in Marta."

"Have we? In what way?"

"Fred very much wants her to know the truth about Jan and Petro, if and when he can discover it. You've clearly been in love with her for years…"

"I suppose I have," Gerald replied. "And you?"

"Sometimes I think I'm nothing more than a nosey cow, grubbing around in Marta's past, just to occupy the time. But I hope there's more to it than that."

"I'm certain there is."

"Are you? So, what do you think it is?"

"I've told you before; I think it's to do with friendship. That means getting to know a person really well, and caring about them warts and all. If we're not interested in doing that, it's not proper friendship. I reckon many people go through life and never have one proper friend, just a bunch of acquaintances." He paused, conscious of sounding portentous. "Oh, I'd better shut up now," he said. "I'm beginning to sound like *Thought for the Day*."

"No, don't belittle yourself, Gerald. I think what you're saying is spot-on. It makes a lot of sense to me."

"I'm glad about that. Anyway, here endeth the lesson."

That night Alison had a dream. She didn't dream often, or if she did the dreams were quickly forgotten. But this one stayed with her. She was still trying to make sense of it at work the next day and during her train journey to and from Leeds.

In the dream she was standing with Marta on the towpath at Hirst Lock. The boy with the rummage sale was there, but instead of the usual tatty paperbacks and old DVDs, he was only selling brand new black and white photographs out of a large wooden box. Marta was looking through them and laughing; Alison couldn't see who or what the photographs portrayed and this was making her feel impatient and a little cross.

All of a sudden, a large black dog escaped the control of its owner and bounded up to Alison. The dog was so powerful that it knocked her clean off her feet and she fell straight into the lock pound, but before she hit the water, many feet below, Marta managed to grab her by the wrist and hold on. Alison looked up into Marta's face and noted the familiar high cheek bones and the resolute stare from the slightly slanting eyes. Despite her advancing years Marta seemed to have remarkable strength, and Alison was soon pulled back to the safety of the towpath. Only then did she notice Gerald and Fred standing together on the opposite side of the lock pound, Fred in his Lycra cycling gear, Gerald with his hands deep inside his raincoat pockets. Fred gave her a little wave; Gerald remained motionless. Someone who looked like Ed was there too, but he had turned away, ignoring the scene, and was busy texting. Marta helped Alison stand upright on the towpath and dusted her down.

"Well now, Alison," she said. "I think I may have saved you from drowning." And at that point Alison had woken up.

CHAPTER SEVENTEEN

Dr Ulrich Fassbinder relished this work. What especially pleased him was the opportunity to leaven his academic research with examples of how specific individuals had been affected by catastrophic events. Not every historian approved. For some, including some of his colleagues at the Institute, such an approach smacked rather too much of kowtowing to the prevailing fashion for "history-made-simple." Was his ambition, they sometimes asked with wry smiles, to have a digest of his work serialised in some popular newspaper? Or perhaps a TV series, in which he would be seen earnestly pontificating about the horrors of the early 1940s against a background of Polish villages and Ukrainian farmlands? If pressed, he would possibly have admitted that such a scenario, however unlikely, was not without its attractions. Writing for a small coterie of scholarly historians might well make him acceptable to the purists, but popularising history by introducing a strong human-interest factor could lead on to fame and fortune. And what was wrong with that?

So, when he was approached by an Englishman called Fred Nicholson to delve into the personal history of one Petro Semeniuk during the war years, Ulrich had leaped at the chance. Correspondence via email and letters came first.

After that, Fred had visited him in Berlin on two occasions, and they had visited Krakow together. They became friends.

Fred was very keen to discover what had happened to Petro and Marta during the war, and Ulrich quickly found that this enthusiasm was contagious. But he was also surprised by Fred's lack of real understanding of the complexities of the conflict. Although Fred had Polish ancestry he seemed to know next to nothing, for example, of the forced removal of tens of thousands of Poles to Kazakhstan and Siberia, soon after Soviet troops had invaded the eastern part of Poland in the autumn of 1939, nor how those who survived this terrible exile were then conscripted into the Allied forces in 1941, after Hitler had reneged on his non-aggression pact with Stalin.

Fred tended to see everything in black and white – fiendish Nazi brutes versus noble Allies; the forces of righteousness and light locked in mortal combat with those of darkness and implacable evil. Ulrich had to explain patiently that things were rarely that straightforward. Circumstances often caused people to change their allegiances – sometimes more than once – in order to have any chance of survival. So it was perfectly feasible that a Ukrainian, like Petro Semeniuk, could have co-operated first with the Soviets, whom he hated, then with the Germans whom he likewise detested and feared, then with the loathed Soviets again. Everything – absolutely everything – depended upon time and place, Ulrich said. Life in Poland or Ukraine had been complicated and dangerous beyond belief in the 1940s. It was Ulrich's job, as a professional historian, to try and ensure later generations understood that. Exploring Petro's and Marta's experience was his way of doing it.

And what had he discovered so far? Very recently something which, his scholar's caution notwithstanding, had made him quite excited; something which he would need to communicate to Fred as soon as its veracity had been confirmed, if that was possible. He did not want to raise Fred's hopes if this new information was just another red herring, *ein Ablenkungsmanover.* (How Ulrich loved that word!) In this line of work, false trails, blind alleys, mischievous lies were all legion. One had to proceed with circumspection. And that suited Ulrich perfectly; he was precisely that kind of a man.

Initially Ulrich had been sceptical about using social media as a research tool. His younger relatives and acquaintances, of course, regarded such a method of communication as indispensable. Life without it was unthinkable; life before its inception was unimaginable. It had taken some time for Ulrich to appreciate that it could be used for more important things than mere narcissistic self-preening and the exchange of idle gossip. So he had used it to send out a simple but well-crafted advertisement: did anyone have knowledge of a Ukrainian called Petro Semeniuk and his very young daughter, Marta, who had lived in Poland – possibly near Krakow – during the latter part of the war and who later lived in England? A good number of responses came back to him. Of course much was totally irrelevant, and some replies were from cranks, or even lunatics, but among the heaps of dross and garbage were occasional pieces of gold.

And the brightest piece was from a woman who claimed that her grandmother (now deceased) had spoken to her more than once about being rescued from a Nazi camp and then sheltered, with others, in the cellar of a ruined hotel. The grandmother had a harrowing tale to tell. She had literally been seized off the street by the Germans. Her brother had suffered the same fate. It was intended that they be moved onwards from the camp to work as forced labour elsewhere in the Reich, but this was the winter of 1944-5, and events were moving quickly. By January the Russians were fast approaching, and the Germans abandoned the camp, shooting many of the inmates and forcing the rest to march westwards.

What happened next, the grandmother said, almost restored her Catholic faith, long replaced by Marxist orthodoxy. Certainly, it had all the trappings of a miracle. Instead of being killed, or forced to march until they dropped dead with exhaustion, the grandmother, her brother and a handful of other prisoners were freed from the camp by a Ukrainian *Hilfwilliger*. He had a young woman, perhaps his wife, with him and also a child called Marta, who may have been their daughter. She was about four years old. The grandmother remembered the little girl because she was exceptionally pretty, with blonde hair and an unusually intense way of looking at you. Two or three days later the Russians arrived and found the group hiding in the cellar. The grandmother, who later achieved some prominence in Poland's post-war civil administration, spoke up for the Ukrainian and that probably saved his life. Sadly, though, the grandmother's brother died; he had never been strong and he had been badly beaten by a guard shortly before the rescue. The grandmother's name was Krystyna Voynich; she was also known as Krystyna Grabowski.

Although his correspondent was unsure of the name of the Ukrainian miracle-worker, Ulrich felt sure that it was Petro Semeniuk. The clincher was the reference to the little blonde child called Marta. And Ulrich knew for certain that Petro had assumed the identity of someone called Grabowski. The grandmother's dead brother would have had no further use for his name, so Petro had simply taken it. Very sensible.

Ulrich presumed that the young woman was Elsa Muller. His other lines of research had made it clear that she had not accompanied Petro and Marta to England. In late 1945 she had died of tuberculosis in a hospital in the American sector of Berlin. That was something else to tell Fred. Ulrich had so far not been able to discover how the three of them – Petro, Elsa and Marta – had managed to get from an abandoned Nazi slave camp in Poland to the war-shattered German capital. But he was confident he would find that out too.

Marta sat in the sunshine on her customary bench next to Hirst Lock. She hadn't been truthful, telling Alison that she rarely came here; she came quite often, weather permitting. She looked along the canal towards Saltaire. There were no barges or pleasure craft on the water yet; it was still too early in the year. The Easter holiday would make a difference. Boats would then be queuing to go through the lock, and the swing-bridge beyond would be constantly opening and closing to let them pass. But just now four Canada geese and a pair of swans were the only things on the water. She could see a solitary heron too, motionless on the opposite bank of the canal. Once, years before, she'd seen a kingfisher, like a flash of blue light, go darting over the water near the lock just for a few seconds, then it was gone. Another time an excited man with binoculars around his neck had stopped her on the towpath and informed her, breathlessly, that he'd spotted a pair of goosanders. She was unsure what he was talking about, so she had just smiled and walked on past him.

Seated on her familiar bench, Marta thought about the photograph, the one that Alison had found and returned to her. How embarrassing that had been! What kind of a state must she have been in to lose it right here by the lock! And, of course, it had meant that she'd had to tell more lies to Alison; ones that were probably not very convincing. Alison was perceptive; not the type to be easily fooled. What must she think of her? With luck, only that she was an old woman who was losing some of her marbles and could get a little confused.

And there were other things she'd not been truthful about. She'd told Alison that she couldn't remember anything before she and her father came to England. There was much she'd tried to forget, it was true, but the doctor in the clinic had told her it was unwise to repress bad memories. She had to try and remember all the bad things and talk about them; that way she would gradually get over the trauma. At first she'd not believed him. How could she possibly talk about the murder of her father? Her stillborn child? Her runaway husband? But the doctor had helped her, and bit by bit, over the months, she'd found that she could talk about everything, and talking about what happened in 1969 enabled her to go on and talk about her early life as a child in another country. All manner of memories emerged that she'd thought were buried so deep that they would never come to the surface again.

Nowadays it wasn't really all that painful to think of those childhood days. What could she remember? She could quite clearly recall the day that she was playing with Aunt Elsa and Pluto in the woods. There had been a sudden big bang which shook the trees and frightened her. It made her cry and Pluto had started to whimper. And she could remember that later Aunt Elsa looked after her in a little wooden house when her daddy was at work. Pluto lived with them, but he was old and when he died they buried him in the garden, next to the fence. She'd missed Pluto and wanted another dog. She knew that there were dogs in the camp where daddy worked; she'd seen them in the distance. But daddy and Aunt Elsa told her that they were not nice dogs, like Pluto, and they often bit people and hurt them.

What else? What else? Ah, yes, she could remember hiding in a cellar with daddy, Aunt Elsa and some other people. Who were they, those strangers? They were all hungry, and some were not well, but what was clearest in her memory was how badly they stank, as if they had not washed themselves for months. Daddy went and found some food, and she'd helped Aunt Elsa to hand it out to the poor people. Sometimes she had to pinch her nose so she wouldn't retch.

Then she was ill herself, but that was later, after daddy and Aunt Elsa had taken it in turns to carry her through the snow to a tumble-down farmhouse near some woods. She remembered there was a goat that lived in a hut, and when she got better Aunt Elsa taught her how to milk it. That was good.

A man in a soldier's brown uniform, with a belt and a cap, came and said he would take them to a big city; he had to report for duty there. He helped them to climb into the back of his lorry and they drove away. It took many days because the roads were badly damaged and often there were columns of thin, shabbily-dressed people walking along and blocking the way. Once, late at night, the man in the uniform stopped the lorry, got out of the cab and made Aunt Elsa go with him into a clump of trees beyond the road. That made daddy sad and he cried, and so she cried too, but then daddy told her it would soon be all right, and they must be brave and not cry anymore. Then Aunt Elsa came back. She just climbed into the back of the lorry without saying anything, and the man in the brown uniform buckled his belt and got into his cab and they drove on. Daddy tried to talk to Aunt Elsa, whispering things which were hard to hear or understand. Nobody did anything for nothing, he said, not at awful times like these; there would always be a price to pay. Then he said over and over that he was sorry, but Aunt Elsa wouldn't speak to him, and when they got to the big city with all its broken buildings she simply got out of the lorry and walked away. They never saw her again. She had a very bad cough. Oh, daddy!

Jan had left her too. Was it guilt or cowardice that made him do it? Though in a way she continued to love him, she also grew to despise him. Whenever a killer is at large, they say some women start to half-suspect their husbands or brothers of being the person responsible. After Petro's murder Jan was interviewed twice by the police. Fellow workers at Salts Mill started to avoid him. Gossip and rumour were rife. And for a time Marta was unsure. It was only natural, wasn't it?

Some months after the murder a priest and another man came to the house in George Street. Jan refused to let them in and the conversation, initially in softly-spoken Polish, took place on the doorstep. Marta could only hear snatches. It seemed that the two men were urging Jan to accept money and he, in turn, was steadfastly refusing to have anything to do with it. Then the discussion became more voluble, and Jan, as was his way, got upset and angry. He told them to leave. This they did, but as they walked away down the short garden path, the priest turned back and said, "No matter. We'll just pay it directly into your bank account anyway. You deserve it." Jan chased after them as far as the gate, but by now curtains were twitching in neighbouring houses, so he didn't follow them into the road. They climbed into an old Ford Consul, and Jan watched them drive away up George Street towards Bradford Road. Marta could see that he was trembling.

Then Marta lost her baby, and for the next six months – or was it longer? – she was stranded in a numbing haze of powerful anti-depressants. She had to spend some time in a private clinic too, where one day the fog in her head cleared a little, enough anyway for her to realise that Jan had stopped visiting her. She asked a nurse and was eventually told that he had left the area. There was no letter of explanation and no forwarding address. She got one only when a solicitor from Reading wrote to inform her that Jan intended to petition for a divorce. And there would be a substantial sum of money paid to her. Oh, Jan!

It was pleasantly warm in the sunshine, even though it was still only March. In a few weeks it would be Marta's birthday and she would be seventy-six years old. She wondered if she should have a little celebration. She could invite Alison and perhaps Gerald. She could tell he liked her. It was always flattering to be admired by men, she thought, even if their admiration was not necessarily reciprocated. It was good for one's self-esteem. She knew that Alison had been attempting a little match-making, and that amused her. Gerald seemed a nice enough man, but he wasn't really her type – a little too conventional, rather – how best to put it? – too plodding. Oh, he would doubtless have been kind, loyal and affectionate towards his wife, she thought, but what would they have found to talk about? How their respective days had gone? Where to spend their annual holidays? What wallpaper to choose for the lounge? She realised that she was being unkind. After all, Jan had not been the cleverest and most cultured of husbands, yet there had been a passion and an energy about him that she had found totally captivating. But they had been young. Would she have still felt the same now, fifty years later?

Fifty years later and a birthday in the offing; better get back to planning her party, she thought. Should it be at her house or at a restaurant? If the latter, it would make sense to plump for *Freddy's.* The Christmas lunch had been such a success. Since then she'd spotted the owner, Fred, on a number of occasions, twice in shops on Gordon Terrace and once in the 1853 Gallery at Salts Mill, where she'd noticed him in front of Hockney's watercolour, *Trees Near Kilham*. He reminded her so strongly of Jan, even though his head was almost shaven, whereas Jan had always possessed a mane of swept-back black hair. She knew that Alison was friendly with Fred. Should he be included in her birthday celebrations? Perhaps she could do some match-making of her own. The thought of this made her giggle, and a passing dog-walker gave her a sidelong glance, as if recognising that here was one of those batty old women who sit alone on benches, talking to themselves.

In fact, Alison and Fred were together at that very moment. He'd told her that he owed her an apology for his behaviour, though she was uncertain what he was referring to. Not phoning her that time? Storming off when she'd asked if Jan was his father? Making that clumsy sexual advance in her kitchen? Perhaps all three. Anyway, to make amends he wanted her to have lunch with him at *Freddy's*. And just to demonstrate her assertiveness Alison had declined, offering instead to buy him a snack and a beer at one of the small bars which had in recent months sprung up in Saltaire. He'd rather grudgingly pointed out that a bag of crisps in a converted shop was hardly the same thing. But he'd accepted her offer nonetheless, as she knew he would. She told him she was working from home again that day and could only spare an hour. He countered that he should really be at his restaurant anyway; Friday lunchtimes were always busy.

"Not much scope for entertaining me then," she said "I'd have been sitting on my own in a corner while you ran around handing out menus."

"No, no, it wouldn't have been like… what's that you're eating?"

"A pork pie. They're very good. You should try one."

"I've never eaten a pork pie in my life," he said, a feigned mixture of pity and disdain in his tone.

"Don't be so snooty. I bet you have."

"Perhaps, but only when I was totally ignorant about food," he said.

"Ignorant about food? I've always imagined you were chasing Michelin stars right from primary school."

"Well then, I may have eaten one at a time when I was too poor to afford anything better," he said.

"You told me you'd inherited a pile of money as soon as you were eighteen."

"All gone. Spent on fine wines, fast women and designer drugs," he said airily. He laughed and swigged his beer from the bottle. Then he scrutinised the label, noting that the beer came from a local brewery in Saltaire. "Hmm, that's rather nice. It would go down well in *Freddy's*. I must ask where the brewery is," he said, turning to survey the surroundings. "Better get a pie too, if they are as good as you say. Don't want to miss out, do I?" And he rose and went across to the small bar.

Alison was pleased and relieved. If they could exchange this kind of silly banter, then it meant that things were all right between them. She'd recently been concerned that she might have over-stepped the mark in her desire to find out all she could about Marta's life history. Gerald had reassured her up to a point, but he was probably equally keen to discover the truth about Marta. If Fred was the key to it all, if he was on some kind of quest, then Alison knew she mustn't do anything to scare him off. Perhaps she should even... no, bad idea.

Fred came back to the table, holding a bottle in one hand and a warm pork pie, on a plate, in the other. He sat down and grinned at her before he tucked in. Alison picked up the bottle of beer and took a drink.

"Is this one German?" she said.

"Apparently," Fred replied through a mouthful of pie.

"Nice," she said, putting the bottle back on the table.

"And that reminds me," Fred said, and he wiped his mouth with a napkin and swigged some more beer. "Have I told you about my German friend, Ulrich?"

"No, I don't think so."

"Well, he's been doing some research on my behalf. He's an academic historian. Lives in Berlin. Anyway, he emailed me recently. He thinks he's got something for me about Petro and Marta during the war; what he calls a 'breaking-through.' I think he means a breakthrough."

"How exciting!" Alison said. "What is it he's found?"

"I don't know yet. He's flying over tomorrow to tell me. I'm to meet him at Leeds-Bradford Airport, off the Düsseldorf flight. Fancy coming with me?" Alison noticed that, despite the wipe with the napkin, there were still some crumbs of pastry sticking to the stubble on his chin.

"Yes, I would," she said. She tried hard not to sound too eager.

CHAPTER EIGHTEEN

Gerald Cranley had always prided himself on his good memory. They say that your powers of recall diminish with age, but Gerald didn't believe that. His memory for facts and faces had certainly helped him during his career as a detective, and he had been meticulous in his record-keeping; more than once magistrates had congratulated him on the clarity and precision of the evidence he had given from the witness box. He was also one of those people who found it very difficult to throw anything away; his wife had never understood why he would insist on trundling boxes of old notebooks – items she regarded as so much redundant junk – into the removal van whenever they moved house.

"You never know when they might come in useful," Gerald used to say if she remonstrated with him about his reluctance to deposit the notebooks in the local tip. True, some of his official pocketbooks had of necessity been retained by the various police forces where he had worked, but Gerald had always kept a pile of more informal records at home.

He had never told anyone, not even his wife, why he had insisted on keeping this dog-eared collection. He had felt too diffident to admit that they constituted the raw material for a project which he had nurtured almost from the outset of his career. After he retired he intended to write his memoirs: *A Copper's Life*. Why not? What was so odd about that? That's what he would tell himself whenever the idea seemed too fanciful. Sometimes, though, he had thought it a foolish and rather pretentious ambition. Who did he think he was, attempting to write a book? Who would possibly want to read it?

Nevertheless, the notion had never gone away, and when retirement drew near he purchased a good dictionary, a Thesaurus and a self-help guidebook for the novice writer. He had even drafted an introduction to his book, but before there was an opportunity to go any further his wife had become ill and caring for her had taken up all his time. After she died, he no longer felt any incentive to continue with the book. Perhaps the whole thing had really been nothing more than an unconscious desire to impress her – to show her that he had more strings to his bow than she'd realised; he was not merely the dutiful but rather dull husband which he suspected was her view of him. So the notebooks – those personal logbooks and journals, recording the ups and downs of his career – gathered dust in a cupboard in the spare bedroom. But at least he had kept them; he hadn't taken them to the tip.

And now he was surrounded by them, spread out on the carpet in the lounge of his house in Baildon. He knew that somewhere in one of them was the briefest of references to something which he could only dimly remember; something important which was connected with… what? And that, in turn, might shed a glimmer of light on… what?

"So, you're going to meet him off the plane? That should be very interesting. I've been doing a bit of digging around myself. I'd got this bee in my bonnet about something an old chum of mine mentioned, but I couldn't put my finger on why it mattered. I've been going through a lot of old, oh… diaries and suchlike, trying to give my memory a jog. I wasn't sure what I was looking for. It was at it for hours, and I was beginning to think I was wasting my time. And that's when I found what I was looking for and the penny began to drop"

"Go on," Alison said. "This all sounds very interesting."

"Do you remember the day of the Christmas carol concert in St George's Hall? Of course you do, but later on you bumped into me near your friend's restaurant. It was raining, I think. I'd been having a quick drink in the pub…"

"…with an old friend. I remember. You were waiting for a taxi," Alison said, impatient for him to get to the point.

"That's right. Now, the friend was a chap called Phil Batty; an ex-colleague. I used to work with him in the old days. He ended up as a sergeant. He always worked here in Yorkshire, but we kept in touch when I moved away; Christmas cards and that kind of thing. Then, when I retired and came back to live in Baildon we used to meet for a drink now and then. That time when I saw you, I'd been in the pub with him for a pint and we'd been talking about old times, like you do, and in and amongst he mentioned that Craig Metcalfe had died. The name rang a vague bell, but I made no connection at the time, and we went on to talk about other stuff."

"So who's Craig Metcalfe? Or should I say, who was Craig Metcalfe?" Alison said. She hoped Gerald wouldn't notice that she was becoming just a little exasperated by this lengthy preamble to the story. But he was an old guy, and old guys were often long-winded. She resolved to make more of an effort to be patient.

"Craig Metcalfe was a pain in the neck, years ago, when Phil and I were young coppers around Shipley and Bingley. I'd forgotten all about him till Phil mentioned him; and just recently I haven't been able to get him out of my head."

"Why is that, do you think?"

"I didn't know at first. That's why I started going through some old notes and diaries that I'd kept. The thing is Metcalfe wasn't a hardened criminal or anything like that; he was more of a nuisance, as well as being not quite right in the head. He was a good-looking chap and a bit of a charmer who could attract women, but he had a terrible temper on him. He used to hit anyone he thought was so much as looking at his lady friends, and that's when we sometimes got involved. Usually we'd just warn him or keep him in the cells overnight to cool off. Twice he was charged with common assault and he was up in court. A fine and bound over to keep the peace was what he got the first time, if I remember rightly.

"Well, the second time he was up in court one of the more forward-looking magistrates wanted to delve a bit deeper, so she sent him for a psychiatrist's assessment. Phil, who'd arrested him on that occasion, thought it was a complete waste of time, that all he really needed was a good kick up the backside. But back comes the shrink's report, and it said Metcalfe was suffering from something called morbid jealousy, and he was in need of treatment."

"Morbid jealousy? I've never heard of it," Alison said.

"Neither had I, but it sounded interesting, so I wrote it down in my notebook. And that's what I've been doing all afternoon – trying to remember those two words and what else I knew about Metcalfe. I've been combing through all my old…"

"You'll have to tell me what morbid jealousy actually is," Alison said, interrupting him, so he wouldn't start on another lengthy digression.

"It's extreme pathological jealousy," Gerald replied. "Whenever Metcalfe had a girlfriend he was so possessive and jealous he'd make her life a complete misery. Like if she went through the check-out at Morrisons, and it was a bloke on the till, he'd accuse them of making an assignation, and there'd be a nasty scene. At home, he wouldn't let her lock the bathroom door, because he suspected she'd be signalling to a secret lover out of the window. He'd always check her underwear for… what shall I say?....traces of activity, even though she'd not been out of his sight. It was all crazy, obsessive stuff like that. Of course, the women always left him, and usually sooner rather than later."

"I'm not surprised. It sounds awful."

"It was. He used to get drunk and disorderly as well. After a time it all got so bad that he had to be sectioned. He was in and out of High Royds."

"What's High Royds?" Alison asked.

"That was the big psychiatric hospital near Guiseley; an old-fashioned loony-bin really. It closed down a few years ago. There's an estate of posh houses there now."

"So why are you telling me all this stuff about Craig Metcalfe and his morbid jealousy?"

"Because there's a link to Petro. It's taken me hours to remember and work it all out…"

"And what is it, this link?" Alison said, interrupting him again.

"Craig Metcalfe was Kathleen Riley's cousin."

"Kathleen…?"

"Kathleen Riley, the woman Petro visited on the night he was killed. She lived near Hirst Lock."

"Ah, I see. So you think Craig Metcalfe might have been morbidly jealous of Petro, because he was seeing Kathleen, and so he killed him. Is that it?"

"Well, that's what I've been wondering…" Gerald said.

"So, was there anything… sexual between these cousins? Had they been an item, or something?"

"Not that I know of."

"I see. Well, I have to say it all sounds…"

"A bit far-fetched?" Gerald finished the sentence for her.

"Well, yes. And surely you, the police, would have interviewed Metcalfe, wouldn't you?" Alison said.

"No, not as far as I remember. He was never in the frame. Anyway, it was assumed that he was in High Royds when Petro was killed."

"And was he?"

"I don't know. I don't think we ever checked."

"God, Gerald," Alison said. Just as she'd long suspected, Gerald and his colleagues had scarcely been in the same league as Poirot or Sherlock Holmes. But she said nothing.

"I know, I know. Don't blame me, Alison. I was just a rookie."

"Do you think he was the murderer?"

"I never thought about it till Phil mentioned his name. All those years and it never occurred…"

"And what do you think now? Now that you have remembered him?" Alison said, interrupting him again.

"That it's a possibility, but like I said, he's dead now, so there's no chance of a confession. I don't suppose we'll ever know."

"For what it's worth, Gerald, I think Craig Metcalfe as the murderer makes a bit more sense than your other theory that Petro was an early victim of the Yorkshire Ripper, but even so…"

"Perhaps you're right." It was his turn to interrupt now. He was finding Alison's scepticism a little hard to take. He had wanted to impress her – astonish her even – with his keen memory and astute analysis, and here she was, dismissing both his theories almost casually.

"And what about Jan?" she said, after a pause. "I'm not sure about him at all."

"Me neither. I used to be convinced he was innocent, but now I'm not," Gerald replied glumly.

"I told you about the letter Fred showed me, didn't I?"

"You did. Inconclusive, you said."

"It was. The one thing that bothered me was the money that Jan seems to have received. Would he have taken it if he were innocent?"

"What's Fred's opinion? Does he think his dad was guilty or innocent?"

"He doesn't know what to think. Obviously he wants to believe his father was innocent, but…" Alison didn't finish her sentence; she shrugged instead.

"Difficult for him," Gerald said. "Maybe this chap from Germany will have some answers. You will keep me in the loop, won't you?"

"Of course I will. Look, I'm going to ring off now, Gerald. I've got to go."

"Very good. See you soon, Alison."

Leeds Bradford Airport has grown over the years from a sleepy old aerodrome, with only a few arrivals or departures, to the usual modern but bland facility to be found close to every conurbation in Europe. Its location, essentially on the flat top of Otley Chevin, makes the airport the highest in the UK, and as a consequence it can be adversely affected if there is snow in winter or fog in autumn. When Fred and Alison drove up Hollins Hill to meet Ulrich on that Saturday in early spring, however, the weather was fine and the flight from Düsseldorf arrived, with impressive Teutonic efficiency, exactly on time, leaving Fred wondering for a surreal moment if Ulrich himself might have been the pilot.

They didn't have to wait long for Ulrich to clear customs and immigration. Soon he was walking through the double doors to meet them in the Arrivals area. Fred greeted him quite effusively, and there was much hugging between the pair. There was no hug for her though; just a polite handshake and a rather formal bow. Understandable, really.

Half an hour later the three of them were seated in the pleasant lounge of the Hermit Inn, on the fringe of Ilkley Moor. It was there that Alison began to realise Ulrich was not yet prepared to disclose any dramatic findings – certainly not to her. He was courteous, it was true, and he engaged her in the usual kind of conversation – though rather stilted, Alison thought – when Fred was buying drinks at the bar, but she had enough emotional intelligence to realise that he would probably have preferred to be alone with Fred. She began to feel she was intruding, and when Ulrich excused himself to visit the gents, she voiced her concern to Fred.

"Oh, Alison, please don't think that," Fred said. "As far as I'm concerned you are not intruding at all. Why do you think I asked you to come along?" She felt reassured by this. "Look," Fred continued. "Perhaps he's a bit unforthcoming just now, but I'm sure he'll relax soon."

"So you don't want me to clear off and leave you two to get on with it?"

"Certainly not. I want you to come to my house so we can all sit down and listen to what Ulrich has to say. I don't want you to miss it; God, no."

"Thanks, Fred," Alison said. Then after a pause, "How long do you think he'll want to stay here in England?"

"I don't really know. I think he wants to do a bit of sight-seeing while he's here. He's never been to Yorkshire before. He's keen to eat at my restaurant too. (I told you he was intelligent.) Oh, and that reminds me, I'd better ring to check that today's lunches are going okay." He took out his phone and pressed some buttons.

"Control-freak," Alison said softly. Fred replied by pulling a face at her, and then he held a short conversation with someone at *Freddy's*.

"Everything's apparently going very well," he said, ending the call and putting the phone back in his jacket pocket.

"Probably because you're not there," Alison said.

"You could be right. Ah, here comes Ulrich, back from the loo. Odd little chap, isn't he? I was beginning to think he'd got lost. Shall I get some more drinks?"

———

"Is that you, Alison? Oh, good. Now, my dear, I want you to do me a small favour. It's my birthday soon and I want to celebrate it with a meal. I want to go to *Freddy's* again. We had such a nice time at Christmas. I wondered if you'd book a table for me. Would you do that? I thought that perhaps Gerald could come too, if he's free. And maybe your friend who owns the restaurant? Yes, Fred. Do you think he'd want to come? Is it etiquette to invite someone to have a meal in their own restaurant? I'm not sure about these things, you see. I'm thinking of requesting something rather special. I'll be seventy-six, by the way. It does sound rather old, doesn't it…?

———————

"Gerald? Can you hear me okay? Ulrich arrived on the dot this morning. I've spent most of the afternoon with him and Fred up at Fred's house in Ilkley. We had to stop off at the Cow and Calf rocks on the way for Ulrich to get out of the car to admire the view and take photographs. I was starting to wonder if he did have anything worthwhile to tell us; maybe he just wanted to stay with Fred and do some sight-seeing. But once we got to Fred's he started to open up." She paused for breath before continuing. "Now, did Jan killed Petro? Well, if he did it as revenge because he thought Petro was some kind of war criminal, then he just might have killed an innocent man."

"Really?" Gerald said.

"Yes. Like we suspected, Petro did work for a time in a camp – not a death camp as such, though it must have been horrible enough. But then it gets complicated; for a start, Ulrich says there could well have been more than one Ukrainian guard in the camp called Petro Semeniuk; it's not an uncommon name in Ukraine.

"That would definitely muddy the waters, wouldn't it?"

"It would indeed. But the next bit is really fascinating. According to Ulrich, a guard who was almost certainly called Petro Semeniuk actually helped a group of Polish slave-workers to escape from the camp when all the inmates were being killed off. It was just a few months before the end of the war. Everything was in turmoil."

"How did this Ulrich chap find all this out?"

"Bizarre as it sounds, the Nazis kept meticulous records. Most of the ones for this camp seem to have been destroyed when it was abandoned, but not all of them. There are a few remnants he found in an archive. But Ulrich has got most of his evidence from relatives of people who'd been prisoners. Survivors must have told their children and grandchildren about what had happened."

"Some would have done that; others would never speak about it, I suppose."

"I agree. Anyway, Ulrich managed to trace some people, one in particular, who knew about the rescue. He's been to the site of the camp as well, but there's virtually nothing left now. Just a field."

"If he's right about all this, it makes it even harder to get at the truth, doesn't it? I mean, guards with the same name? Which one was Marta's father? Was he a killer or a saviour?"

"I know. Anyway, whichever one it was, he managed to get to England somehow or other. Ulrich's not sure about all the details, but he does know that Elsa, the young woman in the photograph, never made it; she died of tuberculosis in Berlin. But get this. Petro wasn't Marta's real father anyway. Ulrich has found out that Petro adopted her after her real father was killed. Marta was not Polish, possibly not even Ukrainian. How about that?"

"God, it just gets more and more complicated."

"And speaking of Marta, it's her birthday soon and she's asked me to book a table at *Freddy's* for a special celebration, and she wants you to be there. You see, I was right. I knew that she'd taken a shine to you. You will come, won't you? I think it will mean a lot to her…"

In the early years of the twenty-first century, once the Soviet Union was no more and the Warsaw Pact had been dissolved, a well-known American hotel chain discovered that the new Poland offered all manner of exciting possibilities. The Hotel Lew was rebuilt – or rather a brand new hotel was constructed on the site of the old one. Apart from the cellars, which were more or less intact, everything had to be built from scratch. The clean-cut young man in charge of the project likened the new enterprise to a phoenix, rising from the ashes. Indeed, for a time the hotel was going to be called the Phoenix, but the American company eventually decided that the original name should be kept; company policy was that some gesture, however flimsy, should always be made to the quaint traditions of the area which was going to benefit from the arrival of a modern hotel. The last thing the company wanted was for their European hotels to look and feel as if they had been transplanted *en bloc* from Cincinnati or Buffalo. Whether this admirable ambition was always achieved was another matter.

So the Hotel Lew retained its original name, and a certain amount of local timber was employed, especially in the restaurant and bar areas, in an attempt to create the atmosphere of a charming traditional Polish hostelry. The rooms, the facilities, the food were all of a suitably high standard, and those guests who could be bothered usually gave the Hotel Lew a more than satisfactory rating on the customer-feedback questionnaires which were conveniently placed in every bedroom.

The hotel management was especially proud of the modifications made to the cellars. A fitness suite, with state-of-the-art machines, had been installed, along with a steam room, a Jacuzzi and a small swimming pool. The steam room occupied the precise space where, in early 1945, a group of desperate and starving people had sought shelter from the Nazis. No mention of this was made in the Hotel Lew's leather-bound information brochure, and neither was there any reference to the hotel once providing hospitality to distinguished guests of the Third Reich. Likewise, there was no memorial marking the spot near the hotel's main entrance where, again in early 1945, the corpse of a young man, possibly called Tomasz Grabowski, had been cremated, using petrol siphoned from a Soviet army truck.

According to the information in the brochure the countryside around the Hotel Lew offered excellent opportunities for relaxing walks. One path led through the woods to a large meadow which, in late spring and summer, was filled with flowers – musk mallow and wild marjoram in particular. There was nothing to inform the hotel guests who might stroll there that a transit camp for slave-workers had been on that very site just a generation or so earlier, nor that all the terrified inmates had been brutally murdered – all, that is, except a handful who had been rescued by a camp guard called Petro Semeniuk and a young woman called Elsa Muller.

CHAPTER NINETEEN

It would be foolish to compare Bradford Cathedral to some of the world-famous churches with which the North of England is blessed; places like York Minster, or the breath-taking pile which is Durham Cathedral. Nevertheless, Bradford Cathedral has its points of interest, including a tower, which was used as a strong-point during the siege of Bradford in the early months of the English Civil War. At one time every school child in Bradford learned how the townspeople had hung woolsacks on the tower to ward off the Royalist cannon balls, and they would also have been familiar with the story of a ghost – a spectral woman – who was said to have visited the victorious Royalist commander in his bedchamber in the middle of the night to beg him to "Pity poor Bradford."

Gerald entertained Alison and Marta with all this as he drove them from Saltaire to Bradford for the Easter concert. The mood in the car was cheerful.

"So why weren't these Bradford people loyal to the king?" Marta asked. "Were they all traitors?"

"No," Gerald replied. "They were all Puritans. They believed the king was a secret Catholic, and they didn't like that."

"Pah," Marta snorted. "That's religion for you. It makes people fire cannon balls at each other."

"I think they also objected to paying too many taxes to the king," Gerald said.

"There you are, Marta," Alison said. "Yorkshiremen being tight with their money. Nothing has changed."

"Just be careful, or you'll be going the rest of the way on the bus," Gerald said. They drove past Lister Park, its broad expanses filled with thousands of spring flowers, still visible in the fading light of early evening.

Fifteen minutes later the three of them had joined the other members of the Titus Salt Community Choir in an ante-room of the cathedral. The choirmaster addressed them *sotto voce*.

"Right, I think we are all gathered," he said. "Now, in a few minutes we'll go out and get into position. The first two items are solo organ pieces, old favourites that you'll recognise – the cathedral has a fine organ – so we'll have to keep as still as possible for ten minutes or so. No yawning or head scratching, please. Then it will be our turn. I'm confident we'll do it just as well as in rehearsal, so long as we concentrate and you keep your eyes on me all the time. When we've finished and lapped up the applause, I'll give the signal to move off, and there'll be another short organ piece accompanying our exit, so walk out nice and orderly. Any questions?"

There were none. The choristers had become used to being addressed in this way; they appreciated that the choirmaster spent his days in an inner-city school, attempting to inspire reluctant teenagers with his own passion for music, so they always made allowances for his officious schoolmaster's manner. He looked at his wristwatch. "Right, let's go. Just follow Arthur. I'll bring up the rear."

The choristers left the ante-room and assembled in front of the audience in the nave of the cathedral. Standing next to Marta with the sopranos, Alison was acutely aware of the silence and stillness. Then she experienced a shiver, coming from somewhere deep inside her, as the organ filled the cathedral with the magnificent opening notes of Bach's *Toccata and Fugue in D Minor*. Of course it was an old favourite, as the choirmaster had said, but that was of no consequence. If ever there was a piece of music which might dent her long-established atheism, especially when played in a church, this was going to be it. She closed her eyes and concentrated all her attention on Bach's masterpiece.

As the fugue reached its finale and the last echoing notes from the organ faded, there was silence for a few seconds, and then a burst of applause ascended from the nave. Alison opened her eyes and looked at the audience. Rather to her surprise she noticed Fred and Ulrich sitting together near one of the huge stone pillars which supported the cathedral roof. She hadn't expected them to attend. Fred was clapping enthusiastically and looking directly towards her, but Ulrich was looking heavenward, his head tilted upwards, so that the light which shone from above was reflected on the lenses of his spectacles. He looked enraptured. Well, he would, wouldn't he? Being a German, he was bound to be a music-lover, thought Alison. Hitler had been a devotee of Wagner, and Reinhard Heydrich, the SS "blond beast," was reputedly a skilled violinist… Alison stopped herself there, conscious that she had embarked upon an unworthy train of thought. She tried to dismiss it by looking again towards Ulrich, and she contemplated the discoveries he might have made about Marta's past life – Marta, the woman standing next to her; Marta, her friend.

Now that the organ piece was at an end, it was their turn. As at the Christmas concert, the performance – quite well-executed – seemed to last hardly any time at all and soon all the members of the Titus Salt Community Choir had returned to the ante-room. They were replaced on the chancel steps by a renowned choir from Wales whose members were to perform the remainder of the evening's programme, including Mascagni's *Easter Hymn,* the *Lacrimosa* from Mozart's *Requiem* and a beautifully sung rendition of the duet from Pergolesi's *Stabat Mater.* But Alison's attention had started to wander away from the music by now, and before long she had slipped out of the ante-room through a side door which led into the cathedral close. Bradford Cathedral stands on elevated ground, and from where she stood, quite alone, Alison could look out over the nearby city centre, where scores of lights from buildings and street lamps lit up the cool spring evening. A cigarette, just now, would be quite wonderful, she thought.

Applause came from the cathedral. The Easter concert was over, and before long the audience started to leave the building. Fred spotted her. He came over and kissed her on the cheek; Ulrich hung back and offered a small formal bow.

"Excellent stuff!" Fred said. "Well done! Your choir was very impressive. In fact the whole concert was… what can I say? Terrific. Yes, terrific," he concluded, unable to think of a better epithet.

"A most rewarding experience," Ulrich said in his cool and precise way. "I think your choir's attempts were quite creditable, but Welsh choirs! Ah, they deservedly have such a high reputation all over the world." No flattery there, then, Alison thought; we were second-best, according to this purveyor of the unvarnished truth. Before she could fashion a suitable reply, they were joined by Gerald, who had come out of the ante-room.

"You are all going to catch your death of cold, standing out here" he said. Then, recognising Fred, he stretched out a hand. "Ah, I believe we have met before, sir. And this gentleman," he said, facing Ulrich, "must be your friend from Germany. Am I right?"

"Fassbinder, Ulrich," the friend from Germany said, with another small formal bow, and he held out his hand for Gerald to shake.

After these introductions there were more polite comments about the pleasure they had all derived from the concert, at which point Alison began to wonder where Marta might be. She asked Gerald, and he replied that he had left Marta inside, chatting with the choirmaster and the ever-faithful Arthur. Then, rather shyly, he drew Alison to one side. Fred and Ulrich had by now turned to survey the view over Bradford, and Gerald saw his chance.

"Look, Alison, I was wondering… seeing that Fred is here… I wondered if… and I hope you don't think… but perhaps you could… oh, dear," he mumbled. It was too dark to see, but Alison guessed he might be blushing like a gauche schoolboy. She came to his rescue.

"If you want to take Marta home without me, it's perfectly fine, Gerald," she said softly, and she gave his arm a reassuring squeeze. "I don't mind you palming me off on these two."

"Thank you, Alison. I appreciate that," Gerald said, palpably relieved. "I'm only intending to take her for a drink, you understand. Nothing more elaborate."

"You must do whatever you feel like…" But he had already turned away and was striding back towards the ante-room, where presumably Marta was waiting for him. Alison watched him go and chuckled to herself.

"Perhaps we'll have to ask Marta herself. We could say, 'Hi Marta, was your dad one of the Petro Semeniuks who killed prisoners in the camp, or was he the one who saved them?' Hmm, perhaps not," Fred said, as he drove them along Manningham Lane towards Shipley.

"Besides, she claims that she remembers scarcely anything before she came to England," Alison said from the front passenger seat. "Anyway, how could we…?"

"I know," Fred said. "I was just being silly." They heard Ulrich, sitting alone in the rear passenger seats, give a sigh. Was it one of exasperation or just simple weariness?

"With great respect to both of you, I think that you are in danger of missing the point," he said. They waited for him to continue. "I think it is clear that the man who is said to have rescued a group of prisoners was the same one who appears in the photograph, a copy of which Alison has on her computer; the photograph with Marta as a child and the woman Elsa Muller, known to Marta as Aunt Elsa. I believe that the same man came to England after the war, bringing Marta with him, as his daughter. Elsa Muller came only part of the way; unfortunately she died in Berlin. It is beyond belief that it was another camp guard, another Petro Semeniuk, who took care of Marta and brought her to England…"

"Well that fixes it, then," Fred interrupted, halting the car at the traffic lights near the Norman Arch. "Our Petro, my dad's father-in-law, was not a war criminal after all. He rescued people. He deserved a medal…"

"Not necessarily, my dear Fred. We do not know what vile acts he might have committed in the camp prior to his noble act of rescue…"

"Oh, but come on," Fred said, as the traffic lights turned to green. "He had a child that he cared for and loved. Marta remembers him as kind and gentle."

"Do you think that some of the worst sadists and mass-murderers in the Nazi camps did not go home at night to the bosom of their families? That they didn't kiss their wives and play with their children after completing their daily duty of dealing out torture and death? Of course they did." Fred and Alison were silent; they had to admit that what Ulrich said was most likely true.

"And I suppose someone could have taken Petro's identity. That must have happened all the time," Alison said.

"Indeed. That also is possible," Ulrich said. "Personally, I do not think that is what happened, though I have no proof."

"So what do you think did happen, Ulrich?" Fred asked. By now the car had passed through Frizinghall and was approaching Shipley.

"We cannot know what Petro Semeniuk did before he performed the rescue. All we know is that he served in the camp under the auspices of the SS. Neither do we know why he suddenly decided to help some of the inmates. Was it a spur of the moment decision? Did he have a sudden conscience about what he had witnessed and perhaps even been a party to? We must not forget also that the camp was in chaos and the Russians were fast approaching, so could he have perhaps planned to use the freed prisoners as a bargaining tool with the soviets?

"To save his own skin, you mean?" Alison said.

"Precisely," Ulrich said. "We must not fall into the trap of thinking that Petro – or any other person, at a desperate time like that – would be acting purely out of the highest altruistic motives. Petro was human. His predicament was horribly real, not a screenplay for a Hollywood movie."

"And you are not able to say whether or not my father killed him?" Fred asked, changing gear and touching the brakes as they approached the junction with Otley Road. "And if he did, why?"

"No, I regret to say that I cannot really help you with that conundrum," Ulrich replied. "It may be that some group of Polish nationalists in exile – some extremists, we might say – persuaded your father to commit an act of vengeance on behalf of Poland. Alternatively, your father may have had no connection at all with the murder, even though some kind of reward money clearly came into his possession. That could have been an error on the part of the nationalist group who made the assumption that Jan had done what they asked. That being so, why should he return the money? Do remember too that Jan would not have been in a rational state of mind at that time. Guilty or innocent, he was close to a person who had recently been savagely killed."

At this point Ulrich had rather adopted the style of an academic chairing a seminar, and Alison's interjection, with a pertinent question, was almost as if she were one of his students.

"So if for a moment we assume Jan was innocent, who might be guilty?" she said.

"Who knows?" Ulrich replied. "Petro may merely have been in the wrong place at the wrong time; a victim of a random and meaningless act of violence."

"Like the violence he must have often witnessed," Alison said softly.

"Ah, now you are playing the philosopher, Alison. But on the whole I rather agree with your sentiment."

"So what do I tell Marta?" Fred asked, as he made a right turn into Victoria Road.

"The truth," Ulrich replied. "What else? You must say to her that you have sought answers, as your father requested in his final testament, but you have not been able to find many."

"And when and how do you think I should tell her?" Fred said, sounding depressed and reluctant, as if he had been ordered to defuse an unexploded bomb using nothing more than a bicycle puncture repair kit.

"That's where I come in, I think," Alison said brightly. "Marta has asked me to book a table at your restaurant for lunch. A special meal, not your normal menu. It's her birthday coming up. She wants Gerald and me to join her." She paused in order to generate a suitable effect. "And, for some reason she wants you to be there too, Fred. Not as a restaurateur, but as a guest. At her party. You could tell her then. It's a golden opportunity."

"What?" Fred said, and such was his astonishment at hearing Alison's words that the nearside rear wheel mounted the kerb as he attempted to steer the car into Caroline Street. A man coming out of the off-licence on the corner felt obliged to take minor evasive action.

"Would you like to come too, Ulrich?" Alison asked sweetly, turning round in her seat and ignoring Fred's inept driving. "I'm sure Marta would be happy with that."

"I would like that very much, but I'm afraid I must decline the offer," Ulrich said. "I am returning to Berlin in two days' time." The car drew up outside Alison's house.

"Ulrich wants us to visit Bolton Abbey tomorrow," Fred said mournfully. "I think I might just walk up to the Strid and jump in."

"What is this Strid?" Ulrich asked.

"It's a notorious whirlpool on the River Wharfe, near Bolton Abbey. Very dangerous," Alison said. She buttoned her coat, picked up her bag and opened the door of the car. "Anyone falling in is more than likely to be swept away and drown. Take no notice of Fred, Ulrich. He's not being serious; it's just his warped sense of humour. Good night." And with that she got out of the car.

The nice lady came every week, usually on a Friday morning. It was something to look forward to because she always said such kind things when she looked through the work you had done. She always smelled of spring flowers, not like Miss Medved who usually smelled of coffee and old cigarettes.

"Let us see what you have for me today, shall we? My, but you have been busy, haven't you? Your handwriting is so neat, and Miss Medved says that you are learning new words all the time. That's very good. And what lovely pictures you've drawn, haven't you? Let's look at them together. Is this your dog? And you've written his name. Does it say Pluto? Like in Mickey Mouse? No? Oh, I see. What a shame, still I'm sure you'll get another one before too long. And what have you drawn here? Yes, it's a goat, isn't it? Does she have a name? She doesn't have a name, I see. Let me look at the next one. Oh, that is good! That must be your mummy, yes? Oh, your aunt, of course. Aunt Elsa. I was forgetting. She looks very nice. And this one is your daddy, isn't it? How neatly you've written daddy underneath. Can you remember coming to school with your daddy to meet Miss Medved and myself? That was the day when you first arrived. And here they are again, daddy and Aunt Elsa, standing next to a lorry this time. You have drawn the lorry very well, haven't you? And who is this other man? Is he the driver? He looks like a soldier to me, with his boots and his cap on. Perhaps he is a friend of your daddy's and Aunt Elsa. Now let's look at this one. Let's see… ah… lots of people sitting or lying on the floor. People in stripy… clothes… I see… and behind them, some burning buildings… soldiers with guns running about over here… all kinds of things happening. A very busy picture. Do you want to tell me about the picture? No? Well, perhaps a little later, then. Goodness, but you do draw so well for someone your age. Do you know, I'm going to ask Miss Medved to let you start painting? Would you like that? We have some paints for making water colours in the cupboard. Brushes as well. And you can wear an apron so you won't splash any paint on your nice clothes."

That's how it was. You showed your writing and the pictures you'd drawn to the nice lady every week and she asked you questions about them. Sometimes it was easy: sometimes hard. Talking about Pluto was hardest because he was dead now and daddy had buried him in the garden that time. You missed Pluto very much. And Aunt Elsa. You missed her too. She'd gone away in the big city with the broken buildings, and that had made you almost as sad as when Pluto died. It was hard to talk to the nice lady about

Aunt Elsa. Talking about the other people you drew – the soldiers with guns and the smelly thin people in their dirty stripy clothes – you didn't bother with that, because you didn't know who they were. Easiest was talking about the pictures you drew of daddy, because he was still with you. He wasn't dead, like Pluto, or in a place far away, like Aunt Elsa. Of course, you were grown up enough to know that Pluto had been really old and that's why he died, but it was still sad. Aunt Elsa wasn't really old, and you thought that she liked you, so why she'd walked away was a puzzle. You'd asked daddy about it, but he'd got cross and upset, so you didn't like to ask him again.

Just yesterday you'd drawn a picture of a train, with you and daddy sitting inside one of the carriages, but today the nice lady hadn't even glanced at that one. You'd wanted to tell the nice lady all about the train, how you and daddy were going to catch it at the railway station in Reading, and how it was going to take you to a new house in a place you'd heard daddy call "Up north." Did he mean you would be living near the North Pole? Would there be Eskimos and polar bears? Perhaps daddy would get you another dog. Perhaps it would be one of those you'd seen in a picture-book, pulling a sledge across the snow. That would be fun! And daddy would have to tell the teachers in your new school that from now on you must paint with water colours, not just draw with crayons.

CHAPTER TWENTY

Fred rose to the challenge all right, but not without some protest. The menu for Marta's highly eclectic birthday lunch was not at all straightforward, and it required him to have lengthy discussions with his kitchen staff and visit various Bradford markets to ensure that all the correct ingredients were assembled. Alison acted as a go-between.

"Are you sure this is what she wants?" Fred asked her more than once.

"I'm certain it is. She specified that precisely," Alison replied each time. "It's her birthday. Give her what she's asked for." And Fred would groan.

"Some of this stuff is designed to sustain peasant farmers through harsh east European winters, not old ladies in Saltaire. At her age it could be lethal."

"Nonsense," Alison said. "She will probably outlive all of us. Anyway, you must use your skill, so it's not too heavy. You're supposed to be an expert chef, aren't you? Do your stuff." Fred sighed, but he did as he was asked.

"You see, I've had to make the soup into more of an *amuse-gueule,* because it's so hearty that…"

"An amusing what?" Gerald asked.

"An *amuse-gueule.* A taster, a savoury aperitif before the meal. It is lovely, the borscht, no doubt about that, but it's a meal in itself. They say that Ukrainians like it so much that they don't mind having it three times a day. And apparently it's not unheard of for people to get up during the night to help themselves to some more. Can you imagine that?" Fred said.

"It sounds good. And what's this we're drinking?"

"It's a Hungarian wine that Marta specifically requested; apparently it's from the Badacsony region."

"Hungarian?"

"Yes. Don't ask me why she asked for that one, or how she knows about it anyway. I'd never heard of it, myself."

"It's certainly very nice," Gerald said, dipping his nose into his glass for a sniff, then swishing the liquid around, as if he were a wine connoisseur.

"And where is our woman of the moment?" Fred said, looking nervously towards the door of the restaurant.

"Don't worry. Alison is coming with her," Gerald said. "On foot. I offered to pick them both up in my car, but I got short shrift from Marta on two counts. First she told me that she was perfectly capable of walking here from her house, even if it was uphill. Then she more or less ordered me to leave my car at home, because I wouldn't enjoy the lunch if I had to worry about driving. 'Perhaps you want to be like an American and drink milk or Coca-Cola instead of wine,' is what she said. Quite scathing, really. Anyway, I did as I was told. I got a taxi."

"Very wise," Fred said. Then, after a pause: "I wonder where they are?"

Where indeed? Alison, as arranged, had gone to call for Marta so that the two of them could walk up to *Freddy's* together, but Marta's door had been locked and Alison knocked and rang the doorbell several times to no avail. Risking her best stilettos on the damp soil of the small garden, she went and looked through the window into the lounge. Marta was there all right, sitting on her favourite sofa, facing the window. She was quite still and her eyes were closed, her cheeks very pale. Was she fast asleep? Or – good God! – was she in fact dead? Alison felt a lurch from stomach to throat, especially when she noticed what looked like a bottle of spirits and a miniature pill bottle standing together on the small occasional table next to the sofa. Surely not…?

"Marta? Marta? Are you all right?" she called out, and she banged quite forcefully on the window. That did the trick and she was mightily relieved to see Marta stir and then slowly open her eyes. She looked puzzled at first, then a little cross, as she came to full consciousness and saw Alison staring at her through the window pane. With some effort she heaved herself up from the sofa and made for the entrance hall. Alison went back across the flower beds to the front door and waited for admittance. Less than a minute later she was in Marta's lounge.

"What's all this? A pre-lunch nap?" she said, disguising as best she could the deep anxiety she was feeling.

"I must have dropped off for a minute," Marta said, yawning. "Why were you knocking at the window? Why not ring the doorbell? That's the usual custom, I believe."

"I did, more than once, but there was no answer," Alison said. She suddenly realised that Marta was not dressed and ready for the impending luncheon date at all. She was wearing slippers and a housecoat over a dress which Alison knew was only kept for everyday use, not special occasions. And Marta, unusually, was wearing no make-up. Had she perhaps fallen asleep on the sofa just a little earlier that morning? Or had she not been to bed the previous night? Alison needed to find out.

"Marta, sit down for a minute," she said.

"Oh, but I must get myself ready. We don't want to be late. That will never do."

"We won't be late. Sit down. Please," Alison said. There was a firm tone in her voice, although in reality she was feeling anything but firm.

"Very well, my dear. If you insist," Marta said, and she sat down again on the sofa. Alison sat opposite her on one of the expensively upholstered chairs. She was beginning to feel calmer now. And a little stronger.

"Tell me the truth now, Marta. Did you go to bed last night?"

"Of course I did," Marta replied, with some show of indignation at what she clearly considered to be an impertinent question. Alison, however, was not to be deterred.

"Did you?" she repeated. "Or have you been on that sofa all night? And what about the bottle of vodka on the table?"

"Just a little nightcap," Marta said, less indignant now. "I only had one glass, that's all." Alison reached over and lifted the bottle, so that they could both see it was more than half empty.

"And the pills?" she said.

"Paracetamol. I had a slight headache," Marta said. All traces of defiant haughtiness had by now evaporated.

"Hardly surprising, after half a bottle of Zubrowka," Alison said, a little more acerbic than she had intended. She was aware that she had adopted the role of a parent investigating the misdeeds of a wayward teenager. Still, she remained resolute and carried on. "So what's been going on, Marta. Tell me the truth now." And she waited for a reply.

What happened next took her by surprise, for Marta suddenly crumpled. She began to sob, her shoulders shaking. Alison quickly swapped the role of stern headmistress for that of concerned close friend, and she moved to sit next to Marta on the sofa. She put her arm around the older woman's shoulders and waited patiently for the tears and sobs to cease, which they did quite soon. Alison offered a tissue, but Marta waved it away, reaching into the pocket of her housecoat to take out a delicately embroidered handkerchief with which she gently blew her nose.

"Oh, Alison, I'm afraid that I have been rather stupid. I started to worry about the lunch today. About meeting Fred…"

"Fred? Why on earth…?"

"I have so many important things which I need to tell him," Marta said, and for a second or two Alison was afraid that she might break down and start to sob again. But she didn't. Instead she blew her nose once more on the handkerchief. Then she sat up straighter and Alison felt able to remove her supportive arm.

"Fred is nervous too," she said. Perplexed, Marta turned to face her.

"What about?"

"About meeting you of course," Alison said. "He has some things he wants to tell you. He's been worrying about it for ages." At this, and very much to Alison's surprise, Marta let out a hoot of laughter.

"Silly boy! Just like his father. He was always a bag of nerves."

So, there we are! Marta had known all along who Fred was; Alison had half-suspected it. Now she began to wonder what else Marta might know.

"You knew that Fred was Jan's son, then?" she said, doing her best to make it sound as if this was nothing other than a mundane enquiry.

"Of course I knew. I may be getting old, but my powers of observation and my ability to make sense of things are still intact," Marta said sharply. Indeed they are, Alison thought.

"And last night?" she asked gently. There was a pause before Marta answered.

"I will tell you the truth," she said, after a couple of heavy sighs and some more work with the handkerchief. "I got it into my head that perhaps it was time to… how best to say it? …time to depart. I even started to make a mental list of the best ways. Should I jump off the platform in front of a train at Saltaire station? No, that would be unfair on the train driver, and the passengers would be delayed. How about if I threw myself into the canal? Appropriate enough, don't you think? Especially if I jumped in near Hirst Lock. But the water is not very clean. I would be fished out by the police like a dirty drowned rat. Not very edifying for any onlookers, gawping on the towpath. I have my pride, as I think you know." Alison listened in silence, unsure if Marta was telling her the honest truth or just an entertaining version of it, for her tone had moved seamlessly from one of earnest gravity to one of almost frivolous good-humour. "So eventually I decided it had to be the pills; an overdose, swilled down with alcohol; the classic method favoured by most women suicides. Did you know that, Alison?" Unable to speak, Alison just shook her head. Marta continued: "I had the tablets in one hand, the vodka in the other." And she demonstrated what she meant, holding each bottle at arm's length. "It would have been easy enough. But in the end, I just drank the vodka; the pills stayed in the bottle." She put both bottles down on the little occasional table before continuing. "But do you know what really changed my mind?" Again Alison shook her head. "Two things, actually," Marta said, quite brightly now. "The first was realising that if I were dead, I would miss my birthday lunch today. I never like to miss a party" And once more she hooted with laughter.

"And the other?" Alison managed to say, not without difficulty.

"Ah, that was much more important." Here she took both of Alison's hands in her own and became serious again. Alison was aware, as on many former occasions, of the way Marta would subject you to a direct and intense gaze, almost as if she was looking right into your head. And she saw again how, despite the absence of make-up, and in spite of her age, Marta remained a remarkably beautiful woman. Today, those high cheekbones and slightly slanting eyes made her look even more exotic than ever. She spoke carefully and slowly: "I thought of you, Alison. That is why I changed my mind."

"That's an unusually kind thing to say, Marta," Alison said, her voice little more than a low mumble. She felt it might be her turn to weep now, but she didn't succumb and the feeling passed.

"You know, Alison, I had not been married very long when I became pregnant. Then, after my father... died and Jan left me, I lost the baby. It was still-born. A girl, they told me. Oh, she would be middle-aged now, my daughter, not a youngster like you." And she squeezed Alison's hands before releasing them and quickly standing up. "But this will not do, will it? We have gentlemen waiting for us. I must make myself beautiful for them, eh?" She laughed again. "I suppose we are allowed to be a little late. As ladies, it is our prerogative." And she made her exit from the room. Alison flopped back onto the sofa's cushions like a rag doll, wondering if her own tears were going to come at last.

CHAPTER TWENTY ONE

Alison phoned for a taxi and she and Marta rode the short distance to *Freddy's*. They were not very late, and soon they were seated opposite their male companions. Fred's culinary expertise ensured that nobody suffered any discomfort from over-indulgence or from the richness of the dishes. Everyone lavished praise on the food; that way none of them had to talk about the various things which were currently occupying their attention. Marta's hangover seemed to disappear as soon as she lifted the first glass of Badacsony to her lips. After her third glass she called for silence and rose from her seat.

"I want to propose a toast," she said, saluting Fred with her full glass and looking directly at him. "To Frederick Nowakowski, son of Jan Nowakowski, my former husband." Fred almost fainted with shock when he was addressed this way. Alison and Gerald, both quite flabbergasted, lifted their glasses as if the toast – and Marta's revelation – were nothing unusual. "You see, Fred," Marta said, "We are practically related." And she beamed at him.

"I don't know what to say," Fred said, unable to meet her eye.

"Then say nothing. There is no need. I know most of what you might want to say to me anyway. Not much would come as a surprise."

"And you clearly know who I am."

"Of course. I knew that Jan had a son from his second marriage, and you look so much like him." Gerald, listening intently, was on the point of confirming this, but then he thought better of it and said nothing. He didn't want Marta to connect him in any way with the decades-old murder investigation. Not if he could help it.

"So, Marta, do you know why I've come to Saltaire?" Fred asked.

"To open this very fine bistro," Marta said, spreading her arms, as if to embrace the room. "Why else? Though I suppose you may have wanted to explore your father's roots too. It would not surprise me if you'd also made trips to Poland to pursue that a little. Am I right?" Here she exchanged a smile with Alison; Fred saw it.

"You are right. Absolutely," he said. "How did you know? Has Alison…?"

"No, no. Alison is not one to break confidences, you know that," Marta said, rather quickly, and to reassure him she reached across the table and laid her hand on his. Alison looked at Fred; she could tell he wasn't convinced, but she reasoned that adding her own protestations at this stage wasn't going to help matters. She had her fingers crossed too that Gerald would not become too loose-tongued once the excellent Hungarian wine began to do its work. "Can you remember your father, Fred?" Marta asked, adopting an almost innocent tone.

"Yes. He died when I was only eight, but I remember him very well," Fred replied.

"And did you think he was a good man?"

"Yes, I thought so then, and I think so now"

"I agree. I think he was a good man." Marta said firmly, then after a pause, "And so was my father. They were both good men. I should know, shouldn't I? I lived with both of them. Here, let me replenish your glass, Gerald. You're not drinking enough. It's my birthday, don't forget." And she gave one of her schoolgirl giggles. Then she said, rather loudly: "I offer a toast to both of them. To Jan and Petro." She raised her glass and the others followed suit, intoning the names in low voices before drinking. "And again," Marta said, even more loudly this time, and she stood up so that she could more easily fill everyone's glass. The waiter, who had been hovering nearby, went away, realising that he wasn't required. It crossed Alison's mind that they might be in for a whole series of toasts, in the East European tradition, perhaps culminating in a hurling and shattering of glasses. (Would Fred charge for them, she wondered?) Already she had noticed that the diners at a nearby table – models of English rectitude and restraint – were giving them anxious looks.

Then the elephant in the room began to stir.

"One thing I will say about my father," Fred said, his speech slightly slurred – not surprising, given what he had

273

imbibed earlier to give him courage whilst waiting for Marta and Alison to arrive.

"And what is that, dear?" Marta asked solicitously.

"He never killed Petro," Fred blurted out. Hearing this, Alison thought of making a run for it. She looked at Gerald and could see that he was contemplating something similar.

"Of course," Marta said, soothingly. "His death could well have been an accident anyway. Who can tell? The police never got to the bottom of it." And here she looked quite deliberately and coolly at Gerald, who swallowed hard and took a hefty swig from his glass in an unsuccessful attempt to cover his acute discomfort. So much for thinking Marta had made no connection, Alison thought. What didn't this woman know? Time for a diversion. Anything would do.

"Have you enjoyed the meal, Marta?" she asked. Marta didn't reply. Instead she lifted her handbag from its resting place on the floor, opened it and started to riffle through its contents. The others watched her with interest. None of them would have been totally surprised, at this stage, if she'd pulled out a live rabbit. But rather than that, she produced two printed brochures, illustrated with coloured photographs.

"I want you all to look at these. I think you may be interested," she said, and she passed them round the table.

The first was rather like an estate agent's flyer, advertising a desirable residence. There was a photograph of a solid bourgeois apartment block, with what might have been an accompanying blurb extolling the manifold advantages of the domicile in question and its neighbourhood. The language was unknown to any of Marta's three companions, but it had similarities to the language on the labels of the birthday wine bottles, so the assumption was, naturally, that it was Hungarian.

"What is this place, Marta?" Gerald asked.

"It is my family home in Budapest. I was born there many years ago."

"Really? Budapest? In Hungary?" Gerald said.

"Yes, Budapest in Hungary, Gerald. Our apartment – the one in the photograph – was requisitioned by the communists after the war, but since they are no longer in power I have been negotiating with the present regime. I wanted to reclaim what my family once owned. This notification (and here she waved a type-written letter) tells me that I have at last been successful. The apartment is now mine."

"Congratulations, Marta," Fred said. "I didn't realise that you were Hungarian; I thought you were a Pole, or perhaps a Ukrainian."

"So I was at one time. Ukrainian, Polish, Hungarian, English. Why do you think we have eaten this meal? This melange of cultures? It reflects what I am; a mixture, don't you see?" They were, Alison thought, all becoming more sober, less noisy. Or perhaps that was an illusion.

"What does it matter what we are?" Gerald said, trying hard to sound full of humanity and wisdom. "We are all humans; surely that's all that matters."

"With respect that is easy for you, an Englishman, to say," Marta said, rather sharply. "You take your nationality for granted. If you lived where I come from your identity might be much more fluid – sometimes you could be told to call yourself Polish, or Ukrainian, then Austrian, or German, or even Russian. It would all depend on time and place."

"Beyond me, Marta," Gerald said, and he shook his head. "I'm just a simple Yorkshireman."

"I know," was Marta's immediate response. Gerald said nothing; he felt as if he'd been put down.

Meanwhile Alison was looking at the other brochure. Unlike the one concerning Marta's apartment, this one was in English. It was an advertisement for the Hotel Lew, a member of a world-wide chain of American hotels. The Hotel Lew, it seemed, was in Poland, in pleasant countryside to the east of Krakow. Newly refurbished, it aimed, said the brochure, to offer the discerning guest traditional Polish hospitality with a modern twist. Snapshots of young and healthy visitors complemented the somewhat overblown description. If the photographs could at all be trusted, it looked to be a very pleasant place to stay.

"So tell me, Alison, will you be leaving us and going back to London?" Marta asked. It was a difficult question.

"I haven't made my mind up yet, Marta," Alison said. She continued stirring the warm milky liquid which passed for coffee in the departure lounge of Leeds Bradford

Airport. "It's a very tempting offer I've had, there is no doubting that."

"You must trust your instincts."

"I will," Alison replied.

"If you go I will miss you."

"And I will miss you, Marta, but London is not too far away. If I move I'll be able to come up here and visit you. Or you can come and visit me." Marta didn't answer. Both of them knew that if Alison went back to London, she would return to Saltaire only infrequently, if at all. Neither of them were the type to attempt to recreate the past, whether good or bad.

And yet, here they were about to board a plane which would take them to Budapest, back to the home Marta had last seen over seventy years ago. And after that they were scheduled to visit the Hotel Lew in Poland. Alison had been both surprised and touched when Marta had invited her to join her on this trip. She could understand Marta's desire to visit her apartment in Budapest; after all she was now the owner. But the Hotel Lew? Choosing her moment she had asked Marta why this was so important.

"To tell the truth I can remember nothing about Budapest," Marta said. "My birth parents do not exist for me. I have no image of them in my head. I don't even have a photograph. I count my life as starting in Poland with Petro Semeniuk as my father and Elsa Muller as my mother, even though I always called her my aunt. She was a lovely person. You would have liked her, I know that. The Hotel

Lew is where I first met them. And Pluto. I was four years old. I still miss all of them."

"We never had a dog," Alison said. "My mother thought a dog would make the house dirty and untidy. She was always obsessive about cleanliness,"

"But at least you had real parents."

"Whatever that means. I'm not sure they loved me like Petro and Elsa loved you," Alison said. Marta made no reply; instead she responded with a shrug and changed the subject.

An announcement informed them that the flight for Budapest would soon be boarding, and that passengers should make their way to the appropriate departure gate. But Alison wanted to ask Marta one final important question before they got caught up in all the tedious paraphernalia of a flight departure. Marta had risen to her feet in response to the announcement and was ready to move off, but Alison gently restrained her with a hand on her arm.

"Plenty of time, Marta," she said. "The plane won't go without us. Sit down just for a minute; I have something I've been wanting to ask you." Marta sat down again and waited for the question. As ever, she subjected Alison to an intense gaze.

"What do you want to ask me?"

"Perhaps I shouldn't," Alison said, more than a little inhibited by the older woman's steady scrutiny, and uncertain if now was the right time and place.

"Oh, do come on. We are friends. You can ask me anything you like," Marta said with a quick grin of encouragement. Very well, thought Alison, summoning up all her courage. Here goes.

"It's about your father's death."

"Yes. Well, what do you want to know?" Marta said.

"Do you actually know who was responsible?" Alison said. "For the killing?" The words spilled out in nervous haste, and once uttered, the question sounded not only intrusive but somehow fatuous. Just for a second – no more – Marta looked like an old woman who had suffered pain beyond belief, but her gaze never wavered and the moment soon passed.

"I think I know. I think I've always known," she said quietly. "But the past is past." Before Alison could respond there was a second announcement, requesting passengers for the Budapest flight to move as quickly as possible to the departure gate. Marta stood up. "We must be going," she said. Her voice was cheerful again. Alison watched her walk briskly away. So that's that, she thought, as she rose to follow. She did not understand Marta's answer, but she wasn't going to pose the question again, or ask for elucidation; if this was a mystery without a solution, so be it; she would have to accept it.

Immediately before boarding, and just as she was about to turn her phone to flight-mode, Alison received a call from Ed. She'd almost forgotten he existed. His call went straight to voicemail.

"Hi Ali, long time no speaky. Thought I'd talk direct, seeing that you never respond to texts and you don't appear to be on any social media at all. What's with it up there? No electricity? Snow not melted yet? Or have you gone fucking native? Smoke signals and talking drums only, hee hee. Anyway, my big news is that I've landed a gig doing restaurant reviews for a blog that Nikki's just launched. Not mainstream joints, y'understand. No way. I've been looking at pop-ups. That's the big scene down here. Know nothing about cooking, can't even boil an egg, but Nikki says not to worry about that. Anyway, thought you might like to come down and join me sometime for some freebie…"

And so it went on until Alison deleted the message.

A little later, as they queued to go up the steps into the aircraft, Alison made a decision. She turned to face Marta, who was immediately behind her.

"I won't be going back to London," she said. "I'm going to live and work up here in Yorkshire."

"Excellent," Marta said, and she kissed Alison on the cheek.

The Boeing 737 pulled back from the terminal building, before turning and taxiing towards the end of the airport's main runway. Alison and Marta pretended to pay attention to the safety demonstration, then, as advised by the aircraft captain, they sat back and relaxed to enjoy the flight.

"Okay, Marta?" Alison enquired.

"Very much so," Marta replied. "You must remind me to send a postcard to Gerald when we get to Budapest. He is such a nice man."

"Do you know his address, Marta? All I know is that he lives in Baildon."

"Oh yes, dear, I know perfectly well where he lives," Marta said. She patted Alison's arm and gave her girlish giggle. Then, more seriously: "And Alison?"

"What?"

"Thank you. For being my friend."

"No, Marta, I should be thanking you."

"Why ever should you thank me?"

"For saving me."

"Saving you? From what?" Marta said, puzzled and amused.

"From drowning," Alison said. Marta shook her head and laughed.

At the end of the runway the aircraft turned and paused for a moment, then with a roar the full power of its two jet engines was released and the plane accelerated along the strip of concrete and rose into the sky. Within seconds they were approaching Ilkley and the plane, all the while climbing, banked quite steeply to the left so that it flew over Baildon and then Shipley. Alison, who was sitting in the window seat, looked out as Yorkshire unfolded beneath them. She thought she caught a glimpse of Saltaire, and

Salts Mill and the shape of the canal far below, but perhaps she was mistaken.

DEUS EX MACHINA –
AN EPILOGUE

In the spring of the following year Father Benedykt Kaczmaryk lay on his deathbed in a hospice for aged Catholic clergy in Headingley, not far from the cricket ground. Father Benedykt was very old and close to the end. When he asked to see a policeman as well as a priest, the members of the hospice staff were perplexed, but they wanted to treat his odd request as sympathetically as possible. Father Benedykt had been with them for many years. It was Sister Marie who came up with a rather neat solution. She knew of a priest, Father Walsh, who had a parish near Wetherby, and before training for the priesthood he had, she believed, spent several years as a policeman. Two birds with one stone....

Father Walsh arrived at the hospice that same evening to hear what Father Benedykt wanted to tell him.

"He is quite lucid at the moment," Sister Marie whispered, as she moved a chair nearer the bed for Father Walsh. "But sometimes he goes off into a world of his own and doesn't make much sense." Father Walsh nodded his understanding and seated himself next to the dying man. He leant as closely as he could to hear his confession. The old man's voice was scarcely audible; there was just a hint of a Polish accent.

"Bless me, father, for I have sinned. I cannot recall how long it has been since my last true confession."

"Don't worry about that," Father Walsh said gently. "Just tell me now what you have to say."

"Many years ago this happened. A young man – someone I knew at the time – came to my church and confessed that he had done a terrible thing. One night he had lain in wait for a man and killed him by beating him over the head with an iron bar, or some such weapon. Then he had pushed the body into a canal and fled. Every day for months he expected the police to come for him, but they never did. Eventually the feelings of guilt became so hard to bear that he felt compelled to turn to me, even though his faith had lapsed long before. I asked what had driven him to commit such a dreadful deed, and he replied that it was love. Yes, love! Just imagine! I asked what kind of love it was that would drive a man to commit murder, and he replied that it was love of his country. He was a patriot in exile, he said. Just as I was…"

Despite his efforts to continue, Father Benedykt was forced to pause at this point, and for a moment Father Walsh thought he might have fallen asleep. He waited patiently, and before long the old priest began to speak again, but now in a less coherent fashion, almost as if he were becoming delirious. "It made me feel so guilty…" he said at last.

"Guilty? But you had done nothing except hear his confession. You were innocent in all this…" The old man interrupted him by suddenly gripping Father Walsh's fingers; he seemed to be trying to sit up.

"Innocent, was I?" he hissed, then he lay back once more and released his hold. "It was autumn. The evenings were getting darker," he said. "Dark enough to hide wicked deeds... I knew we should never have tried... to persuade... we should never have offered money... thirty pieces of silver... that's what the Pharisees gave to Judas... we were not innocent... I was not... innocent."

"What do you mean?" Father Walsh asked.

"Never innocent."

Father Benedykt's voice had become fainter now. His eyelids drooped and his breathing was shallow. Father Walsh bent right over the bed, but it seemed unlikely there was anything more to be heard. He lifted his head and turned to face Sister Marie who was sitting further off, next to the window. She rose and came to the bedside in response to Father Walsh's puzzled expression.

"What is it, Father?" she whispered.

"I think he may be near the end. It's hard for me to follow what he's talking about," Father Walsh said.

"Is there anything you want me to do, Father?"

"Tell me, sister, has he been saying anything about a crime... a murder... and about feeling guilty?"

"Sometimes, when he starts to ramble, yes," Sister Marie nodded.

"And about money?"

285

"Oh yes. About Judas and the betrayal of good men and taking pieces of silver. When he gets anxious and confused, that's the kind of thing he talks about."

"And what do you make of it?"

Sister Marie paused before answering. "He's old, Father," she said. "Close to the end, like you said, God love him," and she gave a slight shrug as she began to turn away.

"Of course. Forgive me for asking." He turned back to the dying man. Father Benedykt was not going to speak any more. His eyes were fully closed now, and his breathing was becoming even more shallow and irregular. Soon it would stop altogether.

Father Walsh stood up and stretched himself to ease his aching back. He felt a great sadness. Was it his policeman's training, or just his long experience as a priest? He couldn't say, but he was not only puzzled by what he'd been told – he was sceptical too. This story of the young man confessing to murder – was Father Benedykt wanting somehow to shift the blame? (How often priests had done that down the years, Father Walsh thought.) Then, when he had started to drift away, had the mask started to slip? Father Walsh looked down at the old man. What had he really been sharing with his fellow priest and confessor? Someone's terrible guilty secret? Or was it really his own?

Father Walsh became aware that Sister Marie had now joined him at the bedside again. She handed him a small leather case from which he slowly began to extract what he required to perform the last rites.

****